Thank you,
Hannah, for
reading my story
and having me
as a speaker

J.D. is a former high school, adult ed. and college adjunct history instructor. He has published articles and letters in two major newspapers and magazines and won a Fellowship from the National Endowment for the Humanities. J.D. received a BA from the University of Maryland, an MEd from the University of Virginia and an MA from Georgetown University. J.D. is a veteran of the 82nd Airborne Division and a former court-appointed humane investigator. He lives alone in Alexandria, Virginia.

Dedication

In loving memory of Marilyn and the hundreds of rescued animals. Also, the military dogs and their handlers from WWI, WWII, Korea, Vietnam, the Persian Gulf War, Kosovo, Afghanistan and Iraq.

J. D. Taylor

BEAUREGARD: CANINE WARRIOR

AUSTIN MACAULEY
PUBLISHERS LTD.

A CIP catalogue record for this title is available from the British Library.

ISBN 9781786298447 (Paperback)
ISBN 9781786298454 (Hardback)
ISBN 9781786298461 (eBook)
www.austinmacauley.com

First Published (2017)
Austin Macauley Publishers Ltd.
25 Canada Square
Canary Wharf
London
E14 5LQ

Acknowledgments

My everlasting gratitude to the following people who made this story possible: George Mayer, Barbara Zenker, Joanne Petras, Bill Greenleaf, Dr. Kenneth Wenzer, Dr. John Cook, VDHA, Allen Richburg, Joseph O Connor, Bill Greenleaf, David Yarrington, Sr., Robert Stanley, Kurt Stadenraus, Jim Arrington, and the U.S. Army Corps of Engineers Archives, Ft. Belvoir, Va.

Author's Note

In June 1967, "Turk" was being returned to the United States by presidential fiat in order to cheer his comatose handler, SFC Richard Castle.

While en route, Castle passed away and this war dog was unfortunately returned to Vietnam where he died in combat.

In the early dawn of December 4, 1966, "Nemo," the most celebrated canine warrior to serve in Vietnam, thrust himself at Viet Cong infiltrators assaulting Ton Son Nhut Air Base in South Vietnam.

Despite being shot through his right eye and nose, "Nemo" crawled to cover the battered body of his wounded handler, Airman Robert Throneburg, saving his life. "Nemo" came home to Lackland Air Force Base in Texas to heal and was placed in a plush retirement kennel. "Nemo" died in December 1972. His memorial kennel and stone stand in his honor.

"Nemo" and "Turk" were German Shepherds.

Two other lionhearted canine warriors need to be venerated at this juncture: "Sgt Stubby" and "Chips." "Stubby," a Boston Bull Terrier of World War I fame, was the only service dog nominated to the rank of

Sergeant in connection with the Smithsonian Institution exhibit.

"Stubby" did 18 months of combat duty with the 102nd Infantry Regiment of the 26th (Yankee) Division in Germany. He saved troops from mustard gas attacks, comforted the wounded and at one point, grabbed a German machine gunner by the seat of his pants, holding him until the German was captured.

After the war, "Stubby" met Presidents Wilson, Coolidge and Harding. He was the center of attention in parades. In 1921, "Stubby" attended Georgetown University with his owner, Conor; "Stubby" became the Georgetown "Hoya" mascot forever more.

A German Shepherd-Collie-Siberian-Husky mix named "Chips" became the most decorated war dog of World War II. Trained as a sentry dog like "Nemo," "Chips" deployed to North Africa, Sicily, France and Germany in 1942 with the 3rd Infantry Division. His handler, Pvt John P. Powell and "Chips" were on guard at the 1943 Roosevelt-Churchill Conference.

After being pinned down by an Italian machine gun squad, "Chips," growling, broke from his handler and leaped into the pillbox forcing the enemy to cease and desist until they were captured.

For his efforts, "Chips" was awarded battle stars, a theater ribbon, an arrowhead and an honorary Purple Heart for his eight campaigns.

Upon his homecoming, "Chips" was greeted by his owner, Edward J. Wren of Pleasantville, New York.

INTRODUCTION

Beginning with World War One, America has employed more than 30,000 military dogs in many capacities. They were used to carry messages, first-aid supplies, and trained to detect booby traps, land mines, and trip wires. These dogs were also taught to guard equipment and perimeters, to locate enemy tunnels and to alert ambushes. The war dogs' final act of heroism often resulted in giving their own lives to protect their beloved handlers.

Prior to the Korean War, a small number of war dogs were assigned ranks and medals. But the policy was later revoked because the Pentagon thought that this "cheapened" decorations and ranks advanced to two-legged warriors.

It was service in Vietnam, however, that earned canine warriors their place in American history. War dogs in Southeast Asia completed 88,000 missions which resulted in approximately 3,800 enemy soldiers killed in action and another 1,200 or more captured. This effort, according to the Vietnam Dog Handlers Association, saved at least 10,000 American lives.

Long gone are the 4,000 or more military dogs that served in Vietnam. Yet, their legacy lives on with the veterans whose names are chiseled on the Wall. Fewer than 200 dogs came home. More than 500 died in combat. But the majority were shamefully abandoned by the U.S. government because they were classified as "expendable equipment." My story is about one of those canine soldiers that returned as a hero.

It is a well-known fact that a number of dog handlers extended their tours in order to remain with their canine companions. "Leaving my dog was the hardest thing I ever did in my life. I can never forget the look in those soulful eyes," was a common refrain by the many tearful veterans interviewed.

Someone once said that war is organized political anger and the final refuge of hatred. Perhaps someday dogs will be used more for therapy than for war. What a pity men have to destroy one another. But it is far more dispiriting to inflict such violence on devoted and faithful canines inspired only by love.

From a political perspective, the two leaders of South Vietnam, Diem and his brother Nhu, wanted the U.S. out of Vietnam as early as 1963. But JFK had no intention of retreating at this time. Historians insist the president intended a phased withdrawal, but only after his 1964 re-election.

The Pentagon Papers make it clear that the administrations of Truman, Eisenhower, Kennedy, and Johnson were all committed to a divided Vietnam notwithstanding the 1954 Geneva Accords.

JFK eventually decided that Diem and Nhu had to be removed from power. With the knowledge of the late president and the CIA, the South Vietnamese military murdered both men in a Saigon Catholic Church. Soon thereafter JFK himself was assassinated. And LBJ faced a Hobson's choice: withdraw or escalate.

'Veet-nam, that damn pissant country.'

President Lyndon B. Johnson

'If you want a friend in Washington, get a dog.'

President Harry S. Truman

PREFACE

(A BACKSTORY)

New Orleans was once a sinking French outpost in the southern crescent of the Lower Mississippi Valley, sometimes called the accidental city. New Orleans was purchased from Napoleon (1803) as part of the Louisiana Purchase – an unconstitutional deed by President Thomas Jefferson. The French-Canadian Jean-Baptiste de Bienville established a tobacco colony (18th Century) on this site in order to wean Frenchmen off English tobacco. A Creole community eventually emerged from the descendants of the colony, a racial mix, including free blacks. Later on, sugar production became a thriving industry based upon slave labor supporting a New Orleans aristocracy. Irony, paradox and confusion ruled the day in terms of New Orleans history.

On the periphery evolved a society known as the "swamp people," engaging in the mercantile trade of coon skins, beaver pelts (employing the cruel steel-jaw trap), as well as alligator hides. Worse yet, a small segment of these people bred and sold fighting dogs (pit bulls) and operated a nefarious puppy mill for greedy, vampire capitalist profit.

Many of these incestuous low-life rednecks belonged to the National Rifle Association. Their ramshackle, smoke-filled shacks contained no indoor plumbing or other essential amenities of normal living. But, above the fireplace and on the mantle their Bibles and guns were evident to any casual observer along with a tattered photo of the NRA president and his best seller: *Guns, Crime and Freedom.* These people were truly the proles of humankind. There was little or no civility among them. "My ideas of civility were formed among heathens." – Charles Dickens

Pierre Lanuit, a stumpy sadistic Hydra who was semi-literate, an alcoholic, obese, an NRA devotee, Bible thumper, ex-convict and child molester who also lacked sartorial splendor, owned and operated this top-down criminal enterprise. Dollops of green guano sometimes trailed him while he pleasured himself.

Never out of sight or range was his 15-year-old Creole demirep, a runaway whom he picked up in the French Quarter of the city promising her the world. She was pretty as a field of clover, dressing meticulously with a woebegone look on her round face most of the time. Lanuit's convict days were spent in Angola Louisiana State prison, the worst penal institution in the United States in the 1950s and 1960s, according to the F.B.I. Cruel and unusual punishment was a quotidian occurrence at Angola, a direct violation of the 8th Amendment of the U.S. Constitution. Male rape, a common activity du jour and prison guards bought and sold sex slaves. Blacks were brutalized. Racism was a hairball in the stomach. A number of Black Panthers were incarcerated. Their platforms then and now: Schools, hospitals, housing and equal justice under the law, especially during the Vietnam War.

The shadowy, forbidding, low flying clouds and angry horizontal lines hovered over the Louisiana swampland, a wooded vine-covered area with an unpaved muddy road where morning fog trumps the sun.

In the distance, rambling down the road was a rusted-out, back-firing early 1950s DeSoto pickup truck. Ear-splitting lyrics of *Howlin Wolf's Evil Fade In* echoed between the trees. Driving the truck was an obese man in his forties, smoking a cigar and steering with his knees while thumping out the tunes on the dashboard. Next to him was a thin, immobile, 15-year-old Creole girl, with straight black hair, chewing *Black Jack* gum and emotionless.

From not too far away, headlights blinked three times. The DeSoto blinked back. A small truck approached. Faded black letters on the DeSoto read: "Pierre Lanuit Enterprises." Another read: "NRA Forever." Yet another: "Jesus Saves."

Spinning wheels and throwing mud everywhere, the truck backs up to the DeSoto. Inside the DeSoto hangs a silver cross swaying back and forth with a cheap pine scent of a naked female air freshener; hanging below the rear-view mirror, a statue of St. Christopher is also visible.

A perfunctory "bonju" and a "koman sa va?" verberates between the two bearded and seedy men. Pierre loads two emaciated pit bulls onto the other truck bed in two fecal-covered, rusty kennels. Cash is exchanged. Pierre stuffs the bills into a dirty shirt pocket and then downs a mouthful of White Lightning moonshine whiskey.

Another small puppy cage is handed to Lanuit but he has trouble handling it because he suffers from *cortico-basalganglionic* degeneration causing him to lose the usefulness of his hands from time to time. At the moment he needs to take a leak. While bending over to set the kennel down, he fumbles (because of his girth as well), the cage door opens and a black and tan Dobie puppy darts into the marshes. With an open fly, Pierre starts running after "Puppy Beau" yelling "Salope," "Merde," "Fils de putain," "Pic kee toi," "Tortue," and finally, "Fuck you, ya little bastard," while losing his lower dentures.

The clouds opened up! Lashing rain, wind, thunder and lightning frighten "Puppy Beau." With a pounding heart, he runs toward the deadly teeth of a cruel, Medieval steel-jaw trap, closer and closer!

Keeping the Dobie puppy in sight, Pierre gains ground, but is nearly exhausted. "Puppy Beau" takes a sharp left turn, just missing the ugly trap. Pierre, however, is not so damn lucky. The din of his screams can be heard over the howling wind as he goes sprawling onto the turbid sediment.

Coming out of the swamp, soaked by rain and swamp water, covered in black mud, cut by flint and briars, stung by nettles, and dehydrated, "Puppy Beau" collapses on a curb at the end of the sidewalk.

Meanwhile, a 17-year-old paper boy delivering the *Times-Picayune*, throwing the papers close to the doors, spots "Puppy Beau" struggling. Jumping off his 1954, Red Schwinn Phantom Bicycle, allowing it to fall to the grass, he runs over to the dog. "What's happened, boy?" with angst in his voice. Picking him up gently, he runs home with "Puppy Beau" cradled in his arms.

Upon arrival, he pushes the doorbell, yelling, "Mother, mother, come quick." Together with Mrs. Toutant (a scion of P.G.T. Pierre Toutant Beauregard of Civil War fame), they drive to their vet hospital while listening to Doris Day's "Que Sera, Que Sera" (What Will Be, Will Be).

From that moment on, "Puppy Beau" and young Charles Toutant were bonded forever.

"Puppy Beau" grew to a handsome, mature Doberman and eventually was donated to the U.S. Air Force to be trained as a sentry war dog that would be deployed to Vietnam, America's war of aggression.

He was named "Beauregard" after General P.G.T. Toutant Beauregard.

The rest is history. Enjoy his story!

"They wrote in the old days that it is sweet and fitting to die for one's country...for no good reason." Ernest Hemingway's *Notes on the Next War*

Chapter 1

Private First Class Juan Martinez dropped to one knee beside Beau, keeping a tight grip on the dog's leather harness. The Doberman's eyes probed the shadows at the far edge of the clearing. Beau stood rigid, ears erect, head cocked to one side, listening. Holding Beau's harness, Juan felt tension rippling through the dog's body.

"Easy, fella," he whispered.

The five-man patrol from Bravo Company, 62nd Engineer Battalion, had been pushing through bamboo and thorn-covered vines for hours. As usual, Juan and Beau walked point. They were looking for a rest stop.

To the human eye, there were no signs of Viet Cong, even though Beau had already alerted several times. Juan felt certain Charlie was nearby. He also knew Sergeant Jackson was losing his patience. The squad leader made no secret of his repugnance for so-called scout dogs.

"I won't have a goddamn dog makin' decisions for me," he told Juan the night before.

Juan glanced back over his shoulder and saw that the men behind him had also stopped and dropped to one knee. Sergeant Jackson signaled him to move ahead.

Juan's gut churned. Beau was still in a state of alert—strongest of the day—his ears perked forward as he stared across the field. With renewed tension, Juan felt Beau's trembling as his lips skinned back from his teeth. Juan followed the Doberman's gaze, and then, suddenly, he saw a ripple in the murkiness. Beneath the triple jungle canopy, something moved stealthily through the grass.

Seconds ticked by. Sweat ran down Juan's neck and under his collar. He could taste it in the corners of his mouth. He had been perspiring all day, but now Juan felt slippery with a different kind of sweat—the sweat of fear.

Locked and loaded, Juan ran his thumb over the selector switch of his M-16, just to make sure it was on full automatic. He glanced back again, signaling with his hand that he had seen something. Jackson was paying no attention. Shaking his head with disgust, the squad leader stood up. He raised his hand to signal. The patrol moved across the opening. The rapid *whack-whack-whack* of an AK-47 broke the still air. Jackson's left shoulder exploded in a mist of blood. He was driven backward, twisting and turning like a rag doll.

Before Juan had time to utter a prayer, another machine-gun burst caught Rob Pierotti, the radioman who was next in line behind Jackson. Tiny puffs of dust

24

snapped from his fatigues as the rounds stitched him from shoulder to crotch. By this time, the other patrol members were hugging Mother Earth.

Controlling Beau's leash, Juan moved crabwise to the left into a clump of elephant grass. Then he made a crouched run toward one of the large old trees that bordered the clearing. The AK-47 fire was constant. Juan could hear bullets tearing up the ground around him. Just before reaching cover, something that felt like a hot fireplace poker tore into his left thigh.

"Fuck, that hurts!"

Throwing himself behind a tree, he lay gasping, nearly paralyzed by shock and pain. Gritting his teeth, he managed to push his back against the tree and pull his legs out of harm's way. Hearing a cry, he looked back in time to see John Allen clutching his leg.

Beau whined and tugged on the leather leash, his back muscles and haunches visibly tensing with the urge to charge the enemy on the other side of the meadow. Beau was fearless, and Juan felt a surge of pride and affection for his four-legged partner.

Juan knew it would be suicide for Beau to enter that green. He didn't want automatic rifle fire ripping his dog apart.

"No, boy!" Juan pleaded. "Down!"

Still whining, his body trembling with pent-up tension, Beau settled down beside Juan.

Juan lifted his M-16 and tried to shift sideways so he could fire around the tree trunk. The movement brought a hot flare of pain up his leg, and he was gripped by an instant of vertigo and nausea.

Losing blood, he thought, staring at the torn cloth and gouged flesh where he'd been shot. Blood was flowing everywhere, soaking the ground. *I've got to stop the bleeding somehow.*

Then something crashed into the brush beside Juan. Craning his neck, he brought the M-16 around before he saw that it was Pete Shepard, Juan's best friend in the 62nd. Over the past few months, Juan and Shep had spent long hours talking about home and their families. Shep was engaged to an alluring brunette; they planned to marry after he returned from Vietnam.

There would be no wedding for Shep, or anyone else. Much of his throat had been shot away. He clutched Juan's arm, his hand waxy and warm with blood. He tried speaking. Only a bloody spray blew from the gaping hole in his throat. Then a terrible sucking sound came from the wound, and Shep flopped over onto his back in the tall grass. His body convulsed, then lay still.

More firing erupted from the trees beyond the clearing, diverting Juan's eyes away from Shepard's lifeless body. He scanned the surrounding area, looking for Jackson and Allen. Were they dead? Jackson had been hit in the shoulder and Allen in the leg. They were doing just what Juan was doing: lying low and trying to cope with the pain—not that it mattered. Charlie would find them. Assistance would not arrive in time, even if Pierotti had called for help—which Juan doubted—and Juan had seen first-hand what the VC had done to American POWs.

Maybe this is just a bad dream, he told himself. *I'll wake up in a minute, and—*

Startled by the singsong chatter of voices coming from the clearing, Juan opened his eyes: Instant silence, then a sharply spoken command. Juan knew for sure there were many gooks in the area. Beau growled.

"Quiet!" Juan whispered, his bloody hand tightening on the dog's leash. *What a stupid way to die—stupid, stupid.* They had walked right into this ambush. (From an officer's point of view, "ambush" was not an acceptable term, especially for General Westmoreland.)

Beau whimpered and shook his head from side to side.

"This isn't your fault, boy. You did your best." Juan looked down at the Doberman and realized that he, too, had been wounded. His left hind leg was oozing blood, probably from a ricochet, and his left ear was a bloody flap. Juan touched Beau's leg gently just above the wound, and Beau flinched with pain.

"I don't think it's broken, boy," Juan whispered. Tears welled in his eyes, blurring his vision. He unhooked the leash from the harness. "You're the only one that has a chance to get out alive, boy. Get the hell outta here!"

The dog turned to give him a worried, questioning look.

"I'm done for, but you might make it," Juan said as his chest tightened and wet teardrops rolled down his cheeks. "Go back! Go back!"

Beau, seeming to understand, rose on three legs. He licked the tears on Juan's face, reluctant to abandon his master.

"Go back!" Juan whispered urgently. "Get outta here, Beau!"

The dog hesitated a moment longer, then turned and vanished into the darkening jungle in the general direction of base camp.

Juan leaned back against the sturdy tree and closed his eyes. He had lost a lot of blood, and he knew it would be easy to drift. His life was in turmoil.

The snap of a twig brought him back for a moment. He glanced sideways around the tree trunk and spotted an enemy soldier less than twenty feet away. Charlie was wearing black pajamas and a soft camouflage hat. Beyond the high elephant grass, Juan could hear the movement of VC vultures coming to check their road kill.

May as well take a few with me, he thought to himself.

Despite the intense pain, Juan shifted his weight and braced the M-16 against the tree trunk, trying to keep steady aim on approaching gooks. Charlie turned just as

Juan fired a burst that tore into Charlie's face and blew the contents of his skull against a nearby tree. Another VC went down as Juan swept his gun to his side, firing until the magazine was empty.

Several AK-47s opened up, and Juan felt the tree trunk shudder against his back as bullets slammed into the other side. He then heard the distinctive sound of an M-16 to his left. He knew that either Jackson or Allen was still alive and firing.

Juan reached for another M-16 clip, then decided he didn't have time for that. Instead, he plucked a grenade from his web belt and pulled the pin. He leaned sideways just far enough to toss it back into the clearing, then pulled another. A bullet creased his helmet, knocking it back on his head, stunning him.

The grenade exploded, and he heard a scream.

"Eat that, you bastards," Juan muttered as he hurled another.

He was aware of more firing to his left, then ducked low as bullets began kicking up dirt around him and shredding tree bark. He soon realized that at least one or two VC had circled around to come at him from the right side.

Juan reached for his last grenade and pitched it toward a moving shadow. It exploded, but he was certain they had stayed clear of the blast zone. There were moving shadows out there, closing in for the kill—easy pickings.

Here it comes, he thought. *Please, God, let it be quick.*

A shaft of sunlight found its way through the canopy and illuminated the area around him. Juan stared up at it, far up to where the beam of light outlined branches and leaves in a prismatic glow, caught in a moment of hope that God had answered his prayer after all, as if he expected to be pulled into that beam of light, directly to heaven—

With the impact of bullets tearing through his shoulder, he was knocked over onto his side. He lay looking at that ray of sunlight, and felt as if he were falling through a great, empty space. Dimly, he heard a shouted order, and the firing stopped.

He thought of his hometown of Carolina in Puerto Rico, his seven brothers, two sisters, his mom and dad. He realized the day he boarded the flight to Vietnam that maybe it was the last time he'd ever see his mother.

"I'll be just fine," he had promised, hugging her and feeling her warm tears on his neck. "I'll come back, Mom, don't worry. I love you."

Juan could never forget his first impression of Vietnam. After arriving at Tan Son Nhut Airbase, an airline stewardess reminded him to "have a nice war." Then, upon deplaning with his heavy, green duffel bag, he was greeted with a hundred-degree blast of scorching, odoriferous air and drenching humidity. Juan could still feel his sweat-stained khaki uniform clinging to his body. To him, this place smelled like a dead urinal.

Sorry, Mom, he thought. *I did my best.*

Approaching enemy soldiers were talking among themselves. He expected to feel more bullets rip through his body. He hoped for a quick ending. His helmet was off. One well-placed shot would terminate his misery.

Death was not ready to embrace him—just yet. He looked up through eye slits at six or seven young VC gathered around him. More VC were rustling through the surrounding area checking other bodies.

"Get your fucking hands off me," said someone to his right. Jackson's voice, he thought. "Cocksuckers—ouch, goddammit—"

Then one of the soldiers near Juan barked an order, and two others bent to lift Juan. They weren't going to kill him right away—and Juan knew that his torment had only begun.

Please, God, just let me die, he begged silently.

The shaft of sunlight was gone. His time was short. Juan's brain was no longer capable of processing pain. It was Beau's image that filled his parting thoughts—that magnificent black and tan Doberman, his treasured companion.

I hope you make it, boy. Goodbye!

With glazed and vacant eyes, Juan gazed intently at the open sky. He had stumbled into a killing zone of an ambush. Beau's brief in-country scout-dog training stint had failed to teach him not to follow trail odors marked by strong herbs, spices, and other olfactory irritants, a VC tactic to divert dogs on point.

Thick, razor sharp, saw-tooth elephant grass, twisting vines, and hovering trees appeared to be wrapping their long tentacles around his limp body. Nineteen-year-old Juan Martinez was crossing swords with life itself. Breathless and with a burning in his gut, he fell lifeless.

#

Beau limped painfully through the wooded area. His wounded ear stung as though it were being attacked by a dozen angry wasps. He shook his head from side to side, slinging blood into the ear canal.

While Beau made his way through underbrush and thickets, elephant grass and stinging plants lashed him. Adding to Beau's misery were bloodsucking leeches, which left swollen and itching spots on his wounds. Fleas, ticks, and other insects also gnawed at his crippled, bloodstained body. Snakes were a more deadly enemy.

Approaching a familiar stream he had crossed that morning, Beau paused long enough to drink his fill and bathe his cut pads in the cool, brackish water. Though his thirst was quenched, Beau was weakened by hunger.

As shadows deepened into night, Beau worked his way through dense trees. He reached the edge of the tree line. Beyond were a hedgerow, a ditch, and an expanse of low grass. The checkerboard pattern of green rice paddies looked familiar, and he knew that he was traveling in the right direction, but his damaged leg and weakened condition made it difficult to walk.

Beyond the ditch, a narrow, curving road circumvented the rice paddies. Coming down the road was a herd of quacking, waddling ducks followed by a lone farmer. He was wearing black, baggy trousers, a white shirt, and a conical straw hat. Around the first bend in the road, another farmer carried two noisy ducks tied upside down by their feet and laced to the rear rack of his bicycle.

Beau hobbled out from between the trees, across the paddies, and into the next patch of jungle. From treetops, cavorting monkeys screamed at him. It was time to rest again; his weariness merged into a troubled sleep.

He awakened in the misty, early dawn and proceeded on his way as dark and ominous storm clouds gathered over the fog-wrapped mountains. Beau continued to search for safety without his adored master.

Chapter 2

Corporal Jim Chivington awoke instantly, rubbing sleep from his eyes when Platoon Sergeant Mack Wilson barged into the tent, pushing aside the bug net, and shouting, "Get your asses out of those cots, you motherfuckers! You've been chosen for a rescue mission."

Chivington's dream about being home in Tuscaloosa, Alabama, ended abruptly. It was a pleasant fantasy about a birthday party. Everyone was there— even Felicia, the dark-haired princess with doe-like eyes he dated through most of his senior year in high school. After graduation, Felicia had moved away, and he had lost touch with her. He heard later that she'd married a salesman in Virginia. The dream brought back sweet memories from a past that seemed a lifetime ago.

Specialist Four Pete Maddox, in the cot beside him, arose yawning. "What's goin' on?"

"Rescue mission," Wilson responded. "Op Center cannot locate Jackson's recon patrol. Captain Wojtacha wants us to find 'em."

"Oh, shit," Chivington muttered. His peaceful dream was now lost from memory. "Jackson's patrol?" Juan Martinez had gone out with Jackson. Martinez was one of only three dog handlers at Phan Rang; their mutual love of animals had kindled a friendship between them.

"Right," Wilson said grimly. "I need you at the point." His eyes moved to Maddox. "Move your ass, Maddox. You're our radioman. C'mon, Mitchell, hit the deck!"

"Ah, shee-it, Sarge," Private First Class Stan Mitchell complained. "I'm a truck driver and heavy equipment operator, not a fuckin' grunt."

"Get off your cock and into those socks," Wilson barked, "and make sure they're clean, 'cause you've got a lot of humpin' to do today, soldier." He paused, his eyes returning to Chivington and narrowing a little. "Hey, Chivington, are ya up to it?"

"Up to what, Sarge?" asked Chivington. He and Mack Wilson had been at odds ever since Chivington had arrived at the base three months ago. He didn't understand why. Perhaps it was his Southern demeanor.

Wilson stared down at him. The slender, handsome sergeant had a chiseled face, a black, narrow mustache, an aggressive jaw, and a commanding voice. His skin was the color of dark chocolate. "The boonies, asshole, the boonies. Now you'll see what the 'Nam is all about."

"Why us, Sarge?" Mitchell asked. "We ain't got no experience for a patrol into gook country."

"We're trained, same as anybody else over here. Everyone's got a first time out. C'mon, assholes, move it! I want to see all of you in front of the Command Post at 0700, after chow."

Chivington turned and poked Private First Class Cecil Walker who lay in the cot beside him. Walker couldn't possibly still be asleep—not after Wilson's whip-crack voice. "Get up, goddammit! We're on for a patrol." Yawning, Walker sighed and rolled over. "Yeah, I heard. Where are we goin'?" Chivington thought Walker was the toughest man on their team. He was tall, lean, and taut; he looked as if he were constructed of knotted wires in various gauges.

"I've got no idea," Chivington said. He pushed himself to his feet, stretched a crick out of his back, and started dressing. "Same place Jackson went, I guess."

"Wonderful." With a heavy sigh, Walker threw his legs over the side of the cot and sat up. Running a hand over his frizzy, red hair, he added, "Helluva way to start a day."

Bravo Company, the newly arrived advance group of the 62nd Engineer Battalion from Fort Leonardwood, Missouri, was camped at Phan Rang Base in II Corps. It was August 1965. The base was located about thirty-five miles south of Cam Ranh Bay and nine miles east of Phan Rang City which had a population of about twenty-four thousand. The deep blue emerald waters of the South China Sea and the lush, verdant rice paddies and green jungles tinged with a carbonate of copper highlighted a scene almost too perfect for a war zone.

Yet it was definitely a war zone. The 62nd Engineers had been deployed to build a tactical air base and a cantonment area for the 1st Brigade of the 101st Airborne Division.

Lieutenant Colonel Geno Ricci, battalion commander at Phan Rang, had his work cut out for him. Chivington didn't know the colonel well, but he thought that if anybody could build an air base here, it was Ricci. He had a reputation for getting things done. He was also known to be a fair and able leader.

With so many North Vietnamese (NVA) in the area, one of Colonel Ricci's greatest challenges would be to maintain a secure perimeter. That was why the colonel had ordered five-man recon patrols into the surrounding area to map trails and locate enemy strongholds in order to preclude surprise attacks. Like his most revered historical hero, Winston Churchill, Ricci also maintained a large selection of war maps.

That was what Jackson and his men had been doing, but it was clear—they had run into some serious trouble. Recon teams were not authorized to engage the opposition; they were supposed to identify the enemy's location in order to direct well-placed air strikes against their positions.

Base camp had lost touch with them. That meant they were more than likely ambushed. Juan Martinez and Beau would have been walking point. Beau's senses should have alerted the patrol to any potential danger. Had Beau failed them? Chivington hoped not. The black and tan Doberman was so eager to please. Unlike the other dogs at Phan Rang, Beau was versatile, companionable, and intelligent.

Whatever had happened out there, Chivington could only hope that Beau was not roasting over a gook fire pit.

#

Minutes later, Chivington and the others emerged from the tent, slapping at sand flies and scratching raw mosquito bites. They wore cotton olive drab fatigue uniforms with deep side pockets. The U.S. Army black and gold nameplate appeared above the heart. Rank was visible on the jacket sleeves which were rolled high over the elbow. Their footgear included brown leather combat boots resembling the vintage WWII double-buckled boot. These boots were uncomfortable for jungle wear because the feet could not breathe. Chivington noticed that Wilson wore an early version of a canvas "jungle boot" which could be found on the black market.

An irritating heat rash caused many GIs to discard their underclothing. A number suffered from open sores near the buttocks because of exposed flesh. Chivington, however, decided to keep his boxers intact.

After using a cut-in-half fifty-five-gallon drum latrine, they washed and followed the aroma of hot coffee and bacon and eggs trailing from the mess tent.

Wilson came over to share breakfast. While eating and sipping coffee, he chatted with his men. Chivington remembered soon after arriving at Phan Rang how mercurial Wilson was—affable one moment and chewing your ass to a bloody rag the next.

"Plan on four days of rations. By the way, blacken your faces." Wilson grinned, showing a row of strong white teeth, and began laughing while the others joined in. "We'll be going into hostile free-fire zone. That means you can shoot first and ask questions later. Enjoy your hot breakfast. There may not be another for a while," he snickered. "Be thankful you're not eatin' a gook breakfast. You'd have to eat noodle and onion soup with fucking chopsticks."

Shoot first and ask questions later. Chivington's stomach knotted. He'd lost his appetite. He had no idea how he would react when faced with having to kill an enemy soldier. He knew that he might not have a choice, that he might have to kill or be killed. He'd hoped that being assigned to the 62nd Engineers as a heavy equipment operator would keep him out of combat situations. *So much for that*, he thought.

Chivington, pushing aside his food and looking out toward the perimeter of the base, realized that somewhere out there, beyond the rolls of coiled razor cable and tangle-foot barbed wire piled six feet high, something dreadful had happened to Jackson's recon team, and within a few minutes, Chivington would be leading another patrol through the gate, into hostile territory, where men and women in black pajamas awaited them. Violent death haunted Chivington.

Some of the men enjoyed cigarettes with a final cup of coffee. After dunking their mess kits in fifty-five-gallon drums of hot, soapy, then clear, water, they met at 0700, grouping in the shade of the watchtower closest to the gate.

"Fall in," Wilson ordered. After forming a straight line, he inspected each man's canvas rucksack. Typical patrol equipment and web gear included a ten-pound flak jacket made of fiberglass and nylon, a coil of rope, a flashlight, a rifle-cleaning kit, and eight to fifteen clips of M-16 ammo. Also included were four fragmentation and two smoke grenades that were attached to the ruck straps, a first-aid kit, Claymore mines with C-4 explosives, a Gerber Marks II survival knife, C-rations, two one-quart plastic canteens of water, an entrenching tool, and the all-important P-38—the little key with an eyelet used to open C-ration cans.

Personal items included things like a round mirror for an occasional shave, extra bootlaces, sunglasses, a pen and paper for writing home, a toothbrush, toilet paper, a clean pair of socks, reading material, a soft camouflage "boonie hat" with vent holes, and condoms—just in case opportunity knocked for "boom boom." Green dragon rag towels would help them deal with heavy perspiration.

Maddox, the radioman, lugged an added burden. The handset, radio, and long and short antenna all weighed about twenty-five pounds. He would also carry extra smoke grenades and flares to direct a rescue medevac helicopter.

Chivington, at the end of the formation, was the last to get inspected. The sergeant grunted once or twice as he went through his rucksack. Wilson found nothing amiss. He then stepped in front of his men to impart words of wisdom, using his strong, authoritative voice.

"We're all strangers to this land and its people. You've gotta remember what ya learned in basic training about survival: Keep your ass down. That's rule number one. Stay low and get somethin' 'tween you and Charlie. When enemy rounds come in, there is no such thing as too much cover. Charlie has lots of weapons at his disposal—"

"Hey, Sarge," called the observer in the watchtower. "There's a black dog approachin' camp. He's lame. Looks like he's hurt real bad."

Chivington grasped the significance immediately. Dogs were not common in Vietnam, and most dogs on the loose soon ended up in a pot or roasting over an open fire.

He hurried over with the others to the open gate, a movable barricade of steel and barbed wire.

"I'll be damned!" Wilson said. "That's Martinez's dog…and sweet Jesus, where's the rest of 'em?"

The perimeter beyond the gate was mined with M-18A1 Claymores and trip flares. Startled, Chivington saw the Doberman limping right into them.

"He'll never make it," Walker said. "He's gonna hit one of those Claymores and get blown to doggie heaven."

Before he knew what he was doing, Chivington sprinted through the open gate, running full speed toward the faltering Doberman.

"Hold it!" he heard Wilson bark.

Chivington ignored him. More than a hundred yards out, the dog collapsed. Within a few seconds, Chivington angled past the Claymores and reached Beau. He fell to his knees beside the dog and saw instantly that Beau was in trouble. White foam oozed from his bloody mouth. Beau's swollen left hindquarter was nothing but a mass of raw meat blanketed with flies and leeches; his left ear—what was left of it—was even worse.

Still kneeling beside the Dobie, Chivington turned and shouted, "We need a stretcher out here!"

"Fuck that!" said Wilson as he glared at Chivington. "We ain't bringin' a stretcher out here for a fuckin' dog. Corporal, what in hell do you think you're doin'? I told ya to stop back there—"

"Sorry, Sarge," Chivington said, turning his attention back to the wounded Doberman. "I didn't hear—"

"The fuck you didn't—"

"Besides, I think Colonel Ricci would want us to do whatever we can to save this dog," Chivington shouted back.

Mack Wilson went silent. Chivington knew that Wilson was weighing those words and their implication. It was rumored that Colonel Ricci was a dog lover. He was the one who had managed to secure three dog teams for Phan Rang. He wouldn't like it if Beau died because Sergeant Wilson refused to give him medical care.

At some point, Wilson reached the same conclusion. He turned and gestured at the GIs standing at the gate. A moment later, two stretcher-bearers came out of the gate and shuffled toward Beau. "Stay clear of the mines!" Wilson shouted.

With Chivington's help, they hoisted the panting, 120-pound dog onto the stretcher and headed back into the compound.

"This dog is barely alive!" Chivington yelled at the medic. "Move your ass! Get 'im over to the aid station and douse 'im with cool water. That'll bring his temperature down—"

I know what to do, Chivington," the medic said. "Don't tell me my job, man! Besides, it's just a fuckin' dog—"

"He isn't *just* a dog," Chivington shot back. "He's probably a better soldier than you—"

"Knock it off," Wilson snapped before the medic could respond to that. "We don't have time for that shit."

Once outside the aid station, cool rainwater from a fifty-five-gallon water drum was applied to the dog's body. Beau moved his head, and his panting gradually eased. He lapped at a small pail of water set before him.

Chivington removed blood-soaked insects and leeches from Beau's wounded leg, then washed his face and cleaned around the mangled ear.

"Where's Juan, boy?" Chivington asked. "Where's the rest of your team?"

"I guess he isn't talkin'," Wilson said with a sneer. "You must be a real dog lover, Chivington. I've never been able to figure out why people like the slobbering, crotch-sniffing fuckers so much."

Chivington remained silent. His lips were sealed. From one of his favorite history classes, he remembered a sign hanging over the teacher's desk that read, *"Now that I know men, I prefer dogs."*

"He ain't gonna make it," said the medic. "I don't know why you're wastin' your time—especially with a mutt that sure as hell led his patrol right into a fuckin' ambush—"

"Is that what happened?" Chivington said, turning to face the medic. "Are you psychic, asshole? Have you been lookin' into your crystal ball? Because I can't figure out how else you'd know what the fuck happened out there."

"All's I know," the medic insisted, not backing down, "is that only one of 'em from that patrol made it back—and that's this dog."

"Enough!" Wilson interjected. "Let's save 'im, if possible. The Old Man worked hard to get these dogs here. What do we have to do?"

The medic shook his head, looking disgusted, but after seeing Wilson's stone face, he decided to keep his mouth shut. "He's gonna need a medical evac to Cam Ranh. They have one Air Force vet there with a half-assed animal hospital. Maybe they can keep 'im alive. He needs antibiotics, fluids, and some serious medical care on the leg and the ear."

"I hope they can save that leg," Chivington said, stroking Beau's neck and back.

"That's iffy, at best," replied the medic. "Look at the swelling, man. It's full of infection."

"All right," Wilson said. "Let's radio Cam Ranh for a medevac."

"For a dog?" the medic said. "They're gonna love that."

Wilson nodded. "Let's not tell 'em it's for a dog."

Muttering under his breath, the medic left to make the call.

"We'd best get the rest of those ticks out of his fur," said Chivington as he rubbed his hand over the dog's back and behind his ear. "Look how big these fuckers are." As he pulled a tick from Beau's ear, it burst into a spray of blood. Chivington was repulsed. "These bastard blood ticks are at least ten times the size of ticks back home. My God in heaven, I've never seen anythin' like it. This is the *Twilight Zone*."

"Nope," said Wilson. "It's just the 'Nam."

Chivington completed removing ticks from Beau in time for the medevac. He was relieved that the attendants didn't squawk about taking a dog. In fact, they went out of their way to make Beau as comfortable as possible, stroking him and talking to him in gentle tones as they prepared him for the flight back to Cam Ranh Bay.

"Christ, he's gettin' more attention than a two-legged GI would," Wilson muttered, standing beside Chivington.

Chivington nodded, "Everyone loves dogs." Then he glanced at Wilson. "Well, *most* people do."

Beau was muzzled, placed onto a basket stretcher, tied down, and whisked away. The Huey medevac helicopter ambulance, marked with red crosses in front and on the right side, disappeared as quickly as it had arrived.

#

Chivington's mind was still on the wounded dog when he joined the rest of Wilson's patrol team in front of the Command Post (CP) tent. By now, it was mid-morning and hot as hell.

If that leg is broken, they'll put 'im down, Chivington thought. *They won't even consider trying to save 'im.* To the Army, dogs were military equipment. Use them until they are spent; then throw them away and get new ones.

Wiping sweat from his brow with a dragon rag, Wilson continued his interrupted lecture.

"Listen up! The VC in this area are some bad-ass motherfuckers. They don't give a fuck about the Geneva Conventions, and they aren't takin' prisoners. If we run into any of 'em out there, don't hesitate. Blow their asses away. Don't give 'em a chance to shoot back. Is that clear?"

A few murmurs and nods. Only Maddox made an audible reply. "You betcha, Sarge. We'll waste those cocksuckin' motherfuckers. We'll blow their asses right to gook hell." Maddox was a thin, fair-skinned twenty-year-old with ash blond hair and light blue eyes that peered out through wire-rimmed glasses. He tried to make up for his meek appearance with macho bluster.

Like Chivington, he was a Southerner, but he made Chivington nervous. Despite his bravado, Chivington saw fear in Maddox's eyes.

"When we move out, keep ten-foot intervals between us," Wilson said, glancing at Maddox. "Chivington will be walkin' point. If he suspects that somethin's wrong, he'll signal with a clenched fist like this." Wilson's tightly closed fist shot up like a rocket. "Maddox, you keep your ass close to me at all times. Make sure you stay on an open and changin' radio frequency. You best put those green towels under your ruck. Otherwise, the straps will cut the shit out of your shoulders. And all of you—stay alert! If our asses get caught by a large VC contingent, we're all dead meat. That's probably what happened to Jackson's patrol."

Chivington had already heard various forms of Wilson's lecture, but it never hurt to be reminded. One could die many ways in Vietnam, and if you didn't die, there were plenty of things that could make you wish you were dead. Blood-sucking mosquitoes were everywhere, not to mention stinging sand flies, scorpions, and a large, crawling, furry black spider with a body about the size of a man's thumb. There were also many poisonous centipedes, termites, bedbugs, cockroaches, and a fierce, biting, half-inch-long fire ant whose mandibles felt like an electric needle puncture to both man and beast. A combination of these insects and jungle rot added a great deal of stress to someone trying to stay alive.

"We'll avoid trails," Wilson was saying as Chivington tuned back in. "They'll most likely be booby-trapped, or lead us into an ambush. Whenever we come across one, we'll mark it on our map and then parallel it, if we have to. If you hear or notice movement at night, somethin' out of the ordinary, squeeze the arm or leg of the nearest man to ya to get his attention. Don't start shootin', givin' our position away, unless you're damned sure ya have to.

"Now, for a few final safety reminders about Charlie's toys. Listen up! Especially watch for the punji booby traps. They're vintage Victor Charlie. They have sharp, nasty tips, and they're covered with human shit or poisonous tree sap. If ya step in that hole, you're fucked if ya don't get to a medic like yesterday. Those traps are hard to see, because they're covered with leaves, dirt, and grass, and there are a dozen or more bamboo spikes to a pit. So heads up! Be alert! Charlie is also known to use captured Claymores, dud bombs, and shells as booby traps. Don't ever pick up a soft-drink can. They are usually hooked to a tripwire with a grenade concealed inside. Touch that can and your ass belongs to eternity, and all that Uncle Sam can say to your mama is, 'Sorry 'bout that.' Any questions?"

"Yeah, Sarge," Chivington said. "Why don't we take one of the dogs with us?"

"Right on. So the same thing can happen to us that happened to Jackson's team?" Wilson said sarcastically.

"They were probably ambushed—"

"Well, hell, that's what the dog was supposed to do—detect an ambush, anti-personnel mines, snipers, and booby traps," Wilson said. "Besides, with Martinez and his dog out of commission, there are only two dogs left on base. The Colonel will want to use 'em for sentry duty, I'm sure. We've got too damn much heavy equipment to guard, and it's rumored that there's sapper

49

activity in the area." His eyes moved from man to man. "Everyone ready?"

They nodded.

"All right. Saddle up." They had taped all the snaps and buckles on their web gear. Their rucksacks were in place. Chivington took his position on point and shrugged to shift the weight of his ruck into a more comfortable position. With everyone on the ready, Wilson gave them the signal to move out. The five-man patrol disappeared through the gate.

Chapter 3

Chivington moved with caution, his eyes trying to be everywhere at once. Blades of sunlight lanced through the trees. They had been moving west through bamboo, elephant grass, and single-canopy jungle for several hours, but Chivington felt as if he'd been out there for a week. The heat was stifling. Around them, the vegetation was alive with buzzing and chirping insects.

As point man, Chivington was never more than a heartbeat from sudden death. Surprisingly though, being in the boonies felt almost routine to him. His only experience with a five-man patrol team had been a fifteen-day basic training stint. There, he had studied map reading, hand signals, and other methods of silent communication. He had also learned about the different types of ambush and how to read a trail.

Chivington felt comfortable outdoors, and in some ways this wasn't too different from hunting deer—except, of course, you never had to worry that the deer might be waiting behind the next tree with an AK-47 to blow your ass off.

During basic training, they had been warned to watch out for reptiles, especially bamboo vipers. Chivington was afraid of them, and he was paranoid about a snake dropping from a high bamboo stalk.

The team's movement was deliberate and slow. No one talked. Each member of the patrol had territory to watch. Chivington covered 180 degrees to his front, while Wilson, ten feet behind him, watched the right side. Maddox came next with his radio, paying attention to the left flank. Walker covered the right flank, and Mitchell came last, looking for signs of movement behind the team.

Chivington stopped frequently to glance back at Wilson for directions. Each time, Wilson consulted his field map and Lensatic compass. Chivington gave Wilson credit for keeping them on track. Where they were going there were no street signs or obvious landmarks or gas stations where they could stop to ask for directions. Everything around them looked the same to Chivington, but Wilson could locate landmarks and points of reference that matched the map. Now and then he would gesture Chivington to angle slightly to the right or left.

Five or six clicks (a click is about .62 miles) west of base camp, Chivington spotted several mounds of earth covered with leaves and grass about fifty yards away. He raised his clenched fist. The men behind him froze in a crouched position.

For the moment, elephant grass provided needed cover. Smacking mosquitoes, Wilson motioned for the patrol to come closer.

"Listen up." Somehow, his voice still carried command authority even though he was speaking in a loud whisper. He pointed straight ahead. "See those mounds of dirt? They could be trouble. We're probably in the middle of a dink graveyard...or maybe some kind of booby trap. The VC are known to hide weapons and supplies in empty coffins. Those mounds of earth usually indicate a gravesite. See those urns? They're used to burn incense, and that little hill says, 'Don't step on me.' It's a form of honor for the dead."

Chivington looked at Wilson with new appreciation. Wilson didn't seem like the type who would take time to learn about the customs or culture of the Vietnamese people.

"What should we do?" Maddox asked, looking at the mounds. "Blow 'em up?"

Wilson shook his head. "We can't risk making that much noise." He poked at his map with a finger. "I'll give these coordinates to base camp. They'll send a gunship out to blast it all to hell."

Wilson looked upward and Chivington realized that the shadowy world beneath the jungle canopy had suddenly grown darker. They were standing in an area of fifty-foot cypress trees with mottled gray and white trunks.

"I smell rain a-comin'," Wilson said. He looked down at the field map. "If we're where I think we are, we're pretty close to the last known position of that patrol. Maddox, contact base camp and tell 'em we're at coordinates HA025255. Tell 'em we'll be staying the night here."

Dark clouds released their moisture. A slow, steady rain began to fall, dribbling through the canopy above them. Everyone opened their green camouflage ponchos for cover.

"Maddox, any contact yet?" asked Wilson after a minute or two.

"Not yet, Sarge, just static." Maddox was hunkered down with his handset, trying to make contact with base camp. He pushed his slipping, steamy glasses back on his nose, and then tightened the black elastic wrap that held them in place.

"Damn the weather, and damn these bugs," Wilson muttered as he pulled his poncho over the map.

"Red Rover One, this is Little Red Riding Hood, over," Maddox said into the handset. "Come in, Red Rover. Do you read?" He listened for a moment, then turned to Wilson and made a zero out of his thumb and forefinger. "Red Rover, we're at coordinates HA025255, over." Another pause. "Red Rover, we're halting for the night. Keep a frequency open, over."

He listened for the sign-off, then returned the handset to the loop on his rucksack strap and stood.

"Base camp says we need to go about one click up and one click right, Sarge."

Wilson nodded. "That's what I thought. Secure our perimeter and break out the C-rats. Plaster on the bug juice. Those fuckers will be wanting us for dinner tonight—and be on the alert for snakes. Use your E-tool to dig your latrine and cover it up, like a cat. Otherwise, you'll be leavin' a trail for Charlie to follow."

"Is Charlie good at sniffin' piles of shit?" Walker asked.

"He can tell if you had ham and motherfuckers covered in grease," Wilson said. "Speaking of which, don't eat the grease. That might give you Ho Chi Minh's revenge, and we can't keep stoppin' for somebody to take a dump." He glanced at Chivington. "You've got first watch."

"Sure, Sarge." It didn't make any difference to him. He was so wound up, he wouldn't be able to sleep anyway.

"Hey, Sarge, we can't eat this crap cold," Maddox complained, looking down at his C-rations with distaste. "A little heat would make it easier to get the grease off." He looked around at the other C-rations. "Looks like everyone got ham and limas."

"I got beans and franks," said Mitchell. "You oughta like all that grease, Maddox, being from Mi'ssippi and all." A wolfish grin spread over his face as he looked around at the others. Mitchell was short, just shy of what one might describe as pudgy. One side of his mouth hooked into a slight perpetual half-smile, as if permanently amused by the world and its inhabitants. "When Maddox was a baby, he was so ugly his mother put him in a corner and fed him with a slingshot, and he likes to cover his chow with all that spicy pepper and garlic shit that he carries in his ruck. With dry leaves everywhere, he'd better shit in the river. Otherwise, he'll set the woods on fire and give our position away."

"Buncha fuckers," Maddox muttered as he stepped aside to urinate. "I ain't the only redneck here, and it don't mean nothin'."

"Okay, guys, knock it off," Wilson said. "Go ahead and use a little C-4 to heat those C-rats. Chow down and get some rest. Be sure to take your malaria pill and that salt tablet. Since it gets a little cool at night, you need to dry off a little, especially if you have wet socks. Change 'em, but keep your boots on—just in case we get hit and have to haul ass outta here. Remember, the night belongs to Charlie."

#

After the others sacked out in their hammocks, Jim Chivington took his position on watch. The rain had stopped. The natural canopy above their camp was not heavy. Looking up through the branches, Chivington could see moon-silvered clouds separated by black patches of sky. Moonlight dappled the ground and outlined the shadowy shapes of encroaching trees. From the vegetation around him came the groans and croaks of lizards and occasional grunts from scurrying animals in their nocturnal search for food. Although the insect repellent kept the mosquitoes from biting, he felt them constantly hitting his exposed flesh.

Settling back against a tree trunk, he thought about the comments Wilson had made earlier about Vietnamese culture. How many of the men fighting over here actually knew about the country, or what they were fighting for? Did any of them know or care that Ho Chi Minh admired Thomas Jefferson and the U.S. Constitution?

Chivington first developed an interest in world history in Mr. Lawler's sixth grade class at Central Elementary School in Tuscaloosa. Mr. Lawler had had an amazing ability to bring history to life in his classroom. He had even made the boring history textbook sound exciting. Instead of just *reading* history, they *lived* history through Mr. Lawler's captivating stories, skits, documents, and lovable personality.

Mr. Lawler had ignited a passion inside twelve-year-old Jim Chivington, who until then had been neutral toward school, at best; this fire burned steadily through the completion of a BA degree in history. To put himself through school, Jim worked summers for a local contractor as a heavy-equipment operator. That was the experience that the Army wanted for the 62nd Engineer Battalion. Chivington intended to further his education once he completed his obligation to Uncle Sam—maybe even getting a Ph.D. so he could teach at a university.

To Chivington, it seemed natural to want to know about Vietnam once he knew that this was his immediate destiny. He read everything possible and followed daily news reports as well as the political machinations engulfing his country.

He soon realized that few American soldiers knew the Vietnamese language or culture, let alone the history of their thousand-year struggle against the Chinese, Khmers, French, Japanese, and Americans. Through most of that period, the Vietnamese had fought against better-armed and equipped opponents. With their nationalistic determination and cunning, they had managed to outlast their enemies.

Now, the U.S. was getting a dose of what the Vietnamese had done to other armies who thought they could defeat them.

According to Uncle Sam, Jim Chivington, like everyone else, had been dispatched to Vietnam to stop the spread of Communism. South Vietnam was on the verge of collapse. Corruption was rampant in both the South Vietnamese government and in its army. South Vietnamese (ARVN) battlefield losses were averaging about 750 men per week. Due to low morale, 5,000 to 7,000 ARVN troops deserted each month. The South Vietnamese Army was riddled with spies. Death threats to family members were a common VC tactic. U.S. Army and Air Force installations under ARVN protection were being hit on a regular basis. Even Da Nang, one of the largest bases, was called "Rocket City" because of the constant bombardment of small VC rockets.

Initially, it was an air war which began in March 1965. The August 7, 1964 Gulf of Tonkin Resolution gave President Johnson *de jure* war powers, and it was a *de facto* declaration of war by the U.S. Congress as well. Johnson said that the resolution was "like Grandma's nightshirt—it covered everything." Now he felt that only "his boys," U.S. ground troops, could save South Vietnam. The upshot was massive escalation. Within six weeks of the first Marine landing of 3,500 troops at Da Nang in March 1965, more than 82,000 troops had been sent to South Vietnam.

Troops like Jim Chivington received the daily dose of military propaganda attacking Communism. Throughout Army basic training units going to Vietnam, a "Red-scare" attitude prevailed. A buddy who attended jump school at Fort Benning, Georgia, wrote Chivington about the wild t-shirt logos in the Fort Benning Post Exchange. One read: *Kill a Commie for Mommie*. This was the U.S. perspective on Vietnam.

Henry David Thoreau taught Jim Chivington that the masses live lives of quiet desperation, rarely standing alone and thinking for themselves. That was one reason why the Ku Klux Klan never captured Chivington's attention, even though his father had been a proud and vocal member.

As a little boy, Chivington remembered his father and Uncle Tyrone drinking beer on the front porch and talking about what they would do to all the niggers and queers if they were running the country.

Chivington's father deserted the family long before Chivington's sixteenth birthday, but he had left a lasting impression of bigotry and hatred with his family. This squint-eyed man was a stereotypical tobacco-chewing drunk and bigot who had treated women with contempt. He had often battered his young daughter, Rebecca. Chivington remembered an occasion when his father had caught fifteen-year-old Rebecca with a black boy from her school. They had been working on algebra problems at the kitchen table, but that made no difference. After throwing the boy out of the house, he had told his daughter to drop her pants, sit on the edge of her bed, and spread her legs. Crying and close to hysteria, Rebecca nonetheless feared him enough to do as he had ordered. He had examined her to see if she was still a virgin.

Chivington sighed, his eyes probing the shadows around him, his ears listening for any movement. A shooting star scratched its fire across the sky, and like a child, he wished upon it.

Chapter 4

Chivington was awake when Wilson, who had taken the last watch, began to rouse his men. "Get with it, guys," Wilson said. "Rise and shine. Dig and cover your latrines, just like you did last night. Keep usin' the bug juice on exposed skin."

After a breakfast of eggs and pound cake, the most popular item in C-rations, they policed the area, checked their weapons and gear. Wilson took a compass reading, then said, "Saddle up. Let's move out. Maddox, is your radio on frequency?"

"You bet, Sarge," replied Maddox as he took a final drag, then dropped his cigarette, crushed it, and kicked dirt over the butt.

Chivington took point, adjusted his rucksack, and began moving in the north-northwest direction Wilson indicated. Knowing that they were going into the area where Jackson's team had disappeared made him cautious. Before each step, he checked to the left and then to the right. The others behind him were alert as they walked slowly, their eyes looking for the slightest movement that would suggest an ambush.

In this fashion, they crept through a thicket of green, tan, and brown clumps of bamboo. High above them, small birds chirped as they fluttered from stalk to stalk.

After struggling through the searing heat for close to two hours, they reached a small stream, and Wilson signaled to halt. He then studied his map.

They all took the opportunity to drink from their canteens. At the stream's edge, a dirt bank dropped three feet into clear, slow-moving water. Both sides of the embankment were lined with large cypress trees, their trunks wrapped tightly with vines. Mosquitoes swarmed in the still air between the ridges.

Wilson tapped Chivington's shoulder and pointed to the right, along the stream. They followed its meandering path for about a hundred yards or so, then waded through the shallow water and found a pathway that looked well used.

Wilson gestured to the left, and Chivington knew that he wanted to parallel the trail. It would be a lot easier to use the footpath itself, but they couldn't take the chance. As Wilson said at his morning briefing, VC often laid booby traps along trails.

Farther on, they came to a small clearing that showed signs of human activity. Chivington raised his clenched fist, signaling a stop. He glanced back at Wilson, then pointed at the small structure that caught his attention, some fifty yards ahead and to the left.

"It's a VC shitter," Wilson said, nodding. "Let's take a closer look."

Surrounded by trees and underbrush, they moved in. Four bamboo poles buried in red dirt formed the corners of an outhouse, with woven palm fronds for walls. In the center, Chivington saw four small mounds of earth about six inches high with holes in the middle.

"Stay put and cover me," Wilson said as he moved forward in a crouch. When he reached the latrine, he got down on his knees, stuck his face directly over one of the mounds, and inhaled. "Jesus H. Christ!" he gagged.

Even from ten yards away, Chivington could smell the pungent odor of putrid excrement mingled with the smell of mold.

"What the fuck is he doin'?" asked Mitchell.

"Hell if I know," replied Walker. "Maybe that's how Sarge gets his kicks."

"He's checkin' to see if it's fresh," Chivington said. "That's my guess, anyway."

After Wilson returned to the squad, Mitchell looked at him, holding his nose.

"I know," said Wilson, his voice low. "There's a strong odor of fresh fish and shit in that hole. That's an active latrine, which means that someone is close by. Let's keep movin'."

They advanced another twenty or thirty yards. Chivington spotted what appeared to be camouflaged hootches and thatched roofs 100 to 150 yards ahead. He raised his clenched fist, then pointed.

Wilson elevated his binos for a better look. He took a few moments to scan the surrounding area, then lowered his glasses and said, "Let's move in a little closer."

The village, set near another small stream, looked tranquil, with smoke from cooking fires drifting lazily toward a beautiful cobalt blue sky. Chivington saw children playing, but as the patrol drew closer, the air became saturated with a sick stench. Chivington stopped and looked around. Wilson tapped his shoulder and pointed. Chivington saw something on the ground but had to move closer before recognizing it as a tattered and bloodstained fatigue jacket with a dirty white nametag.

Then the odor, composed of blood, fecal matter, vomit, and human decay, hit with renewed force. Beside him, Wilson made a hissing sound of disgust.

"Jesus Christ, it's Martinez, Sarge!" gasped Pete Maddox, who had moved up for a look. "The fucking gooks—look what they did to 'im."

"Keep your voice down!" Wilson whispered. "Those fucking gooks might still be around here looking for more U.S. meat."

Chivington wanted to look away, but something inside compelled him to keep his eyes on what was left of Private First Class Juan Martinez. The young soldier lay face up. His left hand and part of his scalp were gone. He had been shot in the right shoulder. The wound was infested. So was the socket of his left eye. The eyeball had been gouged out and lay on the ground beside him, its tendons still attached, staring at the bright, blue sky.

Chivington's stomach was dry heaving. He finally broke the spell and turned away, sure that he was going to lose his breakfast, sucking in several deep breaths of air.

The night before Jackson's patrol moved out, Martinez had talked about his family in Puerto Rico. He had several brothers and sisters, and Chivington remembered thinking that it was a strong family, held together by a lot of love and caring. Juan had planned to use the G.I. Bill to study veterinary medicine.

"Mom and Dad are gettin' pretty old," he'd said. "They've done so much for us kids, I want to make some good money so I can help 'em, and maybe they can rest a little."

Chivington felt a self-draining hatred for the Viet Cong who had done this to Juan. They had stolen this young soldier's future, and they had made his final moments an agonizing hell.

"Sons of bitches," he heard Wilson mutter.

"W-why the l-left hand, Sarge?" Mitchell asked, sounding as shaken as Chivington felt.

"Because he was a dog handler," Wilson replied. "The VC have a bounty on dog handlers. A hand and a dog's ear are worth a lot to a VC bounty hunter. These bastards are scared shitless of the dogs. After they cut off the ear, they usually gut 'em, skin 'em, and then put 'em on a spit and chow down. Dog meat is a delicacy here."

"Yeah, but...they didn't get the dog's ear," Mitchell pointed out.

"They were probably still hopin' to get 'im. Or maybe the hand's enough. How the hell should I know?" Wilson turned to Maddox. "I need radio contact with base camp, and...what the fuck's wrong with you?"

Maddox turned away, heaving his guts out. Chivington barely kept his own breakfast down. Martinez was the first serious war casualty any of them had seen, complete with the effluvium of dead flesh, blood, and heat. It was much worse than anything they could have imagined.

"Sorry, Sarge," Maddox said at last, wiping his mouth with the back of his hand. He pushed up his glasses. "I ain't never seen nothin' like this before."

"If you're done puking, get base camp and tell 'em we need a medevac." Wilson turned to Chivington. "Keep your eyes and ears open. We don't want those fuckers sneakin' up on us." Then, to Mitchell, "You and Walker put Martinez in a poncho. Then set 'im aside for medevac—"

"Jesus, Sarge," Walker said, shaking his head, averting his eyes from the corpse. His shoulders drooped, and he didn't look nearly as tough as he had before they'd left base camp. "I can't—"

"The fuck you can't," Wilson interrupted, his voice taking on a hard edge that Chivington hadn't heard before. "This isn't a fuckin' picnic we're on. Get it done, and I mean *now*. Look for the dog tag off his boot. The VC got the one from around his neck. We've got to find the rest of the team."

Chivington stepped back, scanning the surroundings, glad for an excuse to put distance between himself and the dead soldier. With great reluctance, keeping their faces averted as much as possible, Mitchell and Walker wrapped the foul-smelling and bloated corpse in the makeshift body bag and carried it to the edge of a nearby clearing. Chivington heard one of them retching back there, but he wasn't sure who it was.

Maddox finally made contact and arranged for the medevac.

At Wilson's order, they lined up in formation and began inching their way toward the village, their eyes and ears alert to danger. The patrol hadn't gone far before they came upon two naked and decapitated GIs tethered back-to-back to a tree.

None of them spoke as they gathered around this new horror. They had already seen too much.

Chivington knew that the white man was Specialist Four John Allen, and the black one was Sergeant Jackson, and now he knew why the VC were so feared and loathed. They had relocated Allen's white head onto Jackson's black body, and Jackson's black head onto Allen's white body. The black man's bloody organ was crammed in the white man's jaw, and the white man's penis was jammed in the black man's blood-soaked mouth. Their ring fingers were gone.

Chivington pulled his eyes away and scanned the surroundings, listening for any sounds suggesting that the VC were still around.

Wilson was the first to speak. His voice was hoarse with emotion. "Jackson was a brother and damned well respected. Look at his arm...full of cigarette burns. And look at that right hand. Some of the nails have been pulled off. The VC tried to get information about Phan Rang out of 'im. Poor, poor bastard, how he must've suffered."

Stone-like, they rolled Jackson and Allen in green ponchos, making sure the severed body parts wouldn't fall out, and moved their bodies back to the edge of the clearing, laying them next to Martinez.

Maddox called base camp to report the discovery of the two bodies. Now he held the handset out to Wilson. "Captain Wojtacha wants to speak with you."

Wilson reached for the radiophone. "Red Rover, this is Wilson, over." He listened for a moment, then said, "At this time, we have three dogwood sixes and two MIAs, sir. Over."

Dogwood sixes meant dead bodies, Chivington knew, although "dead body" seemed barely adequate to describe what had been done to Martinez, Jackson, and Allen.

"Roger that, sir," Wilson said. "We'll proceed. Over and out." He returned the handset to Maddox and said, "The Captain says that elements of the 274th NVA Regiment are within a few clicks of our coordinates. They're a crack outfit. They also have VC support."

"Then they're the cocksuckers that did this," Maddox said, nodding his head at the three corpses. He adjusted his glasses, which always seemed to be slipping down his nose. "Let's take out a few of 'em and even things up."

Wilson turned to stare at Maddox. "You really think that's a good idea, Maddox, the five of us going up against a well-trained force of unknown size? Is that what we're out here for, so we can all get killed, too, and have our heads and cocks cut off?"

"Well, fuck," Maddox muttered. "We can't just let 'em get away with this."

"Tell ya what, Maddox," Wilson said. Chivington realized that the sergeant was about to explode. "You go after 'em. Make sure you leave that radio with us, though, and don't expect us to come in and save your ass." He shook his head, then turned to look at the cluster of hootches, now only a few hundred yards away. "Captain Wojtacha wants us to take a closer look at that vill." He nodded at Chivington. "You're on point. Be damned careful. Charlie could be hangin' around, waitin' for some more dumb motherfuckers to step into their trap. Watch out for booby traps, tripwires, and any signs of recent movement through vegetation."

Chivington, adrenaline surging, took his place up front, and led the patrol toward the hootches. One step forward, look to the left, to the right, to the front, another step...

By 1100, the heat and humidity had added to the miserable conditions. Everyone except Maddox had removed his fatigue jacket from under his flak vest. They all stank.

The patrol stopped just inside the tree line, about thirty yards from the village. That was when Chivington became aware that the trees around them were especially quiet. He stopped, his eyes moving through alternating patches of bright sunlight and shade, looking for anything out of the ordinary.

He glanced back at Wilson and saw that he, too, seemed troubled by the tomblike atmosphere. Stan Mitchell, bringing up the rear, turned to scan the area behind them, then turned back and made eye contact with Chivington. He acknowledged, indicating that everything looked okay back there.

Chivington looked at Wilson, who motioned for him to move out of the trees and continue on to the village.

Chivington didn't like that idea, but he knew Wilson was right. They couldn't stay here forever just because things didn't feel right.

They had barely cleared the tree line when gunfire erupted from their left. Chivington spun around in time to see Mitchell throw up his hands and go down hard.

"Down!" Wilson screamed.

They all hit the ground as a trail of bullets chewed the earth around them. A vicious storm of stray sounds had them engulfed.

"Back to the trees!" Wilson yelled. "Stay down! Find cover!"

Bending low, Chivington ran to Mitchell and threw himself down flat beside him. Luckily, Mitchell fell into a ditch which provided some cover from the fire. Chivington could detect the scent of fresh blood.

"Mitchell, can you move? This ain't a good place to be."

Mitchell gagged and turned. Chivington was shocked by what he saw. A bullet hit Mitchell in the lower jaw, leaving a ragged, bloody wound. Through it, Chivington could see pieces of shattered jawbone and a few remaining teeth. The rest had been blown out through his cheek. Mitchell's matted hair was bloody and dirty.

"Ca…ca…"

"Don't try to talk," Chivington said, feeling weak and nauseous. *Christ, how can he still be conscious?* "You're gonna be fine, Mitchell." There was nothing Chivington could do for him while they were so exposed. They had to get back to the tree line with the others. "We gotta move back. We're sittin' ducks out here."

Mitchell nodded his head in agreement.

Chivington looked around, taking stock. Heavy sniping was coming from a clump of vegetation and small trees just ahead of them, fifty yards or so away; most of the fire was going into the trees behind them, where the rest of the team had taken cover. Chivington and Mitchell were shielded from a direct line of fire, but that could change at any moment if the NVA changed their position. Chivington knew that if he and Mitchell moved, they would draw attention.

Then something tapped his shoe. He swung around. Gripping his M-16, Walker lay on his belly behind them. His thumb snapped back toward the tree line.

"Get 'im back there," he yelled over the sound of gunfire. "Go straight back. I'll cover ya if any of those bastards start shootin' this way."

It was their only chance to move Mitchell to cover. Chivington glanced over at Mitchell, trying not to wince at the terrible wound. Mitchell was losing blood, much of it pooled under him.

"Can ya do it?" Chivington asked.

Mitchell seemed to consider the question, then nodded. Above the wreckage of his lower face, his eyes looked surprisingly alert.

"All right." Chivington glanced forward through the smoky haze. "Let's go!"

He rose, grabbed Mitchell under his arms and pulled him past Walker. Bent and zigzagging, Walker, on full automatic, poured rounds into the NVA position.

Chivington, fearing death, stopped twice to help Mitchell. They finally reached the tree line and collapsed behind a fallen log beside Wilson.

"Christ," Wilson muttered after a glance at Mitchell. "We gotta stop that bleedin'."

Gasping, still trying to get his breath, Chivington tore off his shirt and wrapped it around Mitchell's head, stuffing extra cloth into the wound area. Whatever inner store of energy that had kept Mitchell going had ended. He was in shock.

Ten feet away, Chivington saw Maddox huddled behind a huge tree and screaming into the handset. "For Chrissake, get us some fuckin' help out here!"

Chivington turned and looked toward the clump of trees and vegetation, spotting three NVA. They were moving to one side, making a concerted effort to get Walker, still lying on his belly, struggling to get behind the tree line. Wilson was firing into another clump of vegetation to his left. Chivington heard bullets smacking into trees around them, ample proof that somebody was shooting back.

Chivington tuned out everything else that was happening around him, focusing his attention on the three gooks zeroing in on Walker. He steadied his M-16 against the tree trunk, lining up the top of his front sight blade on the face of one khaki-clad soldier hiding behind a small tree. The NVA's AK-47 bore on Walker. The gook was still, apparently forgetting in his zeal to take out Walker. The others had made it back to the tree line.

Chivington squeezed off a burst of four rounds, seeing the top of the NVA's head explode in a gout of blood. The body tumbled back and disappeared beneath a sea of green foliage.

Gritting his teeth, Chivington swung the weapon to the spot where he had last seen another enemy soldier, and waited patiently, ignoring the continuing clatter of gunfire all around him. When the man appeared around the trunk of a tree, firing his AK-47, Chivington squeezed off a few rounds that found their mark. The NVA jerked as if he had been hit by an invisible fist, then vanished from sight.

Then, from somewhere in the distance, Chivington heard the *whump-whump-whump* of choppers. That was the sweetest sound. Two Huey gunships were headed in their direction.

Wilson heard them as well. He waited until the sound grew louder, then plucked a yellow smoke grenade from his web gear, pulled the pin, and threw it into the clearing.

Like huge dragonflies, the Hueys glided over the trees. They hit the thicket of trees hard with .30-caliber machine guns and rockets as Maddox, clutching the handset, directed them. The gooks gave up and retreated.

Chivington saw several people go down, torn to pieces by the machine guns, flopping on the ground like beached trout before lying still. Fire, black smoke, and explosions rocked the village. The smell of torn vegetation, blood, and cordite reached Chivington. He knew that since the enemy were using the village, either for shelter or as a staging area, it would be destroyed. He could only hope there weren't too many civilians in those hootches.

Then he saw Walker struggling, trying to make his way back toward the trees. Chivington realized that Walker was wounded. His left arm dangled at his side, dark with blood. His face was pallid.

"Medevac's on the way," Maddox yelled, still holding the handset.

Wilson leaned Walker against a tree. He reached into the first-aid kit and handed Walker a dime-sized morphine tablet. "Don't chew or crunch it. Swallow it whole." He tossed another to Chivington, nodding toward Mitchell.

Chivington laid down his M-16 and turned to Mitchell, wondering how the man could swallow a pill with half of his jaw blown away, but then he realized Mitchell didn't need the pill. He was dead.

With pumping adrenaline, Chivington swallowed hard, still looking at the corpse. He steadied himself.

Finally, he raised his eyes. The gunships had ceased firing, still prowling the area above the treetops. A medevac chopper arrived and drifted toward them. Its nose lifted to slow its speed. With its main rotor slapping the humid air, the pilot lowered the chopper at the last second, kicked up a cloud of dust, and set down on a Landing Zone (LZ) near the edge of the tree line.

Mitchell's body was loaded onto the chopper. Walker was put on a stretcher and taken aboard. Then Wilson directed the medevac pilot back to the clearing behind them, where they had left the three bodies from Jackson's patrol.

"Pick 'em up, then head out," Wilson told the pilot. "We're gonna take a look at that vill."

The pilot agreed. Increasing the pitch on the blades, the Huey slowly lifted off the ground, moving at treetop level back to the clearing, where it landed long enough for the remaining bodies to be boarded. A moment later, it rose again and disappeared in the direction of the Cam Ranh field hospital and the military morgue in Saigon.

To prevent the NVA from returning, the gunships remained in the area. Maddox was in constant communication with the choppers as the three men entered the village. Spaced about ten feet apart, they were wary of booby traps and tunnels.

The village was a disaster area. Many of the thatch-roofed hootches were still burning. Scattered about were several tipped-over jugs of precious rice.

"I hear someone behind that hootch," Chivington said, pointing.

Cautiously walking around to the other side, they found a bony, toothless woman with a black rag covering her head. She rocked back and forth, cradling a naked baby and moaning.

"Con toi, Con toi, Con toi," she wailed.

"Her baby's dead," Chivington said. "She's grievin'."

Beside her sat two small, barefoot boys in dirty white shirts and dark shorts. They looked at the soldiers with large, mournful eyes. A Vietnamese man squatted beside the woman. Balding, with a long, gray goatee, his hollowed eyes were also watery.

Wilson pointed to the old man and asked, "Ba? Ba?"

The old man nodded.

"He's the father," said Wilson.

"Lam on Kiem Bac Si Cho Con Toi," the old man rambled. "VC, VC, VC, bu-ku VC…VC beaucoup dien cai tau… [VC crazy…]"

Feeling oddly emotionless, Chivington turned away, and the three of them continued to inspect the remaining hootches. In the far corner of the village, near the animal pen, they saw the village chief hanging from a tree, his head grotesquely cocked, bare feet almost touching the ground, entrails exposed and rotting, and covered with flies.

"Cut 'im down," Wilson ordered, his voice hard. "This is what Charlie does. He uses fear and intimidation to freeze the minds and hearts of these poor fuckin' people. He terrorizes by selection, and then grabs 'em by the nuts. Their hearts and minds follow, like it or not." He turned to Maddox, who was staring in space. "Get base camp. I need the Captain."

Chivington removed his knife from the scabbard, cut the rope holding the dead body, and stepped back as the body fell in a heap at his feet. Returning the knife to his belt, he bent and straightened out the man's limbs and turned him so that he lay on his back, providing him a small measure of dignity.

Speaking with the captain, Wilson told him that this village was a staging area for weapons and food, and doubtless was a listening post on Phan Rang. It would also be a logical arena for sapper units planning to sabotage or assault the air base.

When he returned the handset to Maddox, he told them that the remaining villagers would be air-evacuated to a new area. Some would be interrogated.

Maddox pointed toward the pen, where the village animals were kept. "What are we gonna do with the animals?"

"Shoot 'em, then burn 'em," Wilson ordered.

Chivington turned to stare at him. "We can't do that!"

"Yes, we can," Wilson said. "Otherwise, the VC will get 'em."

Chivington shook his head. Despite all of the unspeakable things he had seen in the past few hours, this was a line he could not cross. "I can't shoot pigs, ducks, and a water buffalo."

"Goddammit, I'm givin' you an order—"

"Then you'll have to court-martial me," Chivington said, not flinching from Wilson's steel gaze. "Fuck it. I'm not doin' it."

"Son of a bitch, Chivington—" Wilson stopped and shook his head. He glanced at Maddox, who had had the good sense to stay out of it. Then Wilson shook his head again. "All right, turn 'em loose, goddammit, but if Ricci finds out, we're both up shit creek."

Chivington unhooked the creaky gate, and the animals wandered off to fend for themselves. Chivington hoped that a farmer might find them.

"All right," Wilson said, looking around. "I think we're ready to haul ass."

"Aren't we gonna look for the other two men from Jackson's patrol?" Maddox asked.

Wilson shook his head. "There's no tellin' where they are. It's too dangerous to poke around here any longer. A whole company of gooks could be headed this way by now."

"Maybe they've been taken prisoner," Chivington suggested.

Wilson turned and looked at him as if he'd just made the dumbest statement in the history of mankind. "Didn't ya see what the fuckers did to Martinez, Jackson, and Allen?"

"Well, yeah, but—"

"Did it look to you like they're takin' prisoners?"

Chivington thought about that, then shook his head. "I guess not."

Wilson turned to Maddox. "Get us a ride outta here. I'm sick of this fuckin' place."

Maddox spoke into the handset, and the three men headed back to the clearing. One of the gunships touched down, and they climbed aboard.

"We got one more piece of business to take care of," Wilson said. He went up to the pilot, directing him to the spot where they had seen the grave mounds earlier.

After the mounds had been opened up with rocket fire, it was clear that Wilson's suspicions had been correct: The coffins held arms and ammunition. A few more well-placed rockets took care of that, then the helicopter turned toward base camp at Phan Rang.

"As my daddy the preacher man used to say after a bad day," Wilson said, "please, dear God, let me live to see another day…but not one like this."

Amen, Chivington thought.

Chivington leaned back, closing his eyes, reflecting on the events of the past few hours. Only days before, he wondered if he could kill another human being. Then he saw what the gooks had done to his buddies. When the time came, he killed without giving it a second thought. He felt no remorse. It was survival. This war had neutralized his conscience. He doubted whether he could ever be the same.

Chapter 5

Lieutenant Colonel Ricci, battalion commander of the 62nd Engineers at Phan Rang, frowned as Captain Wojtacha, sitting in an armchair across the desk from him, briefed him on Sergeant Wilson's patrol.

"Dammit!" Ricci muttered. All five men in Jackson's patrol were KIA or POW. One of Wilson's men was dead, and another in an Air Force field hospital at Cam Ranh Bay. Losing six men was bad enough—Ricci's worst loss since arriving in Vietnam—but hearing how the enemy had tortured some of them was more than he could bear. "Goddammit! Haven't those bastards heard of the Geneva Conventions?"

"Apparently not, sir," Captain Wojtacha said grimly. He told Ricci about destroying the cache of weapons and supplies in and around the village.

"Well, that's something, at least," Ricci said, leaning back in his chair. "How about that dog?"

Wojtacha stared at him. "The dog, sir?"

"The Dobie. Martinez's dog."

"He's at the animal hospital, sir, in Cam Ranh."

"Is he gonna make it?"

The captain nodded. "The vet thinks he'll pull through, sir."

"Then he'll be comin' back to duty?"

"I don't know, sir. If you'd like, I'll call Doc Blevins and find out."

"That won't be necessary. I'll check on 'im. Thank you, Captain."

After Wojtacha had gone, Ricci sat staring at the stack of paperwork on his desk. Outside, heavy equipment engines growled. His office, inside a bunker that was surrounded by sandbags piled chest high and five feet thick, was small and uncluttered: a neat wooden desk, a green metal filing cabinet, a swivel chair that had seen better days, and the wooden visitor's chair which Wojtacha had just vacated.

Ricci knew that he had to notify the families of the men who were killed in action. He dreaded that. He also needed to visit Private Walker, who was recovering at the field hospital. He had planned to make the short hop to Cam Ranh anyway in order to inquire about available materials at the Cam Ranh Bay Engineer Supply Yard.

Geno Ricci was a stocky, barrel-chested, dark-haired, thirty-seven-year-old Italian-American who loved his men and the U.S. Army. He was not prone to self-analysis, but he knew he sometimes took things personally. His sense of responsibility was almost too keen—a product of his parents' rearing.

He also detested this war. From the outset, he felt that the struggle in Vietnam was compromised by failed strategy—or no strategy at all. A "just war," he thought, was fought for strategic, not tactical objectives, but he couldn't let his personal feelings prevent him from doing his job. Engineers in Vietnam had three major construction objectives: airfields, supply routes, and port facilities. General William Westmoreland considered airfields to be their number one priority. In a nutshell, the 62nd's goal was to improve the mobility of the good guys and impede the mobility of the bad ones.

More specifically, Ricci's function was to build a secure tactical air base. In order to get the job done, he had to stay focused. He had to convince Colonel Remus at the yard that he needed several tents, vehicles, weapons, lumber, and medical supplies. He was likewise hoping for additional sentry dogs to assist in securing the perimeter.

Ricci's eyes returned to the stack of paperwork on his desk and a copy of Churchill's *The Gathering Storm;* he was reminded of the Churchillian admonition: "Never, never give up." Sighing and realizing a sense of urgency, Geno began leafing through it, searching for further understanding of what he was doing.

#

Three hours later, Ricci gave Sergeant Major Will Young a litany of what-to-do instructions. Young was

Ricci's right-hand man. When the colonel arrived at the chopper pad, he had confidence that Young would carry out his orders with precision.

As the chopper lifted and headed north, Geno settled back. From the air, Phan Rang looked like a small, dusty, makeshift peninsula, but it would look more like a real air base before long, complete with a landing strip 10,000 feet long and 102 feet wide.

The cantonment areas for the 101st Airborne and the USAF units were under construction. Plans called for a water tower (already in place), storage facilities, generators, officer and enlisted barracks, showers, a mess kitchen, a supply area, maybe a small gym, and improved drum latrines. Most of the buildings would have raised wooden floors and electricity.

Heavy equipment had already arrived by landing barge; light trucks came by convoy under the code name "Operation Essayons."

Ricci faced formidable roadblocks, such as material shortages. He had requisitioned another shipment of generators, water pumps, water purification units, and spare parts from the Engineer Supply Yard. He'd also authorized the purchase of some of these items in the neighborhood market, but like most American capitalists, the local merchants raised prices based on the law of supply and demand.

At no other period in U.S. military history was the pressure greater on Army engineers than at this time in Vietnam. With the alarming rate of troop buildup at Cam

Ranh Bay, Long Binh, Tan Son Nhut, Bien Hoa, and elsewhere, Ricci knew the U.S. Army Engineer Command Vietnam (18th Brigade) expected the 62nd Engineers to complete their mission at Phan Rang.

The North Vietnam Army would attempt to dissect the country along the Pleiku, An Khe, and Qui Nhon axes. The NVA were doing a damned good job of interrupting traffic and communications along Highway 19, a paved-surface main artery running east-west along this center line. If Pleiku were overrun, the NVA would control Highway 19, as well as the coast of Qui Nhon. That was unacceptable. The onus of prevention fell on the engineers. Of the approximate twenty-three thousand U.S. soldiers stationed in Vietnam in mid-1965, fewer than one hundred were engineers.

To make matters worse, General Westmoreland's "Rotational Hump Directive" mandated that troops leave Vietnam after a twelve-month tour of duty. Brigade and regimental officers moved on after six months of duty. Ricci tried to limit the loss of manpower by extending tours a month or more.

Ricci compared the rotation policy to a football team forever replacing players and never winning. He changed men as a football coach traded players, just to keep a good balance of experienced veterans on hand. To plug holes, Ricci obtained permission to bring in additional replacements with a non-engineering Military Occupational Specialty (MOS).

Base construction called for more seasoned regulars who were capable of handling expensive and complicated equipment. The young draftee with limited training hindered that effort.

Ricci started an in-country training program to train nationals as laborers, carpenters, masons, and mechanics. Candidates had to be screened to avoid fifth-column infiltration. Because of South Vietnam's rural economy, few skilled workers were available in the labor pool; most of them had already been scooped up by civilian contractors such as Raymond International and Morrison-Knudsen.

Adding to the challenge of constructing a base under such conditions, Ricci knew all too well that it was vulnerable to Viet Cong sapper probes. Many in the U.S. military referred to sappers as "ragged little bastards in black pajamas." Ricci understood the threat to his base. He also knew that sappers were skilled saboteurs and terrorists trained to infiltrate fixed installations and base camps like Phan Rang. Heavily camouflaged, sappers were known to take five days to crawl five hundred yards in order to accomplish a mission. Known as *Dac Con* in Vietnamese, sappers were trained in reconnaissance, infiltration and exfiltration, assault tactics, and pyrotechnics—their signature tactic. A favorite explosive device was the "bicycle bomb." For detonation, they used a wristwatch as a timer. They also employed AK-47s, satchel charges, and rocket propelled grenades (RPG).

Viet Cong sappers were Ricci's main concern because water and jet fuel pipelines were vulnerable to attack.

External air base security had not become an issue until the Bien Hoa Air Base was hit by VC mortars in November 1964, killing thirty Americans and destroying five aircraft. To prevent further attacks like Bien Hoa, forty USAF sentry dogs and their handlers arrived on July 17, 1965 to secure these base perimeters. They were the first American dog teams in Vietnam. Beauregard was among them.

A watchtower equipped with high-intensity floodlights, machine guns, and night-vision scopes had been erected at every corner of the Phan Rang perimeter. Claymore mines, trip flares, and booby traps reinforced the sentries. Scoops, dozers, and backhoes were used to clear trees, other vegetation, and to dig drainage trenches around the perimeter. Low terrain and high water tables in most of Vietnam created tough problems for drainage and earth moving.

Another twenty-foot-high observation tower would be coming in from 18th Brigade headquarters by CH-47A Chinook helicopter within the next few days; that would improve security. Ricci wanted additional dog teams, as well as more floodlights and watchtowers.

Part of the 62nd's tactical combat support role would continue to include mine sweeping, recon patrols, and land clearing. These operations were designed to plow through booby-trapped areas to protect the infantry.

Engineers would also attempt to disrupt tunnels used by Charlie to warehouse supplies and ammo, and to shelter wounded troops.

Ricci wanted to do more than provide military support in Vietnam. He wanted to build permanent thoroughfares, not just military roads as the French had built during WWII. He was considering the future of Vietnam and the current pacification process. He was further motivated by Engineer Commander Brigadier General Robert Ploger's *Eight Objectives and Standards* for American engineers in Vietnam. Objective Number Eight read: *Remember, we are seeking to establish a temporary lodging in the homeland of others; that we owe this country and our fellows-in-arms every available assistance in developing a sound economy and improved environment.*

Well-built roads would improve travel between villages and make it easier for farmers to transport goods, thus improving the economic and social lives of these people. Ricci was in Vietnam not to demolish, but to develop—and that brought him to one of his stickier problems. To complete the airstrip and tactical roads, he needed immediate access to a rock quarry. He had become aware of a quarry in the Central Highlands near An Khe, nearly two hundred miles north of Phan Rang. It was the operating headquarters of the 1st Cavalry Division (Airmobile), as well as the historic 7th Calvary Regiment of General George A. Custer fame.

Ricci envisioned the Chinook sling hauling 28,000-pound loads of rock to Phan Rang. The Chinook, or

"Go-Go Bird," could transport CH-54s, 105mm Howitzers, and sling-loaded Hueys.

Getting sufficient wood for construction was a top priority. A serious lumber shortage existed because of NVA and VC activity in the area as well as a lack of a significant lumber industry in Vietnam. Wood had to be imported.

Ricci was interested in an area northeast of the base. It would be a good place for a sawmill. Unfortunately, it was a VC rest area. Ricci could provoke a counterattack on Phan Rang.

The chopper began its descent. They were approaching Cam Ranh Bay. An odd assortment of buses, cars, motor scooters, and military vehicles were traveling in random fashion. Driving in Cam Ranh required survival instinct; only those with the quickest reflexes endured. Beyond the city, he could see the beautiful white, sun-bleached, sandy beaches. It was silica sand (used in glass making).

Cam Ranh was the largest and safest logistical base in South Vietnam. Ricci saw many tents protected by sandbags. There were also many wooden structures: mess halls, a dispensary, the field hospital, a BX, clubs for enlisted men and officers, and the animal hospital. The 35th Engineer Construction group planned to construct a laundry, a concrete runway, a milk-recombining plant, a two-thousand-bed hospital, a library, and a mini-version California-style Gold's Gym.

Ricci heard that Cam Ranh engineers employed numerous South Vietnamese war widows as laborers. Most were under five feet tall and weighed one hundred pounds or less. They were known as "little tiger ladies."

Unlike the city, the base appeared neat and organized. Many combat troop units were temporarily stationed at Cam Ranh, including elements of the 173rd Airborne Brigade, the 101st Airborne Division, the 1st Air Cavalry, the 1st Infantry Division, the 18th Engineer Brigade, and the South Korean 1st (Capitol-Tiger) Infantry Division, who ran their morning miles barefooted. Soldiers and airmen, some dressed in faded jungle fatigues, others in neatly pressed khakis, came and went.

As the chopper touched down, Ricci glanced at his wristwatch and saw that it was a little past 1600. Even though it had recently rained, the air coming through the open windows was onerous, like a steam bath.

Well, I didn't come here for R&R, he reminded himself.

Chapter 6

Ricci stepped out of the chopper onto the sand-like soil that was typical of Cam Ranh after a rain. A jeep pulled up beside him.

"Welcome to Cam Ranh Bay, sir," the young driver said cheerfully, saluting. "Colonel Remus from Brigade headquarters sent me to escort ya 'round the base."

Ricci nodded, tossing his duffle bag into the back of the jeep. "Thanks. I appreciate the lift. Here's my agenda: the field hospital, the animal hospital, and the Cam Ranh Engineer Supply Yard. I'll work out the details later with Colonel Remus."

"Yes, sir." The driver waited until Ricci settled into the seat beside him, then revved the engine, shifted gears, and sped off.

Moments later, the jeep stopped in front of the field hospital, a two-story wooden building with an eye-catching credo above the entrance: *We treat them. God heals them.*

Ricci climbed out of the jeep, told the driver he expected to be only a few minutes, and stepped through the main entrance. The place was clean and tidy, with large fans stirring the humid air. He went to the information desk, explained who he was, and asked to see Private Walker. He was given the ward number and directions.

Twin-sized metal cots lined the walls, covered with white sheets and blue, military-issue blankets. He never liked hospitals, especially after seeing his wife Marilyn die in one. He felt anxious and jittery.

He took a deep, steadying breath before reaching Walker's bed. A blond nurse, her back to Ricci, was changing the bandage on Walker's left arm. Next to the bed was an IV stand, and a clear line that fed fluids into the back of Walker's right hand. He was either asleep or unconscious.

Ricci glanced at the nurse, then did a double-take. There was something familiar about her. He paused. With dry lips, he said, "Excuse me, I'm here to see Private Walker."

She completed her work with the bandage and turned to face him. Ricci, frozen in place, stared at her with widened eyes. It was Captain Barbara Brewer.

Babs recovered more quickly than Ricci. She turned and gave him a fierce hug. "I'll be damned! Geno, you handsome devil. You're a sight for sore eyes. What in the hell are you doin' twelve thousand miles from home in this godforsaken place? This sure is a long way from Fort Bragg. How long has it been?"

"Um, four or five years, I believe," he said, feeling a little flustered. "You're still as beautiful as ever, and Air Force?" This was not idle flattery. Babs was a full-figured, twenty-eight-year-old, startling blue-eyed blond with classic bone structure, from Alexandria, Virginia. She stood about 5'6". Because of her ailing father, Babs had taken a break in service from the U.S. Army, but once Vietnam became a full-blown war, she felt compelled to return, this time as an Air Force nurse.

"It's warm, isn't it?" She wiped his brow with a soft towel, then turned to position a fan directly in front of her patient.

All of a sudden, Ricci remembered why he was here. Feeling a little guilty for the lapse in focus, he turned his attention back to the soldier in bed. Walker's left arm was concealed by the new bandage. His eyes were closed. His chest rose and fell in even breaths.

"How is he?" Ricci asked quietly.

"Not good," Babs said, turning to look down at Walker. "We're tryin' to get the infection under control. The doctor says there's only a fifty-fifty chance that the arm can be saved. He's heavily sedated right now. The next twenty-four hours will be critical. We'll know more then."

Private Walker, Ricci remembered, was only twenty-one years old. "Let's hope for the best," he said.

"We always do," Babs said, turning back to Ricci and reaching out to squeeze his hand. "He's in good hands, Geno."

After Babs completed her rounds, she and Ricci walked back through the ward to the main entrance. Holding her hand, he said, "How about a drink at the officers' club tonight? We can catch up on old times."

"I thought you'd never ask," she said, giving him the sparkling, fetching smile that he remembered so well. "I'm off duty at 1900. Pick me up at the nurses' tent. We can walk from there."

#

I'll be damned, Ricci thought, as the chauffeur drove toward the animal hospital. It had been an unexpected pleasure to see Babs. He had met her while he was a patient at Womack Army Hospital located at Fort Bragg, North Carolina. He'd blown a knee during a parachute jump, and she was a nurse on the ward. They had formed a strong bond during the two weeks he had spent under her care.

They had stayed in touch over the next few months. He remembered taking her to see *West Side Story* at one of the many theaters at Fort Bragg. Later, after his knee had regained its strength, they had danced at the main post officers' club to Percy Faith's "A Summer Place."

Of course, their friendship had been platonic, because Ricci was married, and very much in love with his wife, Marilyn.

In the two years since her death, Geno hadn't looked twice at another woman. Nobody would ever be able to take Marilyn's place. It wasn't something he wanted to think about. He felt guilty that he had asked Babs to have a drink with him.

We're just good friends, he said to himself. *Babs is a good person. It'll be nice to talk with her again.*

As the jeep rolled to a stop in front of the animal hospital, Ricci's mind shifted back to the problem at hand: the well-being of his dog, Beau.

Green grass surrounded the animal hospital, while banana and fan palms provided abundant shade. From an open window, the tail end of a pair of red cotton curtains flapped in the breeze. Sandbags covered the roof and were stacked chest high around the building.

Ricci asked the driver to wait while he walked towards the building's entrance. Along the side were dog kennels under canvas tents. Several dogs tethered to their crates on six-foot chains watched him with interest—and not all of it was friendly. As far as he could see, they were all German Shepherds. The Shepherd was the military dog of choice in Vietnam, especially the Belgian Shepherd, because of fewer cases of hip dysplasia.

Ricci opened the door and stepped into a narrow corridor. The first door to the left was open. When Ricci looked inside, he found a small office. The furnishings were sparse: a burnished oak desk, ladder-back wooden chairs for visitors, and a dark green filing cabinet. A healthy philodendron along the window ledge added a little atmosphere. On the desktop was a nameplate: "Captain Jake F. Blevins."

The stocky airman standing beside the desk looking at a medical chart was much too young to be Captain Blevins. When Ricci knocked on the doorjamb, the man looked up. He seemed surprised to find a lieutenant colonel standing before him. He saluted crisply.

"Good mornin', sir. I'm Airman Second Class Robert Slater. How can I help you?"

"I'd like to speak with Captain Blevins about one of my sentry dogs," Ricci said. "His name is Beauregard, tattoo number A119."

Airman Slater nodded. "The Dobie, sir?"

"Yeah, that's the one."

There was a pause. The airman looked uncomfortable. "Well, sir, the doctor should return at any minute. He's over at the field hospital lookin' for supplies."

"Supplies?" Ricci repeated. "At the hospital?"

"Yes, sir. We use tetracycline for infection in dogs, the same as humans. We also need gauze, bandages, ointments, aspirin…well, ya get the picture, sir. We don't have enough supplies and medicine to do the job."

Ricci thought for a moment. "Maybe I can help. I'll speak to someone about that. Any chance of seein' Beau?"

"Yes, sir. He's crated in the back room, where it's cool." Again, Ricci noticed the uneasy look across the young airman's features.

"How is he doin'?" Ricci asked.

"Not so well, sir. He's thin and full of infection. That leg looks like it might have to come off. If that happens, Dr. Blevins will probably feel that it would be more humane to put 'im down."

Just then, a tall, rumpled-looking man in his early thirties sauntered into the room. "Welcome, Colonel," he said, with a wide, toothy grin. "I'm Dr. Jake Blevins, but everyone calls me Doc. How can I help you?"

Ricci got right to the point. "The black and tan Doberman, Doc. What're his chances?"

The veterinarian frowned. "Hmm, not that good, I'm afraid. He's not respondin' to treatment, which is disheartening, and we don't have all the medication that his wounds require. I scrounge what I can, but that only goes so far."

"I understand, Doc. Let me take a look at the dog and see what we can do."

They stepped out of the office and walked down the corridor to the back room. Ricci saw Beau lying on his side, filling the aluminum shipping crate used to contain him. A small oscillating fan pushed a steady stream of air over his wounds. His leg was bathed with Vaseline-like jelly and wrapped in white gauze. Also bandaged was his left ear, the wrap going around his jaw and over the top of his head. The dog's right ear was uncovered, and Ricci could see the four-letter service number.

As Ricci watched, Beau tried to lick his right front pad, but soon gave up.

"He's lost a lot of blood," Blevins explained. "That's one reason he's so weak, that, and the infection."

What happened out there, fella? Ricci wondered. Whatever it was, it had been traumatic, but there was still some life in the Doberman. When Ricci called his name, Beau's un-bandaged ear perked straight up. The dog lifted his head slightly and turned to look at Ricci. Their eyes met and held for a moment.

There is something special about this dog, Ricci thought.

"He's got some serious problems," said Blevins, consulting a clipboard that Slater had retrieved from his office. Each military dog had an official medical record that contained vital information such as his age, weight, height, where he began military service, his training record, and a picture of his profile. "He's not eatin' well. Even if we save his leg, I don't think his chances are good. His spirit is broken." The veterinarian glanced at Ricci. "I suppose it would be best to have him euthanized—"

"Isn't that premature, Doc?" Ricci said sharply.

Blevins frowned. "He won't be of much use if we have to take off that leg, and even if we save the leg, we don't have the time or manpower to nurse this dog back to duty status."

Flushed, Ricci turned to face Blevins. "What you're sayin' is that Beau is expendable, just like everything else in this fucking war. He's just a dog, and—"

"Hold on, Colonel," Doc said, raising a placating hand. "I didn't say—"

"I'm responsible for all of my men, Doc, including the three dogs assigned to the 62nd. They all count. I'll be goddamned if any of 'em are expendable, including this dog—not on my watch, not by any fucking standard."

"Yes, sir, Colonel," Blevins replied as he put the clipboard aside, "but that isn't the Army's position."

"Believe me, I'm aware of that." Ricci knew it wasn't fair to take out his bitterness and frustration on this veterinarian. Ricci was so damned sick of seeing lives squandered in this war. "If Beau dies, no one will hold a twenty-one gun salute. There will be no military burial, no white cross to mark his grave. Nobody will be giving him a Purple Heart."

Doc Blevins lifted an eyebrow. "You don't buy into that?"

"Hell, no. I'll make the final decision on this dog, Captain. Not you or anyone else. Do you read me?"

Blevins nodded, his lips turning up in a lopsided smile. "Loud and clear, Colonel. You like dogs, I take it?"

"You're damned right I do."

Blevins chuckled. "Then let's see what we can do for Beau." He turned and led the way back to his office. "Have a seat, Colonel. I'll see if I can scare up some refreshments."

Ricci sat on one of the uncomfortable wooden armchairs, drumming his fingers on the arm. A moment later, Blevins returned and sat down in the creaky chair behind his desk.

"Just to set the record straight, Colonel, as the unit veterinarian, I'm responsible for all military dogs that enter this kennel. It's my duty to prevent the spread of disease and treat injuries. So far, my record speaks for itself."

Ricci felt a little embarrassed by his earlier outburst. "I'm sure it does—"

"And I don't like the way these military dogs are being treated any more than you do. They save a lot of lives over here, and a lot of them are dyin' in the process. They deserve better, but I'm not the one who sets the policy. If you want to work with me on gettin' this dog back to duty status, I'll do what I can."

Ricci nodded, relieved. "Glad to hear it, Doc."

Slater returned with Cokes and cookies, and placed them on the desk.

"I have friends in the officers' mess," Blevins explained, smiling.

"It's been a long time since I've had a chocolate chip cookie." Ricci reached for one and bit off a huge chunk, then washed it down with Coke. *Ah, how easy it is to forget the simple pleasures.* "Okay, Doc, let's talk."

"First," Blevins said, "Beau has a shrapnel wound to his left ear. Dogs have a vein that runs around the margin of the ear. It's been hell to stop that bleeding. He keeps shakin' his head. After putting 'im under, I removed a small piece of metal fragment. I sutured and applied a pressure bandage to control the bleeding. So far, the sutures are holdin'. As for his leg wound, it's still infected, swollen, and needs constant cleaning. It's gotta be painful."

"He didn't look to be in too much pain," Ricci observed.

"Because it's abstract. Dogs are unable to communicate pain, but I've been monitoring his behavioral changes. They indicate pain. As you well know, Colonel, pain thresholds differ in animals, man or beast. There are no fractures in the leg—"

"Well, that's good news, isn't it?"

"Sure, but we have to get the infection under control, and for that we need more antibiotics like penicillin or streptomycin. Beau needs an intramuscular injection of cortisone—something else I don't have. As for his front pad, the callus is nearly off. Until a new one is formed, he's ineffective. If this were my San Francisco office, I'd say 'no problem,' but it's so damned hard to get what we need here."

"Enough said, Doc. I get the picture."

"I'm not sure that you do, Colonel," Blevins said. "Besides the medications, this dog will need a lot of care." He waved his hand in the general direction of the kennels outside. "You can see how many dogs we're takin' care of here. There's only so much that Slater and I can do. Your Dobie will need to have his bandages changed daily. He may have to be hand-fed until he gets his strength back. Mostly, he needs somebody who cares what happens to 'im. Once he regains his strength and starts to heal, he'll make it, but Slater and I can't spend an hour or two each day nursin' him back to health. I'm sorry, but that's the way it is."

Ricci frowned. "Surely there's somebody—"

"I don't even have time to look, Colonel. If you want your dog back, I'm afraid you'll have to find someone to give 'im TLC. I wish that wasn't the case, but for that matter, I wish we weren't even in this fucking place."

"You and me both, Doc." Ricci pushed back his chair and got to his feet. "Give me twenty-four hours to see what I can do."

Blevins lifted an eyebrow. "You have something in mind?"

"No," Ricci admitted. "Just promise you'll keep that dog alive for twenty-four hours, okay?"

"Okay, but what happens then?"

"If I haven't got the problem solved, then I'll go back to Phan Rang, and you can do whatever has to be done."

Blevins thought about that, then nodded. "Will do, Colonel—and I wish you all the luck."

#

After leaving the animal hospital, Ricci had time to shower and relax before meeting Babs for drinks.

In his assigned hootch, he tried to take care of some paperwork he'd brought with him along with Churchill's book but was too distracted. Finally, he lay down on his bunk, hands behind his head, staring up at the ceiling as if it might hold answers to his dilemma.

Why the hell was he so fixated on saving this dog? He had an air base to build, and he knew that he shouldn't let himself become distracted by a dog that would probably die anyway.

"You like dogs, I take it?" Doc Blevins had said.

Even after all these years, Doc's words brought back memories of Winston, the black and white mongrel that had been so much a part of Geno Ricci's life when he was a boy on his family's farm near McConnellsburg, Pennsylvania.

In high school, being 5'11" and 210 pounds, Geno had gravitated to the weight room and football field, relying on natural quickness, strength, and agility. He was an honor student and an all-state halfback who was offered full scholarships to Penn State, the University of Virginia, and the University of Maryland. He had chosen Maryland because of the coach and the School of Engineering, not to mention the cultural and intellectual value of the Washington, D.C. area.

Old Winston, blind and nearly deaf, died on the family farm two weeks before Geno's graduation. One of his true lifetime regrets was that he had not come home sooner to say goodbye to his old friend.

Months after graduating with a civil engineering degree from the University of Maryland, Ricci volunteered for military service. The Korean War began on June 25, 1950 and Lieutenant Ricci was assigned as a combat engineer to the Second Infantry Division.

That was where he'd had his first experience with military dogs. More than five hundred war dogs saw action in Korea, and there was no way to know how many lives they had saved. Many of them guarded supply depots, and some were still used to patrol the Demilitarized Zone (DMZ) along the 38th Parallel.

Ricci had witnessed the exemplary work of the 26th Scout Dog Platoon, whose logo read *Hell on Paws*. The dogs and their brave handlers had supported combat operations throughout the war. Like the Viet Cong, the Chinese and North Koreans had an almost supernatural fear of those dogs. The 26th Platoon received Silver and

Bronze Stars for gallantry in action and meritorious service.

After fifteen months in the war zone, Ricci was wounded and spent time recuperating at a U.S. Army hospital in Japan. He later returned to the United States. For his bravery, Captain Ricci was awarded a Purple Heart and a Bronze Star.

To pursue professional football, Ricci took a break in service. He was a member of an all-white Washington Redskins team, quarterbacked by the Little General, 5'7" Eddie Le Baron, whom he had befriended in Korea. He was signed to a short-term contract. This team was known more for its parties than the number of touchdowns it scored.

After three successful seasons with the Redskins, Ricci injured the anterior cruciate ligament in his right knee and decided to hang it up.

While maintaining his military status in the active reserve, he had returned to graduate school. Upon completion of his Master's degree, he had rejoined the Army. He had requested parachute training and was assigned to Jump School at Fort Bragg, North Carolina, with the 82nd Airborne Division.

On his fourth jump, the right knee had buckled, and he washed out of Jump School. The only good thing to come out of that experience was meeting Babs while he was laid up in the hospital.

Ricci was reassigned to Fort Leonardwood, Missouri, where he assumed command of the 62nd

Engineer Battalion. On the fifteenth anniversary of the Korean War, the 62nd was deployed to Vietnam.

"You like dogs, I take it?" Doc Blevins had said.

Yes, he did, but now he realized that his problems with the military went beyond the life or death of a dog. In a way, Beau's predicament symbolized everything that Ricci hated about this war. Having his men ambushed and tortured left him with an empty, angry feeling.

Ricci glanced at his GI-issue Swiss watch. It was late. He had let himself sink into a slump, and now he barely had time to meet Babs at the time they had agreed upon.

He got off the cot, straightened his clothes, and went to a small mirror on the wall so he could comb his close-cropped wavy hair recently trimmed at Phan Rang's jerry-built barber shop.

He recalled his own words to Doc Blevins. *"Beau is expendable, just like everything else in this fucking war."*

He realized then that there was more at stake than life and limb. It was too damned easy to lose one's self-respect over here; he couldn't let that happen.

Still looking in the mirror, he tested a smile, determined not to be morose when he met Babs. After a few tries, he found one that looked almost sincere.

Chapter 7

Ricci arrived at the nurses' tent just as Babs stepped out. The sky was darkening in the east but was streaked with orange, red, and purple light in the west.

"Hey, stranger!" she called cheerily, giving him a hug. "How did things work out at the animal hospital?"

"Not as well as I'd hoped," he said, "but let's not talk about that. Let's just enjoy the evening."

They walked the short distance to the officers' club where they were led to the back of the room and seated at a small, candle-lit table for two. The candle's warm glow added to the shadowy ambience. At one corner of the club, an old-fashioned jukebox worked overtime, playing favorites from the '50s and early '60s.

Both ordered bourbon and ginger ale and made small talk until the drinks arrived, but Ricci had to get something off his chest, so he decided to bring it up without delay. He took a healthy swallow of his drink, then set it on the table while looking across at Babs. "I don't know if you heard about my wife."

"I did, Geno." She reached across and touched the back of his hand. "I'm really sorry. What has it been…a couple of years?"

He nodded. "About two years ago." He offered a tentative smile. "December 22nd, one month after Kennedy's assassination. Long enough to start getting over it, I suppose."

"I don't think a person can ever get over something like that, Geno. Not entirely, anyway, but over time, it'll get easier."

"I hope so." He sipped his drink, wishing now that he hadn't mentioned it. A self-imposed hush hung between them.

"There's something else, Geno," Babs said at last, "something that's bothering you. What is it?"

He sighed. "I guess things are gettin' to me. This damned war, all the death and destruction, and no end in sight. It's all such a waste, Babs. We'll never win this war because the hearts and souls of the South Vietnamese people aren't in it. We're only kiddin' ourselves thinkin' we can save 'em."

She nodded with understanding. "I've been here for five months, Geno. Too many times, I've seen 'em loadin' coffins on the planes that fly out of here. Good people are in those boxes," she paused, her eyes on his, "but I can't stop the war. God knows, I wish I could. All I can do is try to make life more comfortable for the wounded, and to make dying easier for those who can't make it."

"I suppose you're right," he said. "Over here, it's too easy to see the glass half empty."

Another moment of silence stretched out while she studied his face.

"Now," she said, "tell me what happened at the animal hospital. Is your dog too far gone to save?"

Ricci took another healthy swallow from his glass, then set it on the table, clasping both hands around it. "The vet is talkin' about puttin' him down."

She frowned. "That's too bad. The dog must be in pretty bad shape, then."

"Beau is, but Doc Blevins has promised to keep 'im alive for at least twenty-four hours."

"What happens then?"

"Well…by then I'd better have some supplies rounded up, and somebody to nurse the dog back to health. Doc only has one vet tech, and they don't have the time. They've already got more dogs than they can take care of. They have to give their time to the ones that have a good chance."

"So he's just givin' up on Beau?"

"He doesn't have much choice," Ricci said. "Doc's in the same boat as the rest of us—tryin' to get by as well as he can until this damned war is over."

"I don't think that's gonna happen in the next twenty-four hours," Babs said. She reached across the table, covering his hand with hers. Someone punched in

Mickey and Sylvia's 1956 tune, "Love is Strange." The sounds filled the club. "I'll help, Geno. I'll do whatever you need."

He stared at her. "Babs, you've got your own duties to carry out. How could you—?"

"Don't worry about the *how*. To me, Beau is a four-legged GI who needs nursin'. I'll do my damnedest to beg, borrow, or midnight requisition the supplies I need. I'll go to the kennel every day after my duty hours. Just arrange it with Doc."

"Babs, really, I can't ask you to—"

"You don't have to. I'm glad to do it."

While squeezing her hand, Ricci shook his head and returned her smile. "You're the greatest, Babs. Do you remember our first dinner out together?"

Blushing, Babs replied, "You mean the time I used a knife and fork to cut my spaghetti?" They both laughed. "Now you look like the guy I met back at Fort Bragg," she said, smiling.

More music echoed throughout the club. Henry Mancini's "Moon River" moved them to dance, the floor already crowded with nurses, Red Cross volunteers, Donut Dollies paired with ranking officers, and Rear Echelon Motherfuckers (REMF), also known as "Remington Raiders" or those posted to safe areas such as clerks, journalists, and the like.

At the end of the song, Ricci walked over to the jukebox and punched in one of his favorite Elvis tunes,

"Can't Help Falling in Love." It was the last number before closing. He and Babs embraced on the dance floor.

On their return to the nurses' quarters, they strolled under a starlit sky with a full moon beaming over the white sands and slow, rushing waves of Cam Ranh Bay, all the while cognizant of the possibility of incoming 107mm rockets and 82mm mortars.

As they approached Babs's tent, Ricci whispered, "I'll see you tomorrow evenin' about the same time."

She turned and looked up at him. "You'll be leavin' on Saturday?"

He nodded. "I have to return for a field inspection. I'll see Doc in the mornin', then I'll be talkin' to Colonel Remus about materials."

Babs smiled. "I can't wait to see you again, Geno."

He kissed her goodnight.

#

Three hours later, Geno Ricci rolled over on the narrow bunk and tried to find a more comfortable position. He seldom had trouble sleeping, but his mind was too full of the day's events. He couldn't turn it off.

Mostly, it was seeing Babs. She stirred up a lot of feelings, including guilt. He and Babs never did anything

111

to feel guilty about; however, thinking about Marilyn while also harboring feelings of affection toward Babs was conflicting.

Long enough to start getting over it, he had told Babs, but he wondered if he ever would. Even after two years, whenever he thought of Marilyn, the ache of loss was there, thick in his throat—and in his chest and in his eyes.

He remembered Marilyn the last time he had seen her. Her platinum blond hair was cut in a shoulder-length, windblown style that gave her a touch of wildness. Her oval face with soft green eyes, delicate nose and chin, wide full mouth—it was all there, fresh and detailed, as though her image had been permanently imprinted in his brain.

He also remembered how her moods could change, and how deep her feelings ran. She could be laughing and teasing one moment, then in the next moment turn serious about something she had read in the newspaper—an environmental issue, or a story about laboratory experiments on animals.

He remembered the last time they had made love, the night before he had left for a temporary duty assignment in Guam. She had looked lovely that night. It was a sweet memory, clear and focused, one that he never wanted to forget.

It was curious how some incidents were forever etched in one's memory, while most of the details of life were often forgotten. There had been so many loving, gentle moments with Marilyn—images and impressions from the past that swept through his mind like a kaleidoscope, a video of his life and marriage, with a zoom lens going in and out, revealing a variety of shots of him and Marilyn.

Geno never forgot the night of the telephone call. His father had broken the news as gently as possible from a continent away. Whenever Ricci thought back to that time, the words all blurred together.

"Bad accident...two drunk hunters comin' off Scrub Ridge...old pickup crossed the center line...she's in a coma...."

That was the gist of it. None of the rest really mattered. It wasn't right, Geno thought, that an event as obscure as two drunks hunting in the Pennsylvania mountains could have such a devastating impact on Ricci's life. It made him realize there was no such thing as a promise of tomorrow. Human life is fragile, like a tightrope walker precariously perched, with disaster waiting for the slightest mischance.

He had returned to Pennsylvania, rushing to the Fulton County Medical Center in McConnellsburg. He was directed to the Intensive Care Unit, a large room with four beds. Only one was occupied.

Marilyn lay there, almost totally concealed. The only thing not hidden by the oxygen mask covering her face and the bandage wrapped around her head was a stray lock of blond hair and a small bruised strip of her forehead. The rest of her body was fully draped. An IV stand was next to the bed, its two bottles of fluid merging in a single line that led under the covers.

According to the doctor, Marilyn had crashed into the windshield. She had a skull fracture and deep facial lacerations. Skull radiographs suggested subdural hemorrhaging.

Fighting back tears, Ricci had reached under the blanket and touched her hand, then leaned over and kissed it.

The doctors offered no words of encouragement. Yet Ricci had hoped that she would recover, that they could continue with their life.

Later, he and his father had looked at Marilyn's car and the pickup. They had been towed to a nearby body shop. Broken, twisted metal was almost unrecognizable as vehicles. The aroma of stale beer permeated the pickup cab. Shattered window glass and dark, dried blood covered the front seat of Marilyn's station wagon.

Ricci had noticed the gun rack lying across the rear pickup window. A familiar-looking black and red sticker with a resting eagle on crossed rifles above the year 1871 was glued to the left panel window.

Geno recalled the efficiency and cooperation of Pennsylvania State Trooper Paul Bard and his handling of the accident. Most of all, he remembered Bard's kind words: "You-uns be careful now—and my heart goes out to you, Colonel."

Two days later, Marilyn Ricci died, having never regained consciousness.

The following days were foggy. The next frame in Ricci's memory was of a small chapel, the atmosphere heavy with the scent of flowers, the oak coffin standing on a draped trolley, the lid closed tight. The funeral director told Ricci he thought it would be better that way.

During the service, Ricci's family crowded the first pew. Father George had eulogized Marilyn as a loving, devoted wife, teacher, humanitarian, animal lover, and a woman with a marvelous sense of humor.

"Like Jesus," he had said, "she gave out of love to others the most valuable of gifts: her time and energy. She was a fine example of selflessness." Looking at the grief-stricken family members in the front pew, Father George added, "There is never a good time for death. An old English proverb states, 'Death either comes too early or too late.'"

As the congregation sang Marilyn's favorite hymn, "Amazing Grace," Ricci asked God if He really cared. *Are you just too busy? Why Marilyn?*

More than anything else, Ricci wished they'd had children. They had been married for just two years. They had wanted to wait until his career was a little more settled before starting a family. Now Marilyn was gone. It was too late.

Alone, hot, and tired, Geno Ricci slept fitfully, turning and tossing on the narrow cot, his needs and questions unresolved.

Chapter 8

Geno awakened to the "Dawn Busters" over the American Forces Vietnam Network and the redoubtable and irreverent disc jockey, Adrian Cronauer, with a rousing "Goood Mawnin', Vietnam, broadcasting from the Delta to the DMZ." Geno would have preferred hearing a sound bite from Verdi's tearjerker, "La Traviata," a story about the tragic death of Violetta in the arms of her lover.

With the fierce morning sun streaming through the window, things were looking a little brighter.

He made a hasty trip to the drum latrines, took a quick shower, and dressed in a fresh set of fatigues. After breakfast, the young driver took him to the kennel. It was another hot and humid morning. *What else?* thought Ricci.

"Good mornin', Colonel," Airman Slater said. "Doc's in his office."

"Thanks," Ricci said without slowing down. Doc Blevins rose snail-like as Ricci walked in, but Ricci waved him back into his chair. "Sit, I've got a plan."

The chair creaked as Blevins settled back. "As Bugs Bunny always says to Elmer Fudd, I'm all ears, Colonel."

"Captain Barbara Brewer, an Air Force nurse assigned to the field hospital, is a friend of mine. She's volunteered to visit Beau after hours every day possible. She'll feed 'im, change his bandages, and work with 'im until he is well. She also has access to medications you'll need. What do you say?"

Doc Blevins grinned and slapped the palm of his hand against his desktop. "That sounds great, Colonel! Tell your friend to come over here ASAP, and we'll work out the details."

Ricci got to his feet. "Give us some time, Doc. Captain Brewer's TLC will help Beau."

After shaking hands with Blevins, Ricci hopped into the jeep and was off to see Colonel Remus at the Engineer Supply Yard.

#

By the time Ricci returned to his hootch, it was almost 1800. It had been a grueling afternoon, and he'd hoped for some time to relax before meeting Babs. He rushed his shower. His starched fatigues were no longer stiff, but he didn't have time to do anything about that.

118

Twenty minutes later, he and Babs sat at a small table with a flickering candle between them.

"Geno, you look better tonight," she remarked after drinks were ordered.

"You've got that right. Doc's okayed your plan for Beau. He's ready to help, and this afternoon, I managed to get my hands on some cement, nails, and lumber for Phan Rang. They're gonna send it by barge."

"Sounds like you've had a productive day."

"That, I have. How's Private Walker today?"

"He's turned the corner," said Babs. "He's responding well to the antibiotics, and the doctor says he'll be goin' home in a few weeks."

"Wonderful!" Ricci grinned. "And, Babs, you look absolutely captivating. Let's enjoy what time we have left." Pushing his chair back, Ricci walked over to the jukebox and punched in "I'll Never Find Another You" by the Seekers, a new group out of Australia.

Amid the din of romantic music, dancing, and overall merriment, their rendezvous was memorable. Later, after he had walked Babs to the nurses' tent, she handed Ricci a small gift she had purchased at the base BX. It was a sterling-silver unicorn and chain. He smiled and lowered his head as she hung it around his thick neck.

"How did you know I like unicorns?" he asked.

She returned his smile. "Just a lucky guess."

He bent and kissed her on the cheek. It had been a long time since he had felt like this about a woman. What could he say? "Babs, you are a gem, a woman with a big heart. Thanks for goin' the extra mile for Beau. You know what he means to me. I loved this evening, and your gift."

That night, it was Babs who had trouble sleeping. She rolled onto her side, clutching her pillow, pulling it close to her heart, thinking of Geno. Her erotic thoughts seemed all too real. Suddenly she felt her breasts tighten, the nipples growing hard.

Babs! she admonished herself, *you can't let yourself get carried away with this man!*

She remembered how she had reacted the first time she had met Geno when he was a patient at Womack Army Hospital. With their first eye contact, she had felt warm, as if he had touched her physically. Her vibes were intense as her heart fluttered. She had never reacted this way in a man's presence. Some strange chemistry, she thought. She had struggled to ignore her emotions. He had been married, and he had talked openly about his love for Marilyn.

And now…well, the problem was clear: Geno still loved Marilyn, even though she died over two years ago. Would he ever be able to give his love to another woman? Could Babs ever hope to take Marilyn's place?

Agitated, she rolled onto her back.

Another image came to her: the silver unicorn with all its mystical powers and vulnerability, handsomely suspended from his neck.

Besides the erotic significance, she felt that the amulet would protect Geno. She loved the unicorn's charm for its innocent strength and gentleness. *All fitting Geno*, she thought.

Sleepy and drifting, she thought the gift for Geno was just right.

Chapter 9

For Babs, this Saturday's dawn was not like any other morning—except for the ever-present heat, humidity, and the pungent odor of the drum latrines. Babs called them "outhootches." They were constructed of two long, flat boards sitting parallel to one another, running the length of the hootch. The boards rested upon low cinderblock walls. Several round holes were juxtaposed the entire length of the boards. Under each opening sat a modified drum. The inside walls of the hootch were festooned with flypaper strips covered black with dead flies. The atmosphere reeked.

Some users drank coffee while others read the *Stars and Stripes*. All the while, little Vietnamese mamasans wearing straw hats and using straw brooms removed the filled slop pots and replaced them with new containers.

Yawning, stretching, and rising from her narrow bunk, she wrinkled her nose and grumbled, "The shit burners are at it early today."

Her eyes felt gritty. All she wanted to do was go back to sleep, but she had a full day ahead and couldn't afford the luxury. Her mental to-do list included breakfast, ward rounds, sick call (because of the doctor shortage), lunch, and then the dog kennels.

Babs's inspiration for her work came from a French nurse called the "Angel of Dien Bien Phu." Her name was Geneviève de Galard-Terraube, also known as "the flying nurse." She flew with the old Douglas Dakota C-47 medevac aircraft crews. De Galard's WWII work with the French Underground convinced her that she, too, had a duty like her ancestors.

Babs, like her guiding light, felt the same messianic calling. Because of possible VC mortar and artillery rounds, while attending the wounded, Babs often wore a helmet and protective gear.

Morning rounds at the field hospital left her feeling optimistic, as she did her best to ease her patients' pain by making them as comfortable as possible. Private Walker, from Phan Rang, was in good spirits. The doctor had reduced his pain medication. Walker was looking forward to going home soon.

Fixed in Babs's psyche were reminders from one of the many U.S. Air Force field manuals that the Air Force medical service was a supporting branch of the combat arms. In her mind, the job of the Medical Corps was to maintain the health and fighting efficiency of the troops, and she thought this applied to *all* troops, including the canine warriors attached to various units in Vietnam. Her mission: get them back to duty.

With this thought in mind, Captain Brewer, braving stifling heat and humidity on a chrome-bright day, set off on her trek to meet the base veterinarian, Captain Blevins, and Ricci's dog, Beauregard. Cam Ranh Bay was a vast installation, but as luck would have it, the kennel was not too far away from the field hospital.

As her pace quickened, the bright sun reflected off the silver captain's bars attached to her baseball-style fatigue cap, while perspiration cascaded down her brow and onto her sunglasses and between her breasts. More irritating was the dry, red dust that clung to her skin, exacerbated by rolling beads of sweat. Like many of the bush grunts, Babs carried a dragon towel. She couldn't stand sweaty eyes or smudge lines on her glasses. She didn't like the sweat-soaked armpits of her neatly pressed uniform, either, but what could she do? This was typical tropical climate for Vietnam.

Inside the kennel, a young airman stood and saluted her, "Yes, ma'am, may I help you?"

"Airman, I'm Captain Brewer. I'm here to take a look at the Doberman belonging to the 62nd Engineers."

"Hi, I'm Captain Blevins," came a voice behind Babs before the airman could reply. She turned to find a man standing behind her with a toothpick dangling from the right side of his mouth. "You must be Captain Brewer."

"Yes, I am—"

"Good. Please, come into my office. We need to talk."

After Blevins asked Slater to bring Cokes, they sat across the desk from one another. A lone, rackety fan on top of a filing cabinet spewed hot air in their direction. Blevins's eyes dropped momentarily to the dampened uniform hugging her breasts; they didn't linger.

"So, Captain Brewer, what do you think about babysitting a dog in the midst of a war zone thousands of miles from the real world?"

"Captain, I—"

"Please, call me Doc."

She leaned back in the wooden armchair, feeling more at ease. "Thanks, Doc. I'm Babs. Anyway, I told Colonel Ricci that I consider this dog a four-legged GI who needs nursing care like any other wounded soldier. I will do my best, along with your help, to get Beau back to duty status."

He nodded. "That's fine. Let's work out a plan. As I told Colonel Ricci, my supplies are limited. Do you think you could find some extra bandages?"

"I'm sure. What else?"

"How about antibiotics, anti-bacterial ointments, and some anti-inflammatories?"

She thought for a moment. "I can probably get those things."

"Good."

Slater returned with Cokes and two ice-filled glasses. After Blevins poured, they took long swallows.

125

"Colonel Ricci said you would also come and help nurse Beau back to health," Blevins said, returning his glass to the desktop.

"I can try," Babs promised, "but I have to admit, I don't know much about dogs."

He lifted an eyebrow. "As a kid, did you have a dog?"

"Nope, my parents wouldn't have pets in the house," she paused. "Well, I had a goldfish once."

Blevins laughed. "I'm sure you'll have better luck with Beau. You'll need to bond—get him to accept you. That's likely to help his recovery as much as anything."

"How can I do that?"

Blevins took another long swallow of Coke, then reached for Beau's medical file. "There was something in here...I think..." he flipped through a few pages. "Yeah, I thought somebody had left a note about this." He looked up at Babs and grinned. "Beau likes vanilla ice cream and peanuts. That should be a good place to start." Blevins turned his head toward the open doorway and yelled, "Hey, Slater, get the jeep and hit your mess hall with a request for a pint of vanilla ice cream, and tell the Mess Sergeant to get some of those peanuts out of his goodie locker."

"Consider it done, sir." The airman was out the door in a flash.

"Slater's a good tech," said Blevins. "He eventually plans to attend vet school at the University of Georgia.

He knows a hell of a lot about dogs. He treats 'em like they're his children."

Babs sipped her Coke. "If Beau recovers from his physical wounds, will he be fit for duty again?"

"He'll need some retraining, and he'll need TLC to restore his confidence, but I think he'll come back."

"Are the handlers responsible for training their own dogs?" she asked.

"Some of it. The dogs go through rigorous training before they're sent over here, but it's up to the handlers to fine-tune."

"So the handlers are like…dog experts?"

Blevins chuckled. "Not hardly. But they train with the dogs. Overall, I think it's a pretty good system. Dog handlers have told me that over time, the handler and the dog together become a six-legged soldier."

"But Beau's handler was killed. That has to be traumatic."

"Very perceptive, Babs," Blevins said approvingly. "He's used to seein' his handler every day. His handler is the one who fed, groomed, and loved him, and now, when Beau needs him most of all, he's gone."

"That's why Beau's bonding with me is so important?"

"Right. Dobies have an instinctive eagerness to please—in addition to guarding their territory. Not all dogs want to please. Some resist any form of training."

"Will Beau accept me?"

"Probably. Dobies are not necessarily one-man dogs, so bonding with 'em might not be a problem for you. If he goes back to duty, he'll be assigned to another handler, and the bonding process will have to start all over, but by then he'll be physically well. It should work out if Colonel Ricci finds the right man to be Beau's new handler."

"Sounds like you know quite a bit about Dobermans, too, Doc."

He grinned. "I've done a little readin' since Beau's arrival." Blevins told her that the Doberman Pinscher is a noble dog named after a German, Ludwig Dobermann, who believed he could breed the perfect guard dog. This breed also became popular in the U.S. during WWII, he explained.

Blevins jerked his thumb toward the back room. "In that wounded animal, Beau still has all the alertness and aggressiveness that Dobermann envisioned in the ideal dog. In WWII, the U.S. Marine Corps adopted this breed as their mascot and named them 'devil dogs.' At Bougainville in the Pacific, devil dogs fought side by side with their handlers against stiff Japanese resistance."

"That's amazing. I didn't know the U.S. military even used dogs back then."

"Most people don't." Blevins pushed back his chair and pointed to the room in the rear. "Are you ready to meet 'im?"

"I sure am." Babs stood up and set her empty glass on the desk. As they walked past Slater's small desk in the corridor, she noticed a tri-cornered plaque resting near his nameplate. It read: "The Misery of Keeping a Dog is His Dying Too Soon—Sir Walter Scott."

Slater's passion for canines moved her. *Hmm*, she thought, *maybe he can help me.*

The kennel door opened, and Slater walked in holding a dripping container of vanilla ice cream and a small can of Planters Peanuts. "It took a little arm-twistin', sir," Slater said.

Blevins grinned. "That's okay. Sergeant Greenleaf owes me. Leave the peanuts on your desk for now." He motioned Babs toward the back room. "Don't let first impressions scare you off. Dobies generally look at strangers as intruders."

"Why's that?"

He shrugged. "That's just their nature. They are primarily guard dogs. That's how Beau has been trained."

Beau's aluminum shipping crate had three rows of ventilation holes on both sides and an opening for food and water on the right.

As they approached Beau, Blevins yelled, "Hey, Slater, grab a bowl."

Slater opened a small, white-enameled cupboard, picked up a stainless steel bowl and a wooden spoon, and handed them to Babs.

Blevins gestured. "Meet Beau."

As Babs knelt before his padded cage, their eyes met between the holes of his enclosure. She could sense Beau's obedient but cautious watch. One ear was erect, the other covered with a bloodstained gauze bandage that needed changing. Beau shook his head.

"That ear might still be inflamed," Blevins said. "I'd better take a look."

As Blevins leaned over and unhooked the latch, Beau moved his head to the open space. There were no growls or bared teeth. Beau was a good patient.

"Slater, bring me some cotton swabs, clean gauze, and Panalog ointment."

"Yes, sir," Slater replied, already on his way to fetch the supplies from another white metal cabinet.

While Blevins swabbed Beau's inner ear, Babs could see brown wax and dried blood. Blevins put some ointment around the ear canal and re-bandaged the entire area. For now, Beau's head shaking had ceased.

"Shouldn't you give 'im some tetracycline?" Babs asked.

"No, this ear problem must be treated topically, not internally. Tetracycline is good for bacterial infections. In fact, we're out of that drug."

"I'll see if I can find some for you."

"Good. How about some penicillin, as well?"

"I'm sure I can get some of that, too," Babs said. "They're keepin' us well stocked with antibiotics."

"His ear has improved a little," Blevins said. "When I first got here, I saw a number of dogs comin' out of the bush shaking their heads. I assumed that was a form of otitis, a simple ear inflammation that may have been caused by ticks. Tick larvae infest the canal which causes a great deal of pain. Dogs scratch until their ears are bloody. In fact, that was one of Beau's problems."

"How did you treat 'im?" she asked.

"First, I had to remove those ugly bastards from his ears. Then I used Malathion dip to kill fleas. Then I treated the otitis with an antibiotic-steroid combination. But back to my original point, some of those dogs comin' off patrol would have nothing more than grass seeds stuck in their ears, which caused the dogs to react in the same way. I learned real fast."

Babs saw a mucus buildup in the front corners of Beau's eyes. To her, Beau's dark brown eyes suggested intelligence, caution, and at the same time pain. Though he was lean, his massive chest and velvet-black coat with rust-brown markings caught her attention.

Dipping the spoon into the soupy ice cream, she placed it in the slot. Beau licked the spoon clean—then another and another. His white whiskers amused her. She offered Beau another spoonful. While lapping, his tongue passed over her fingers. Babs felt a rush of affection for Beau.

Blevins interrupted the tranquil mood. "That's enough for now. Dogs can't handle too much sugar or milk. They have a problem with lactose, and sugar increases their susceptibility to parasites without any nutritional benefit."

"Does he really taste the ice cream?" she asked.

"To a certain extent. Taste is not one of their acute senses. Not like us, anyway. We have many more taste buds. Dogs discern sweet, salt, or bitter tastes. Anyway, I can see that you've begun to bond with 'im."

Babs smiled. "That makes me happy. Let's map out a feeding program."

"Our dog food inventory is low," Slater said. "We only have a small amount of dry food."

Blevins nodded. "Yeah, I know that, Slater, but I'm expectin' a shipment of Hill's Science Diet."

Slater's eyebrows lifted in surprise. "Really, sir? How'd ya work that out?"

"I've got Army scout dogs from Ft. Benning and Air Force sentry dogs comin' in from Lackland real soon, so I managed to order more food for 'em."

"I'll get some fish and chicken from the mess hall," Slater said. "That will help strengthen Beau."

"How about boiled rice with chicken soup?" Babs asked. "I've seen many a weak patient improve on chicken soup."

"Good," said Blevins. "Make a list, Slater, and take it to the Mess Sergeant."

"That mess hall has everything," said Slater.

"Put eggs on the list," said Blevins. "That will help Beau's iron level."

"And his coat, too," Slater added.

"Hell, those peanuts have biotin, protein, and fat," Blevins said. "That's what he needs, along with lots of water to keep 'im hydrated."

Beau moved as if he wanted to stretch. Babs watched this once-powerful and muscular canine shift in his cramped cage. She could see bare skin splotches from lying in one position too long.

As soon as Beau regains his strength, he'll need to be walked daily, Babs thought.

#

Over the next three weeks, Babs and Beau became an item of interest in the area between the field hospital and the canine kennels. The chicken soup and TLC worked miracles. At the BX she found a brush for Beau's coat. He was mending and becoming a pal. Babs looked forward to their daily walks.

Airman Slater was a good vet technician, and he helped immensely with Beau's recovery, performing his duties well beyond the required standards. Despite Captain Blevins's obvious preoccupation with her bust line, she believed that he, too, provided excellent medical care for Beau and the other dogs.

Geno and Babs wrote to each other often. He told her how anxious he was to see her and Beau again, and she kept him updated on Beau's progress.

Beau's physical condition steadily improved, and after three weeks, Doc Blevins told her that Beau was ready to return to duty. His pads, abrasions, and bruises were healed, and his coat shined. His eyes showed no signs of puffiness, squinting, or being bloodshot. His nose was not dry or scaly. His temperature was a normal 101 degrees, and he weighed a little over 110 pounds— not yet up to his fighting weight, but getting there. His teeth were clean, his nails trimmed. His ears were free of brown wax, swelling, and irritation. Although the wound to his left ear had healed, the scars were still visible and the ear drooped a bit. Babs didn't think it would ever perk up like the other one.

One day, Babs got word that Beau's new handler and Geno would be arriving Friday afternoon. They would return to Phan Rang on Saturday.

The thought of seeing Geno again energized Babs, but at the same time, she felt a little emptiness as she realized that Beau would soon be leaving her care.

Before her introduction to Beau, Babs had known little about canines, let alone military dogs and their life-saving contributions to the war effort. After spending so many hours with Beau, she had a newfound friend. The awakening of such deep feelings toward an animal moved her.

She smiled, thinking that Beau had left emotional paw prints on her heart.

Chapter 10

Chivington's elation surprised no one when Ricci asked him to be Beau's new handler, but working with a trained military dog like Beau would be a challenge.

"Beau won't be your pet," Ricci warned. "He's a trained military dog. You'll be teammates."

"Yes, sir, I understand," Chivington said, but inside, he thought, *Maybe he'll become both a soldier and a pet.*

"You'll have to go through an in-country refresher training course," Ricci told him. "You'll need to learn how to be an efficient handler. Beau will have to relearn how to be an effective sentry/scout dog. He's been through a lot—probably worse than we can imagine. He'll have to regain his self-confidence."

Chivington understood. He managed to suppress the urge to grin, but hiding his enthusiasm was not easy. He did not want Colonel Ricci to get the idea that he wasn't taking this new assignment seriously. "Yes, sir. I'll be pleased to do it, sir."

Chivington had always loved dogs. While growing up his parents had never allowed him to have one. In a way, Beau would be his first pet. Working with a military dog involved a lot of effort. He expected it to be a challenging and exciting experience.

While on patrol, Chivington knew that his life, and the lives of other men, depended on how effectively he read Beau's alerts to booby traps and enemy soldiers. Beau was the one with the keen senses, but it would be up to Chivington to interpret them.

Chivington was issued a military dog-training manual. It contained procedures and illustrations of tools for grooming, voice commands, hand and arm signals, and deployment. He studied the manual carefully, so he would be prepared when he and Beau attended the military dog-training course.

Ricci and Chivington arrived at Cam Ranh Bay and went directly to the kennel. Captain Blevins and Airman Slater greeted them. Blevins asked Ricci and Chivington to follow him.

As they walked past caged dogs, a few snarled viciously. One threw himself against the gate. Chivington wondered about that portal, if it might open accidentally.

"Beau isn't so aggressive," Ricci said, noticing Chivington's doubtful looks at the growling dogs.

"He's a real cupcake," Doc Blevins added. "Babs has spoiled 'im rotten."

Large bags of dog food were stacked high against the walls alongside several large metal wall lockers. Water hoses were connected to pipes at each end of the kennel. Chivington surmised they were used to wash down the cage floors.

Nearing Beau's kennel, Chivington caught sight of an attractive Air Force nurse in starched fatigues holding a leather leash in her left hand. At the end of the leash sat Beau, looking as he did the night before he and Juan Martinez had gone out on patrol. Beau was a regal-looking dog with a beautiful black and tan coat, a robust chest, and a pair of trenchant eyes that fixed on Chivington as he approached. His right ear was erect, but the left one still drooped. Chivington recalled that Beau had been wounded in that ear. Beau exemplified pride, confidence, and control.

Hey, buddy, Chivington said silently, holding the dog's gaze. *We're gonna get along fine.*

"Good afternoon, Captain Brewer," said Ricci. "Lookin' good, both of you."

"He's a winner," Babs agreed.

Chivington's eye shifted to the dog, but he caught Babs looking longingly at the colonel. *Well, that's interesting*, he thought. *More power to 'em if they can find something worthwhile in this hellhole.*

"Captain Brewer, this is Corporal Chivington," Ricci said, maintaining the rather formal tone. "He's Beau's new handler."

"Yes, ma'am," Chivington saluted.

She returned the salute. "I think Beau is as ready as he'll ever be," she said, trembling with visible emotion. "You'll have to get to know 'im. He's a good dog."

Chivington nodded. "I'm sure he is, ma'am." His eyes returned to Beau, who was watching him with interest. *You're a good dog, aren't you, boy?*

"We've all worked hard to cure his medical problems," Dr. Blevins interjected, "but we have to give Babs most of the credit. She also augmented the supplies that helped Beau's recovery."

"Don't forget Airman Slater," Babs turned and smiled at the vet tech. "He's been an excellent instructor to me and a damn good medic to this dog."

Blevins agreed. "You're absolutely right, Captain. Slater is a major link in the operation of this kennel and the care of these dogs. He also keeps flawless records. We've passed every inspection with flying colors."

The young vet tech grinned, blushing fiercely. "Just doin' my job, sir."

"Let's go inside and finalize the paperwork," Blevins said. "Then we'll get this dog back to duty."

"Maybe Corporal Chivington and Beau can use this time to get acquainted," Ricci suggested.

Blevins nodded. "Good idea. Slater, why don't you and Captain Brewer take a walk around the kennel. Let Corporal Chivington walk Beau alone for a while, but keep an eye on 'em."

"Yes, sir," Slater said. He led Chivington and Babs out beyond the immediate kennel area.

Blevins and Ricci walked back to Blevins's office.

"I'm impressed with your kennel management," Ricci said as he pulled the armchair closer to the desk and sat down. "The Air Force does things first class."

Blevins grinned. "Colonel, I appreciate what you say, but the nurse really gave Beau the day-to-day attention that brought 'im around. She got off to a good start with ice cream and peanuts."

Ricci furrowed his brow. "Ice cream and peanuts?"

"He really goes for vanilla ice cream and peanuts," Blevins said, laughing. "Somebody had put a note about that in his file. Give 'im some ice cream and peanuts, and he's your friend for life."

Ricci chuckled. "We'll have to keep that in mind."

"If this dog is to stay healthy, your handler will have to understand a few things about daily maintenance," Blevins said. "Since you don't have a vet at Phan Rang, you guys will have to do the basics."

"No problem."

Blevins leaned forward and opened the manila file folder that lay on his desk. Ricci could see that the papers inside were Beau's service and medical records. Blevins signed a few of the papers, then closed the folder and handed it across the table to Ricci. "He's all yours, Colonel."

Ricci and Blevins returned to the kennel area just as Babs, Slater, Beau, and Chivington reappeared from their walk.

"How did it go?" Ricci asked Chivington.

"Not bad, sir," Chivington replied, "but he's really attached to Captain Brewer. Hell, he couldn't wait to get back to her after our walk. He really tugged at the leash. I could see his stubby little tail wagging like windshield wipers the minute he spotted her."

"I guess we'll have to find some vanilla ice cream and peanuts back at the base," Ricci said.

Chivington gave him a puzzled look. "Sir?"

Blevins slapped the corporal on the shoulder. "You can read all about it in his file," he said. "Now, for some advice before you take this dog back to your base."

"Yes, sir," Chivington said, nodding. "I'll appreciate anything you can tell me."

"Good. First, as Beau's new handler, you've got to keep his ears clean and free of ticks and mites, especially the left ear that was in such bad shape."

"Yes, sir. I know how important that is," Chivington replied. "I'll never forget those fat, bloody ticks we picked off 'im when he was hurt."

"Topical therapy is usually enough with the external ear canal, but be damned careful when using cotton swabs with alcohol, peroxide, or even an iodine solution.

Swabs or rolled tissue can sometimes rupture that membrane."

"I understand, sir," Chivington acknowledged.

"You can use swabs once in a blue moon, but not regularly," Blevins smiled. "Did your mom ever tell you not to stick anything in your ear smaller than your elbow?"

Chivington smiled. "I believe she may have said something like that, sir. What about ear mites?"

"Mites don't burrow like ticks, but the bastards can cause just as much trouble. I'll give you some ear medication for Beau and the other dogs in your unit, but if their ears get infected again, you'll have to get them back here for treatment. I will also check 'em for internal parasites."

"Doc, not long ago, I read somethin' in *Stars and Stripes* that bothered me," Ricci said. "There was conflicting data about two potentially fatal canine diseases affectin' dogs in tropical climates like Southeast Asia. Apparently, they're something new. Have you heard about 'em?"

Blevins nodded. "You're probably talkin' about heartworms and ehrlichiosis. Heartworm doesn't have anything to do with worms. It's a disease transmitted by female mosquitoes. It's a filarial parasite that infects a dog's right ventricle and pulmonary artery, eventually causing valve leakage and cardiac edema. I think it's present in Vietnam but not yet diagnosed.

"Ehrichliosis is a tick-borne sickness identified in the U.S. in 1962. It's a contagious death sentence for dogs unless they're treated with tetracycline. In fact, that's the Pentagon's specious argument for not returnin' the dogs home," said Blevins in a sobering tone. "Unfortunately, most military dogs are out in the boonies when they contract ehrlichiosis, and they don't get the drug in time." He looked at Chivington. "Check 'im often. If you keep the ticks off 'im, he'll be all right."

"I will, sir," Chivington promised.

Blevins nodded. "I know you will, soldier. Beau's a lucky dog. He's got a handler who really cares about 'im."

That evening, at the enlisted men's club, Slater and Chivington guzzled beer and devoured hamburgers while Ricci, Babs, Doc Blevins, and a perky beauty named Sonja savored Dom Perignon champagne, shrimp, salad, and rock music at the officers' club. Like Babs, Sonja was a nurse at the field hospital. She and Doc Blevins had met three weeks earlier and had obviously hit it off.

After dinner and some dancing, the foursome sat around a table sipping drinks, making small talk about hometowns, colleges, and what was happening "back in the world." They all read the *Stars and Stripes* and felt that this was a good venue for the latest exchange of news and gossip.

They were in a festive mood. Ricci predicted that the Cleveland Browns running back Jim Brown would lead the team to the NFL title and become this year's MVP— for the second time since 1957. They talked about Peter Arnett, an Associated Press reporter who was becoming something of a legend in making Vietnam a newspaper and television war. Arnett's apocryphal activities were well known. Reports had him swimming the Mekong River with his stories clenched between his teeth.

Sonja mentioned the latest issue of *Time* magazine, which had Bill Moyers, LBJ's press secretary, on the cover. The article featuring LBJ's twelve-inch scar tickled her. LBJ had exposed it at a press conference held on the hospital's golf course. The doctors had removed his gall bladder and a kidney stone. Holding up his shirt, the president said, "I had two operations for the price of one...I hurt good!"

All four were skeptical of the Warren Commission's conclusion as to who killed President Kennedy. The February assassination of Malcolm X, the more recent Watts riots in Los Angeles, and the civil rights march led by Martin Luther King, Jr. from Selma to the Alabama capital had them all concerned about heightened racial tensions. Commanding officers like Ricci had to be on top of the possible ripple effects that could alter morale in units like the 62nd Engineers.

By night's end, Blevins and Sonja decided to catch a movie, *The Sons of Katie Elder*, with John Wayne and Dean Martin, at the base theater while Ricci and Babs longed for some time alone.

Leaving the club, they walked arm in arm under the spell of another night lit by a crescent moon, grateful that the calm was not shattered by the "squeak and thud" of Charlie's "incoming mail."

"Geno, do you think animals have souls?" Babs asked.

In the darkness, he considered the question. "My Catholic upbringing says no, but I'm not so sure. I guess that's up to God."

"I think they must," she said. "You can see Beau's soul, if you look into his chocolate eyes."

He chuckled. "Really?"

"Yes," she said seriously. "I mean it, Geno. He can let you see it, if he wants to—and it's so beautiful. He's such a wonderful dog." Her voice was starting to break up, as Ricci drew her close. "Geno…someday I want to have a Dobie just like Beau. I've never had a dog before…"

Now she was crying, and Ricci didn't know what to do except to hold her. After a moment, the sobbing stopped, but Babs continued to cling to Ricci, her head on his shoulder.

"Beau is so innocent, so eager to give unconditional love, so willing to accept us just as we are, faults and all."

#

Saturday morning dawned, and a boiling sun soon enveloped Cam Ranh Bay. Ricci, Chivington, and Beau were ready to board the chopper back to Phan Rang.

Babs's lips began to quiver, but she was determined to maintain control over her emotions. After all, she was a U.S. Air Force officer.

As Babs moved toward Beau, his stubby tail wagged. His eyes converged on her as she knelt before him. He licked her face.

"I…I'll miss ya, boy," she said. "Goodbye, Beau."

Rising, she walked over to Ricci. He broke ranks, pulling her close to his chest with a bear hug, and then a long kiss.

"Babs, I love you," he said.

Clinging to him, she responded in a halting voice, "I…I love you, too."

Even the *whump, whump, whump* of the rotors and the hot, swirling sand could not obscure Ricci's view of her as the chopper lifted and headed out over the placid South China Sea.

#

It was a short hop back to Phan Rang. Saturday afternoon meant down time for some of the troops.

Because of recent talk that VC sappers were planning to probe and disrupt construction plans, the base was on a mild-alert status. This forced the other two dog teams to work around-the-clock shifts.

Ricci felt secure about Chivington taking over as Beau's handler. Chivington was likewise pleased with the new assignment. Beau took to him quickly. It was clear, however, that Beau wasn't happy about leaving Babs.

Ricci stepped into bunker headquarters and sneezed; during his absence, the wooden floor had become carpeted with a thick layer of dust. After unhooking his web equipment, including his .45-caliber side arm, he sat down at his desk where Sergeant Young had left a stack of paperwork that demanded his attention.

Even with a small fan on his desk, he could feel moisture trickling down his forehead. While wiping his face and neck, he touched the unicorn.

He sat for a long moment. So why was he troubled? He knew why. He reached into a desk drawer and found a folded letter that he had received at a mail call while in Guam on Temporary Duty (TDY). His hands trembled a little as he unfolded it and began reading:

December 15, 1963

My Dearest Geno,

It seems like ages since your last letter arrived. Govy stays close to me, especially at night. He sleeps at the foot of our bed, which is painfully lonely without you. He is only politely social with the farm dogs. He prefers to be inside where I always leave him while at work.

Teaching elementary students is trying. I have to be mother, father, friend, counselor, and teacher at various times. Some of them have no parental guidance whatsoever.

Your mom's diabetes is about the same, and your dad has just quit smoking. He's trying! Geno, the fall colors were so beautiful. They reminded me of our first date back in high school. You remember that night? It was after the great game you had. I think you ran for three or four touchdowns, and afterwards you asked me out. Boy, the other cheerleaders were green with envy! What a heartbreaker you are (ha ha).

I love and miss you so much,

Marilyn

It was his last letter from her. He had received it just two days before word came of the accident that had put her in a coma. He brought the letter out now and then, as if it might help him maintain contact with her. He had read that letter dozens of times, always wishing more than anything that he could bring back that world it talked about: the happy, comfortable world that had existed for him before those two deer hunters decided to get drunk and drive home.

How, he asked himself, could he love another woman when he still loved Marilyn so much? Ricci remembered reading about a similar dilemma confronting Thomas Jefferson. While in Paris after the death of his beloved wife Patsy, he met Maria Cosway. Maria was only twenty-three, charming and gifted. Jefferson fell in love but was devastated knowing he could never have her. Maria was married and a devout Catholic.

To comfort his aching heart, Jefferson wrote Maria a long letter in the form of a dialogue between his heart and his head, saying in effect that physical separation will not diminish love. Jefferson, like Ricci, had agonized over the conflict between the emotional and intellectual sides of his being, but...well, Marilyn had died two years ago, and he knew that she, of all people, would want him to be happy. She would not want him to carry the burden of her death around with him forever.

Lamenting, he re-folded the letter and returned it to his desk drawer. He could not let personal feelings interfere with the mission to oversee the construction of this air base. He was responsible for the function and safety of his men and their equipment. He had to stay focused.

With a heavy sigh, he reached for the stack of paperwork on the corner of his desk.

Chapter 11

Chivington had no idea why he had been summoned to Captain Wojtacha's bunker office. His concern deepened when he saw Wilson walking in the same direction. Chivington couldn't think of anything he'd done to deserve a reprimand, but with the Army, one could never be sure.

He gave Wilson a questioning look, and Wilson shrugged. Without a word, the two of them stepped into the office and saluted. Wojtacha waved them to chairs.

In typical fashion, he wasted no time with preliminaries. Looking at Wilson, he said, "Colonel Ricci wants you to be a backup handler for Beau—"

"What!" Wilson burst out. "Excuse me, sir, but I don't know the first thing about dogs. Hell's fire, I don't even *like* dogs—"

"Colonel Ricci may not have considered whether this would be something you would enjoy doing," Wojtacha said dryly. "Should I tell 'im you've declined to carry out his orders because you don't like dogs?"

Wilson sagged back into his chair. "No, sir, of course not—"

"Good. Colonel Ricci feels that every dog team should have a reliable number-two quarterback. That's what you'll be. Both of you will be going to the Bien Hoa USARV Dog Training Detachment. You'll have to move out with Beau bright and early Monday morning. That'll be all."

"Yes, sir!" Chivington said, rising to his feet. "Thank you, sir."

Outside, Chivington couldn't hide his pleasure, despite the sour look on Wilson's face.

"Damn, this is the best thing that's happened to me since I've been over here." He paused, then added, "The only good thing, in fact."

"I'm glad you're so happy about it," Wilson said. "I'll tell ya one thing—if that damn dog even looks at me cross-eyed, I'll kick his teeth so far down his throat he'll be shittin' teeth for a week."

#

Chivington spent most of the weekend with Beau. He even gave him some ice cream and peanuts. He knew it would take a while for Beau to fully trust and accept him as Captain Brewer's replacement, but spending as much time as possible together was bound to help. Beau was friendly and docile enough, unlike some of the other military dogs Chivington had encountered. How he would behave in combat situations was unknown, but Chivington felt certain that the spark he saw in Beau's eye promised that he would come through.

On Monday morning, Chivington, Wilson, and Beau boarded a Huey slick for Bien Hoa Air Force Base, located in III Corps on the Dong Nai River near Saigon. The USARV War Dog Training Detachment was in the experimental stages of development. Bien Hoa would become the official training and deployment center for all in-country dogs and their handlers. Chivington was eager to reach the base and begin training with Beau. Wilson kept muttering things under his breath, but he had given up complaining outwardly.

Some military dogs were skittish about choppers, but Beau had no problem. He looked at the helicopter with interest, and willingly complied when Chivington gestured for him to jump aboard.

When they were all settled, the pilot rolled open the throttle and squeezed the trigger switch, turning the engine and main rotor blades. After reaching proper RPMs, the chopper pulled pitch and lifted. The earsplitting *whap, whap, whap* of the rotors permeated the interior of the open-sided aircraft. The nose dipped, and the helicopter roared off toward Bien Hoa Air Force Base.

Beau stood up and leaned forward to stick his head out the open door while Chivington kept a grip on the leash. Beau seemed to enjoy the cool air blowing in his face—until he looked down. Then he scooted back in a hurry next to Chivington and hugged the floor.

Wilson burst out laughing. "I guess the mutt doesn't like heights. Look! He pissed all over the place."

Chivington reached down and gave Beau a reassuring pat on the neck while using rags to mop up the urine. "He'll do fine. He's a smart dog."

"Yeah," Wilson said, "smart enough to turn tail and run when his patrol got their asses kicked."

Hot anger rose in Chivington, but he forced it down. Nobody but Beau knew what had happened during Jackson's patrol. As far as they knew, Beau had done everything he could to save those men, but arguing with Wilson was pointless. Wilson had his mind set. He disliked dogs, and nothing Chivington could say would change that. All he could hope for was to get through the training course without letting Wilson get too far under his skin.

The ride was bumpy, and they spoke little for the rest of the trip. Finally, through the door, Chivington saw that they were approaching Bien Hoa. Noted for its pottery, brassware, and lumber, Bien Hoa City was near the resorts of Vung Tau and Long Hai, and about six miles from the infamous in-country GI jail called LBJ— Long Bien Jail.

For Americans stationed at Bien Hoa before the war, water skiing on the Dong Nai was a popular form of recreation. It was always hot and muggy there during the rainy season.

Soon the airfield and terminal complex came into view. On the tarmac below were fighter planes, helicopters of various types, and sandbagged hangars and retaining walls to house them all.

Upon landing, Wilson, Chivington, and Beau were taken by jeep to the canine training compound. As they approached, they caught sight of a logo in large black letters over the entrance: *Forever Forward*.

Chivington smiled, thinking how appropriate that was. In Vietnam, the military dogs would always be walking out in front of their patrols.

Wilson and Chivington were met by Sergeant First Class Ron Violette, who would be their instructor. Violette was in his early thirties, with dark, curly hair and the face of a genial prizefighter. A small square patch above his nametag showed the black head of a dog against a yellow background. It was, Chivington knew, the patch worn by all military dog handlers. Chivington was looking forward to earning his own insignia through dog training and qualification.

Violette showed them around. The dog kennels were housed in a wooden structure with metal fence siding and a tin roof. Forty dog runs—twenty on each side— were separated from one another by chain link fencing. Chivington was surprised and glad to see that the kennel had been wired for electricity, and that overhead lights had been installed. Empty runs were used to store dog food, supplies, transport crates, and other equipment. Grooming equipment, leashes, collars, and body harnesses were stored in wooden bins.

Several handlers who had arrived earlier were grooming their canines on small wooden tables outside. They talked to the dogs, all German Shepherds, while they brushed and checked them for health problems. The dogs impressed Chivington. They all looked healthy, lean, and muscular. Some were not so friendly as Chivington followed Violette's instructions not to touch. Wilson gave the dogs a wide berth.

Violette assigned one of the empty runs to Beau. He told Chivington and Wilson to get him settled, then report to training headquarters. At this time, they would pick up their in-country instruction agenda, their equipment, hootch assignments, and map giving them directions to the mess hall, dispensary, BX, and airmen's club. He also warned them to be alert for "Eleven O'clock Charlie," who sent incoming rockets into Bien Hoa every night just before or after 2300, aiming at warehouses, barracks, planes, or anything else in sight. Violette finally told them not to listen to Hanoi Hannah's bullshit propaganda over radio Hanoi which came in clearly at night as well as the rockets.

By noon, Wilson and Chivington were on their way to the mess hall. After chow, the handlers assembled for orientation in the training area. During the session, Violette brought them up to speed about dog nomenclature.

"Gentlemen, all y'all listen up. All military working dogs keep their original names. I've already seen too damn many German Shepherds named Duke, King, and Rebel." Turning his eyes to Wilson and Chivington, he said, "This is the first dog I've seen named Beau, I gotta admit. For that matter, it's the first Doberman I've seen in 'Nam."

Chivington heard that German Shepherds were easier to train than other breeds. They worked well in various climates and terrains, but he was determined to prove that Beau was as good or better than any German Shepherd.

"There's a reason for that name, Sarge," he said to Violette.

From the corner of his eye, he saw Wilson turn to him in surprise. "Who the fuck cares, Chivington?"

"Save it for tonight," Violette said. "Meet me at the Pair-O-Dice airmen's club at 1900. We'll tip a few brewskies and get to know each other a little better. Y'all can also tell me more about your dogs, including that big Dobie."

Chapter 12

That night, surrounded by Schlitz beer cans and the rousing sounds of rock music coming from the jukebox, the six new handlers sat exchanging views about hometowns, military backgrounds, and women. Violette and Chivington engaged in a discussion about Beau while Wilson drank silently, lining up empty beer cans in front of him.

"I did a little investigating and found out that Beau was named after Civil War General P.G.T. Beauregard who ordered the firing on Ft. Sumter," Chivington spoke up enthusiastically. "Actually, his name was Pierre Toutant, and the family plantation was called Beauregard. Following Creole tradition, his family signed their name as 'Toutant de Beauregard,' saying, in essence, that they were Toutants from the Beauregard Plantation. Pierre used Toutant-Beauregard until West Point, where he dropped Toutant because he was embarrassed by his hyphenated last name. He then shortened his military name to P.G.T. Beauregard."

"I'll be damned," said Violette.

Snorting, Wilson looked away.

"After graduating from West Point, Beauregard was commissioned a second lieutenant in the artillery," Chivington went on. "Because the engineers were more prestigious at the time, Beauregard switched branches of service from artillery to engineers."

"But how'd your dog get named after a Civil War general?" Violette asked.

"Oh, for God's sake," Wilson muttered into his fifth beer, "who the fuck cares?"

Ignoring him, Chivington said, "A descendent of the Toutant family wanted to continue the family's military tradition, so they donated this well-bred, one-year-old Doberman to the canine procurement process headed for Southeast Asia. The family named the dog after the General and insisted that he be assigned to an engineering outfit. Beau trained at Lackland Air Force Base, close to San Antonio, as a sentry dog. He was among the first military dogs to arrive in 'Nam."

"I've been wonderin' why a Dobie was accepted for 'Nam," Violette said.

"I suppose it was his breeding and intelligence," Chivington said.

"Sounds more like it was the family's political clout," Wilson observed, slurring his words.

"He's the biggest damn dog I've seen over here, that's for sure," said Violette, "and that's not bad. Until we get additional dog teams, Beau, like the other dogs, will have to do double duty as both a sentry dog and a scout dog. It's better to have 'em specialize in one or the other, but there aren't enough to go around."

Violette went for more beer and soon began to catch up with Wilson. Chivington was taking it easy with the booze. He didn't want a hangover on his first day of training.

The conversation drifted into off-color jokes and on to the Confederate battle flag. Violette, a white South Carolinian, defended the flag as an emblem of Southern honor and was damn proud of its flying above the statehouse dome in Columbia. Wilson contended the rebel flag shouldn't be displayed publicly on vehicles, helmet headbands, or state capitols because it symbolized racism and segregation.

Violette stared at Wilson, unruffled but tugging at his upper lip with thumb and forefinger. Then the surface calm rippled.

"Bullshit," Violette said, and Chivington realized that both Wilson and Violette were getting a little carried away by the beer. "Does burnin' the cross of Jesus on hillsides or in front yards make the cross a symbol of evil? I don't think so. Hell, Sarge, the Confederate flag flew over the Southern armies, not over slave auctions."

"The South violated the *Constitution*," Wilson said, pressing the point. Chivington was pretty sure that "constitution" had come out with only three syllables. "Pure and simple treason, that's what secession was—treason. It divided the Union."

Now Violette banged his bottle on the table. Beer foamed up through the neck and ran down over the sides of the bottle. "My great-granddaddy fought for the South. Are you callin' my great-granddaddy a fuckin' traitor?"

"Hell, yes, if he fought for the South. That flag is a skunk, Sarge. It makes a negative statement and should be thrown in the trashcan of history. Hell, it oughta be fuckin' burned, and how 'bout the POW camp for Yankee prisoners at Anvil...Andervil...fuck." He paused, gathered himself, and pronounced evenly: "*An-der-son-ville*. It was ever' bit as bad as the Nazi camps and—"

Violette erupted. Staggering to his feet, his chair falling backwards and clattering to the floor, his fists doubled and arms cocked. He growled, "You're callin' my flag a skunk. You're callin' my flag a fuckin' Nazi flag. Well, you're nothin' but a black cocksucker!" With that, he lashed out with a fist that caught Wilson's jaw. It would have been much worse if Wilson hadn't jerked back at the last moment, and if Violette hadn't been so drunk.

Chivington watched this drama unfolding before him with stupefied horror. He couldn't believe that something as innocuous as a conversation about a dog's name could evolve into a brawl.

Wilson rolled backwards with the blow, but returned in a fury, throwing himself across the table and sending Violette crashing to the floor. Beer cans and beer foam flew everywhere. Landing on top, Wilson pummeled the sergeant twice before Chivington and two other dog handlers were able to get their wits together and pull him away.

The Air Force security police entered the fray, ordering everyone outside. Standing ramrod straight and with arms akimbo, a burly, steely-eyed NCOIC delivered a blistering, ass-chewing lecture, ordering them to sober up, bury the hatchet, and get their sorry butts back to their hootches.

All of which, Chivington thought, was a damned good idea.

Wiping his face, a little more sober now, Violette mumbled, "Shit, I'm sorry, Sarge. Too much damn beer, and my feelings got hurt. Oughtta not said what I did about...well, ya know..."

"'Bout me bein' a black cocksucker?" Wilson offered. Violette nodded, wincing a little.

"Yeah, that. My apology. I shoulda left out the 'black' part, and I'm sorry I hit ya."

Holding a blood-soaked handkerchief to his lip, Wilson muttered, "I'll live." That was as close to accepting Violette's apology as Wilson would go.

"We all need some shut-eye," Violette said. "Tomorrow, I want all y'all standin' tall with your dogs at 0700 in the compound."

#

The hootch to which Chivington and Wilson had been assigned was the typical wooden hut set on a concrete foundation with a corrugated sheet-metal roof. Sandbags were piled waist high around its walls as protection against mortar or rocket attacks.

Wilson sat on his cot, dabbing the still-oozing lip.

"That's gonna be sore for a few days," Chivington said, sitting down across from him on his own cot.

"No shit," Wilson said. "Thanks for the diagnosis, Dr. Chivington."

Chivington sat for a moment longer, looking across at Wilson, thinking he should just leave well enough alone and go to bed, but he couldn't quite do it. He had to have a closer look at that huge chip on Wilson's shoulder.

"What the hell was that all about, Sarge?" he asked.

Wilson fixed him with a hard look. "You were there, Chivington."

"Yeah, but I don't know what it was all about. We were all just drinkin' beer and talkin'. Nobody meant for anything to be taken seriously."

"Anyone who supports hoisting the fucking Confederate flag above a state capitol has got to have some sense pounded into him. That's all."

"You from South Carolina, Sarge?"

"Hell, no. I grew up in the fine, segregated community of Tuscaloosa, Alabama."

Chivington stared at him in surprise. "No shit? That's my hometown."

"No shit," Wilson muttered, looking away.

Chivington was missing something. He just didn't know what it was.

"We're from the same town, and we're gonna be stuck here together in this fuckin' war for quite a while," he said, "so maybe you could tell me why ya act like I'm a piece of shit that got stuck to the bottom of your shoe."

Wilson's eyes, hard as marbles, fixed on Chivington. "We're from the same town, Chivington, but it was a hell of a lot different for me than for you."

"What the hell is that supposed to mean?"

"My daddy was a Southern Baptist minister, and he knew what was right and what was wrong."

"Like what?"

"Like how our ancestors were brought over from Africa to serve as slaves to your white ancestors. He knew that was wrong. I've seen crosses burned on our front yard, and I know that was wrong. I remember water fountains and bathroom signs for whites only, and total exclusion or required balcony seating in movie theaters. That was so you and your white-ass family wouldn't have to put up with seein' us little nigger kids."

Chivington held Wilson's hard stare, refusing to let his eyes drop. "Is that what you're holdin' against me? You're pissed off because I'm white?"

"I remember how my dad cried when the 16th Street Baptist Church was bombed in Birmingham," Wilson went on as if Chivington hadn't spoken. "Do you remember when that happened, Chivington?"

"Hell yes. Four kids were killed—"

"Four *black* kids. The Ku Klux Klan was behind that, but nobody was ever brought to justice for it. Not too surprisin', really. J. Edgar Hoover was no civil rights supporter. He considered Martin an enemy and a Communist sympathizer. The FBI shelved the case. Who cares about four little black kids burnin' ta death, right?"

"That's bullshit, Sarge," Chivington said angrily. "Lots of people care, whether black or white—"

"Sure, they do. That's why they burned my dad's Beulah Baptist Church in Tuscaloosa to ashes. They didn't get any little black kids this time, though. People saw 'em that time, in those fuckin' white sheets and hoods."

Oh, shit. Now Chivington had an idea of what this was all about, and why Wilson had been on his ass from the moment he arrived in this abode of the damned.

"My dad died two months later of a heart attack," Wilson went on, his voice bitter, "but it was really a broken heart. There was no money to rebuild the church. Everything he'd worked for all his life was gone. Of course, nobody was ever brought to justice for that, either," he paused, staring at Chivington through narrowed eyes, "but there were some rumors, and a name that kept comin' up. Chivington, I think it was. Tyrone Chivington, grand dragon of the Tuscaloosa KKK."

Now Chivington's eyes slid away to a shadowy corner of the hootch. "He's my uncle...my father's brother."

"I suppose your daddy was there that night, too. Was he the one that tore out all the flowers my mom had planted in front of the church? Or maybe he was the one that—"

"My father was dead by then," Chivington said, still staring into the corner. "Fucked up his liver with booze."

"How about you?" Wilson pressed. "Were you there?"

Now Chivington's eyes snapped back to Wilson. "Hell, no! I hated those bastards—"

"Sure, ya did."

Chivington was short of breath. He had to pause for a minute and gather himself.

"Listen, Wilson," he said at last, "my father was a drunk. He beat my mother, and he beat us kids whenever we didn't move fast enough to suit 'im. He spouted that KKK shit every day, and he'd slap us hard across the face if we uttered even a word of disagreement. I never shed a tear the night he died. None of us in the family did. We hated 'im, and we hated everything he stood for.

"Tyrone is worse. Even the KKK couldn't put up with 'im when he kept gettin' drunk and braggin' around about all the things he'd done to those 'niggers'— including burning down that church. They kicked 'im out of the KKK and even made 'im leave town. I don't know where he is now, and I don't give a fuck, as long as he never crosses my path again. In college, I joined my black friends in protests and marches. I got the shit beat out of me a few times for it, too."

Wilson pursed his lips, and looked down at his clasped hands. "Yeah, that's what you say," he muttered.

Chivington decided he'd had enough. He got to his feet and headed for the door. He needed fresh air. By the time he came back an hour or so later, Wilson was in his cot, facing the wall.

#

Later, lying in the darkness, sleep eluded Chivington. His thoughts were on what Violette had spat at Wilson: *Are you callin' my great-granddaddy a fuckin' traitor?*

It was likely, Chivington knew, that Violette's great-grandfather had been fighting for a cause he believed in. In that sense, there was honor in what he had done. Chivington's father, grand dragon of the Tuscaloosa KKK, believed only in bigotry and hatred. He'd had no

166

honor, but the Chivingtons had been bred from a long line of intolerance. His great-grandfather had earned the blue ribbon on that score. An ordained Methodist minister, Colonel John M. Chivington had been known as the Fighting Parson. Colonel Chivington's claim to fame was his ignoble engagement in the 1864 Sand Creek Massacre involving defenseless Indian women (many of them pregnant) and children. The six hundred or more Cheyenne and Arapahos had been guaranteed presidential protection.

Colonel Chivington and his seven hundred Colorado volunteers, with the blessing of Colorado Governor John Evans, planned and carried out this brutal slaughter.

This robust and towering bearded bull of a man bragged that he was going to "collect scalps and wade in gore;" that it was "right and honorable under God to kill and scalp Indians—even children." He collected one hundred scalps.

My God, the awful things human beings can do to each other, Chivington thought, his stomach tightening into a hard knot. When would the killing and hatred end in this far and distant land called Vietnam? Haven't we learned anything since the Sand Creek Massacre?

Jim Chivington had no answers, and it took him a long time to get to sleep. The Cheyenne death song haunted him:

"Nothing lives long

Only the Earth and the mountains."

Chapter 13

It was raining the next morning, but that wasn't enough to drive away the sweltering heat. The air was so humid that breathing was difficult. The sky was slate gray.

Violette and Wilson were still hung over. Wilson's upper lip was swollen to twice its normal size. Violette had a knuckle-sized bruise under his left eye, and another on his forehead. It was clear they were also nursing some inner wounds, but nothing was said of the night before. Chivington was grateful for that; he wanted to get on with the business of training Beau.

He also regretted confronting Wilson as he had. Wilson was unusually quiet and subdued, but he said nothing about their conversation.

In the training compound, five student handlers and their German Shepherds lined up with Wilson and Chivington. One of the dogs was in a bad temper, snarling now and then at the other dogs, and once turning and snapping at his handler.

Beau looked around with interest, but he made no aggressive moves. From time to time, Chivington reached down and scratched behind the dog's ears.

Violette grumbled about having to train two handlers for the same dog, but he understood a direct order. Chivington would be Beau's primary handler, with Wilson as backup.

"These dogs," Violette began, taking a lecturer's stance in front of the handlers, "are not *your* dogs. They belong to the U.S. Army, and as far as the Army is concerned, they are just like any other piece of military equipment."

Chivington bristled at that, but decided to keep his thoughts to himself.

"For equipment to function, it must remain in good repair," Violette continued. "This equipment must be maintained. That means daily exercise and regular checkups, including weighing your dog at least once a week to determine if he's losin' or gainin' weight. If he's losin', then you'd better get him back in shape, pronto. A simple check of the dog's ribs can determine weight. Stand facin' your dog. Ya should be able to see or feel a clearly defined waist behind the rib cage. Run your fingers along the rib cage. That'll tell ya if he's over or underweight."

Violette reminded them that this training did not attempt to replicate in detail that of Lackland Air Force Base. Dogs went through a rigid physical exam. Forty-five percent failed. The Lackland dogs also had to go through a twenty-one day temperament test before they were assigned to a permanent handler.

Because of the endurance factor, Violette explained that patrol missions should be scheduled early in the morning or late in the afternoon.

"Dogs work better with frequent breaks and cool-off periods. They won't respond as well to commands in the heat of the day. Unit commanders should adjust their patrols to the dog's pace."

"Right," Wilson muttered, his voice so low that only Chivington could hear, "let's plan everything around the fuckin' dogs. Maybe we can get Charlie to cooperate, too."

"In most cases," Violette was saying, "dogs off-leash work about twenty-five yards ahead of their handlers. While on-leash, the dog should be kept to a minimum of fifteen yards or so at about one to two miles-per-hour pace. At that speed, they'll be able to clear an eight- to ten-foot-wide path—and, gentlemen, don't get attached to your dogs. When you go home (DEROS), your dog stays here. He'll get his discharge when he dies."

"What?" Chivington burst out. "Sarge, you've gotta be kiddin'."

"Afraid not," Violette said. "If a dog handler is killed, wounded, or lucky enough to complete his tour of duty and go home, his dog is reassigned to another handler." He stared hard at Chivington. "That's how you got that Dobie, right?

Chivington nodded. "Well…yeah…"

"These dogs will serve in Vietnam until they die in combat, are killed by disease, or succumb to other unfortunate circumstances. Believe me, Corporal, none of these dogs will die of old age, and some of 'em will die back in the world."

"What the hell do the Army brass know about these dogs?" Chivington fumed. "These dogs are soldiers, not equipment."

Two or three of the other handlers muttered agreement.

"What you or I think about it doesn't matter a whole hell of a lot, Corporal," Violette exclaimed.

Chivington grasped Beau's leash firmly and kept silent, but in his mind, he was thinking, *Beau, I'm gonna do my damnedest to make sure you don't get stuck over here.*

For dog health and care, Violette pointed to Army Field Manual 20-20. "By tomorrow, I want all of you to be familiar with this book. That's homework assignment number one. Y'all learn how to groom, feed, water, and daily inspect the eyes, ears, nose, skin, and feet of your dogs. If your dog gets injured, wounded, or just plain sick, you'll be responsible for first aid until ya can get 'im to a vet. Appendix C will give ya specific details on daily care. You'll have to maintain your dog's Daily Performance Record, and that'll be part of their final scorecard for this course. Chapters Six and Seven in FM 20-20 give ya food rules for maintenance runs and combat missions. These chapters also remind ya to give your dogs the chance to evacuate before any run, combat or otherwise. Any questions?"

"Evacuate?" one of the handlers asked.

"He means take a dump," Wilson said.

"Can we keep our copy of FM 20-20?" another handler asked. "It's hard for me to remember what I read unless I can mark it in the book."

Violette nodded. "No problem, soldier. It's yours. The taxpayers have already paid for it."

Violette went on to explain that the handlers must not add to, drop, or in any way modify the methods, techniques, and procedures of their training. In turn, he said, critical comments and positive recommendations to improve training effectiveness would be welcome.

Violette outlined other key areas of training, such as obedience. He explained that the dogs would have to learn on-leash and off-leash commands by voice or by hand signals, such as *heel, down, stay, come*, and *move out*, but he said a handler should avoid commands too close together, because they would only confuse the dog.

"Never give a command that cannot be carried out," he stressed.

He went on to say that canine training was based on a rewards-correction-praise system, and that a dog sharp in obedience is a good indicator of an alert handler—both essential for survival in 'Nam. He emphasized that the handlers must do the right thing if the dog is to work properly. A well-trained dog would not function well with a poor handler.

"We're fightin' a shadow war with no front lines, rarely facin' the enemy one-on-one. Ten percent of our casualties are caused by mines and booby traps, but ambush takes its toll, as well. So learn and live."

He reminded them that they were here for cross-training, meaning a scout dog as well as mine and tripwire detection training.

"In theory, a handler should never attempt to do things that he and his dog are not trained to do, but under the present circumstances of a military dog shortage, the dogs in 'Nam at this time will have to do whatever needs to be done, and y'all remember that a food reward should never be used for anything but a mine or tripwire detection situation. A dog can hear the wind against a tripwire. That deserves praise and food, but never feed during a correction."

"Why not, Sarge?" Chivington asked.

"'Cause when your dog does what ya tell 'im to do, ya reward 'im right away with praise or food, but if he fucks up, ya don't want to reinforce a bad response. In order to correct 'im, grab 'im by his working harness and lead 'im toward the target. When ya get within two feet of the target, force 'im to sit. He ought to sit there by himself for at least one minute, without a reward. Then give 'im the move-out command. That's correction. That's stayin' alive!"

Chivington nodded. "I see what ya mean, Sarge. That's obedience, repetition, and consistency."

"You got it right, Corporal. To your dog, obeyin' your command means verbal or physical praise, and sittin' in front of a mine or tripwire means a food reward. Save the most powerful reward for that. You're tellin' your dog that his most important response is to sit before a mine or tripwire. Charlie sets 'em almost anywhere, even as high as five feet above ground, especially in tree holes. He uses bark to contour the ordnance where a limb branches away from the trunk. A mine can also be set off-trail behind a bush, a clump of grass, or a vine.

"One more thing: on maintenance runs, hold food back once in a while, because that's the way it will be on a real combat run. Out there in slope territory, you won't always have time to get a food reward out of your ruck and give it to 'im."

One of the handlers raised his hand. "If he don't always get the reward, won't he stop doin' what he's supposed to do?"

Violette shook his head. "Even if ya give 'im the reward once in a while, he'll still want to do what he's supposed to do. In the textbooks, it's called intermittent reinforcement. He'll always be expectin' the reward, but not gettin' it won't stop 'im from hopin' for it next time."

Violette told the handlers not to smoke or talk much while handling their dog because it would interfere with the dog's senses of smell and hearing. The dogs were trained to be quiet, too, and all commands to the dogs would eventually be given silently, with arm and hand signals.

"I guess you're sayin'," Wilson cut in, "that when a handler and his dog are walkin' point in a patrol, it's the dog that's in charge, not the team leader."

If he expected Violette to back down from that, he was mistaken.

"You're damned right, Sarge. The dog can sense danger that nobody else in the patrol can sense. If they decide to ignore what he tells 'im, they're fucked. A lot of men are KIA because of that bullshit ignorance."

Chivington wondered if that was what had happened to Beau's former team members. Sergeant Jackson, he knew, had not been enthusiastic about taking a dog team with him on patrol.

"Maybe we should have the dogs makin' policy decisions, too," Wilson muttered.

"Maybe so," one of the other handlers chimed in. "They could probably do a better job than those fuckin' assholes in Washington."

They all laughed at that. Even Wilson cracked a smile.

"I know what their first order would be," another handler said. "No more dogs in Vietnam."

That brought more laughter, and they all loosened up a little.

"Back to business," Violette said. "A dog will hear sounds you won't hear, and his sense of smell is far greater than yours. It'll be your job to interpret what the dog is tellin' ya, and to act accordingly. The design of their ears allows them to raise, rotate, and tune in the faintest of sounds."

Violette then instructed the handlers not to use punishment as a form of training.

"Punishment teaches fear, and a fearful dog in the bush will get your ass in deep shit. Remember, your dog wants to please, and he enjoys finding the scent. That makes for a good working partner. Instead of punishment, use obedience reinforcement."

"Sarge, how long will we use on-leash obedience training?" asked Chivington.

"Until ya have complete control. Then you'll run your dog through a ten-minute refresher every day or so to keep 'im sharp, with both on- and off-leash commands. Don't wear out obedience commands. These dogs already know the basics, but if ya want to keep 'em sharp, trainin' never stops—even on weekends. Our graphs and records prove that if a dog is inactive over the weekend, he's not as sharp on Monday as he was on Friday."

Chivington nodded. He could understand that. *At least dogs don't drink themselves to oblivion on the weekend and come on duty Monday mornin' with a thumpin' hangover.*

"One more thing: in order to avoid unnecessary injuries, don't ever stake your dog out with a choke collar. Always use a leather collar."

Violette told them they would get twenty-four-hour passes on Saturday for Bien Hoa City and Saigon, which was about one hour's drive by jeep.

"Be sure y'all carry your raincoats with ya, along with your side arms, and try to tone down your ragin' hormones. There's plenty of booze and pussy out there—along with every venereal disease known to man."

#

After retiring their restless, hungry, and thirsty dogs, the handlers were ordered to reassemble for a short meeting before breaking for chow.

They were instructed to review kenneling instructions with the kennel master. Then Violette introduced the vet tech, Specialist Four Larry Williamson, who would tell them about canine first aid, including the proper removal of blood ticks and the procedure for their own routine sick call.

Williamson explained that tick-borne diseases like ehrlichiosis could be prevented if the tick is removed immediately.

"Ticks need protein. That's why they go for the blood. Keep your dog out of tall grass, tree branches, or bushes as much as possible."

"Hey, Doc," a handler called out, "this is Vietnam."

Williamson nodded. "Right, so your dogs will get ticks. If you remove the ugly fuckers early on, they can't hurt you much. It takes twenty-four to forty-eight hours to infect a human, deer, or dog. It's best if you use tweezers to grab the tick's mouthparts as close to the skin as possible. Then pull the entire tick away, slow and easy, with no twistin'. If you twist or snap 'em, you'll leave mouthparts in the skin which will cause infection and the possible spread of disease. Once that happens, you'll get a red rash lookin' like a bull's-eye. Then your dog will start feelin' weak."

He warned them about poison ivy, which in his terminology also included poison oak and sumac. He said that poison ivy is an allergic contact dermatitis caused by the sap of certain weeds that thrive near rivers and streams in humid and warm climates like Vietnam.

"Ivy penetrates the skin within twelve to fifty minutes, and then you've got a rash, redness, swelling, blisters, and a bitch of an itch for at least ten days. You can even get it from touchin' your dog's coat, if he's been exposed."

"Are we always lookin' for three leaves?" asked one handler.

"Over here, you may find it with leaves in groups of three, five, seven, or even nine. Ivy has yellow-green flowers and white berries. It grows as a low shrub or climbing vine. Once you have it, wash your skin quickly without soap, and then scrub under your fingernails and hope the medic has some calamine lotion to spare."

"Why not use soap?" a handler asked.

"Soap can spread the oil from the weeds, which is really the poison that causes the trouble."

Williamson told them the U.S. Army was training most of the vet techs, also known as animal specialists or by their MOS 91Ts, for all the services at Walter Reed Army Hospital in Washington, D.C. The bulk of their curriculum consisted mainly of preventive medicine and canine first aid.

When Williamson asked if there were any questions, there were none, but looking around, Chivington could see doubt on the faces of his fellow handlers. They had been given a lot to take in at once, and he knew they must be feeling as overwhelmed as he was with all the material and training skills they and their dogs would have to absorb in such a short time.

After evening chow, the handlers' hootch resembled a freshman college dorm the night before a final exam: quiet and studious.

During the next few days, the dogs and their handlers were hustled through several phases of training, including the obstacle course.

Each morning, the handlers would have breakfast, then go to the kennel to feed the dogs, refresh their water, and clean the runs.

During the training, each dog handler had to carry a canteen of water, an eight-foot leather leash, a leather collar, a choke chain, a twenty-five-foot nylon leash, a leather muzzle, a first-aid bandage, and a .45-caliber pistol in a leather holster.

Basic obedience was the root of training, and Chivington soon learned that successful preparation was all about repetition and consistency. After mastering simple voice commands, they graduated to voice commands accompanied by hand signals.

One day in the training compound, as handlers were teaching their dogs to get on and off choppers with haste and dispatch, an incident occurred that was hair-raising at the time, yet almost amusing when Chivington thought about it later.

A Huey gunship, losing engine power and trailing white smoke from ruptured hydraulic lines, was almost home free when it had to make a dead-stick emergency landing in the training area. It was clear from the chopper's erratic movements that the pilot was struggling to control the pitch of the rotor blades.

Wilson and Chivington had stopped to watch the situation. Chivington saw that Beau was following the helicopter with interest as it wobbled toward the ground. The vibrating chopper was only a couple of feet above the ground when Beau lurched like a bolt of lightning, yanking free of Chivington's grasp. With leash dragging, he leapt aboard, uninvited.

Rattled by the action of this predator-like animal, the door gunner, wearing his "chicken plate" chest armor, turned around and reached for his .45, yanking it from its holster. In an instant, Beau locked his powerful jaws around the gunner's wrist. The door gunner quickly grabbed the .45 with his other hand and brought the muzzle around to aim at Beau's head.

All of this happened in about five seconds, and during that time the pilot managed to get the chopper onto the ground in a teeth-rattling landing.

Chivington, M-16 in hand, vaulted into the chopper, shoved the rifle in the gunner's face, and said, "Pull that trigger, and you're dead, asshole."

Beau released the door gunner's wrist. The man stumbled backward, lowering his side arm, as his face became deathly pale.

Chivington lowered his M-16 and stepped back, giving Beau the recall command, "Come here. Heel," which he did.

After the chopper shut down and off-loaded, the pilot, Chief Warrant Officer Jerry Webb, dressed Violette up and down for not having better control of his troops and that "wild animal." Webb, a lean, sinewy man with dark brown eyes and matching hair, demanded the name, rank, service number, and the commanding officers' names of both Violette and Chivington, threatening to bring them up on charges.

It was obvious that Webb knew precious little about military dogs and their function in Vietnam. The chopper crew was lucky to be alive, and the puncture wounds on the soldier's wrist didn't bleed much at all.

Toward the end of week one, the handlers and their dogs were put through routine scout-dog maneuvers. Violette prefaced the morning session by explaining the difference between scout and tracker techniques. There were no U.S. tracker teams in Vietnam yet, but Violette said they would be coming soon.

"Tracker dogs take a single scent off the ground, a blood trail, a footprint, or clothing," explained Violette. "The dog needs to follow that scent without engagin' the target."

"Why don't they use bloodhounds for this, Sarge?" asked one of the handlers.

"I don't think they'd make good trackers in 'Nam. They bark, slobber, and thrash around too much. They just like to play. In my mind, black Labs would make the best trackers."

Violette continued discussing how a scout dog will alert to any unfamiliar scent from the air or ground, often upwind from his position, while walking point.

"When your dog alerts while on patrol, your job is to immediately drop down onto one knee and determine why he's alertin'. If no enemy contact is made, ya resume the point position and continue on. If your dog's alert results in contact with Charlie, then you and your dog will move back inside the patrol's main body.

"Once Charlie has been detected, these dogs can follow a scent as old as twenty-four hours. However, I recommend no more than a three-hour delay." On a small chalkboard standing before the group, Violette drew an invisible scent cone in the shape of an arrowhead. He said that when a tracker or scout dog passed through that cone, he was on target and must work the downwind side of the trail. He said troops that trail the dogs should always work on the upwind side of a dog's path.

"What about a no-wind condition?" asked a handler.

"In that case, the scent most often stays close to the target," said Violette. "That reduces the dog's chances of finding enemy targets that are not close to his path. Under a no-wind situation, you'd better follow the path with care, or Charlie will blow your ass off."

"On a windy day, then, it will take longer to find a potential ambush zone," Chivington stated.

Violette nodded. "High wind means the target scent carries further, and you're right about the dog taking longer to find Charlie. Other factors such as heat, humidity, and density of vegetation all affect the ability of a dog to alert."

Violette decided to call it a day. He dismissed them with a final order.

"It's a little early for chow call, but take the dogs back to the kennel, feed and water 'em, clean up, and be ready for some real live ordnance and ambush detection conditions tomorrow. In the next couple of days, you and the dogs will have to pull it all together and get ready for that final exam."

Chivington was hungry, but he attended to Beau first. Before feeding him, he checked the food package for insects. Bugs were everywhere in Vietnam, and it was always a challenge to keep them out of the dog food.

#

That night, Chivington awakened to the blare of barking dogs blasting its way through the mist and humidity saturating the base. He hurriedly pulled on some clothes and bolted toward the commotion with his M-16 in hand.

As he rounded the corner of the building and reached the kennels, his legs suddenly stopped moving as if he were stranded in quicksand. Seeing was not believing! A huge king cobra had somehow made its way into the kennels. It was coiled, its head swaying, tongue flicking, ready to strike. Beau made snarling lunges against the kennel fencing, his ivory-white teeth gleaming in the pale light.

Chivington could see that Beau was doing everything he could to engage the enemy, and it was likely, he realized, that if Beau had not drawn the cobra's attention and raised such a ruckus, the cobra would've buried its fangs into someone before the night was out.

Chivington flipped the selector of his M-16 over to semi-automatic, took careful aim to make sure no ricochet would come back at him or the dogs, and blew off most of the cobra's head with one shot. One more finished the job. The rest of its slithering body went into spastic contortions.

After a deep, audible breath, Chivington regained his composure. He had never seen such a frightful, yet exotic-looking serpent. In a way, he hated killing it.

By now, the hootch had emptied. Violette and the handlers were at the ready with their M-16s. When he saw that the action was over, Violette told them to salvage the remains for dog food.

During breakfast, all talk focused on the incident. Chivington remarked with almost fatherly pride that Beau hadn't backed down. If it had not been for the kennel wire, Chivington was sure that Beau would have attacked the cobra. As for the other dogs, their yelps seemed to be more out of fright than anything else. He thought Beau was majestic.

Chapter 14

A torrid sun baked the handlers and their dogs as they congregated on the training ground for their final sessions.

Violette outlined what they would be doing for the last few days of training. For their scout-dog maintenance runs, some local village children would be brought into the compound, basically to play hide-and-seek with the dogs at various points on the obstacle course.

Violette reminded them that scout-dog teams on point were valuable because of their ability to detect and search out the enemy far more efficiently than a grunt without a dog, but he once again reminded them that a handler and his dog must complement each other in order to be effective.

"That's why you've gotta know your dog and how he communicates with ya. Watch his eyes. Eyes tell it all, and be sensitive to his body language. Watch for his alert to that scent."

Chivington knew that he had to identify clearly when and how Beau alerted, so he would know what Beau's signals meant. He had to know what Beau would do when he sensed various kinds of danger, from tripwires to a VC soldier hiding in a tree.

To Chivington's surprise, Wilson asked a question. It was his first sign of interest in the training. "What happens if the pace of the patrol is not in rhythm with the dog team on point?"

"In that case," Violette said, "if a patrol needs to increase or decrease its pace and avoid fuckin' up a dog's detection ability, then the point man and his dog will regress to the rear of the formation 'til ya get it worked out. Another important aspect of walkin' point is that the point man oughtta have a cover man. A cover man, gentlemen, is nothin' more than a bodyguard. You need somebody else to cover your ass when you're on point, 'cause your main focus will be on that dog."

Wilson turned toward Chivington. Their eyes locked. Chivington thought, *To hell with that bullshit. One eye will be on my dog, and the other will be lookin' for Charlie.* He remembered how Martinez looked after the ambush. *No way that's gonna happen to Mrs. Chivington's son,* he vowed.

#

Later that morning, the first scout-dog maintenance runs began. Each dog would have to work at least two different day and night trails which varied in length from

187

one-half to one mile. Terrain and conditions reflected what the dogs might encounter in an actual combat environment, including VC clothing to teach scent.

Detachment personnel were placed at various junctures in order to grade the dog teams. Dog team scores were based upon both subjective and objective criteria, such as motivation or desire of the working dog, ability to solve trail problems, number of misses, intensity of alerts, response to directional commands, rate of speed, endurance/stamina level, timely fashion of the handler's commands, and the handler's adherence to procedure. Night runs included the dog's reaction to illumination flares and shotgun blasts.

Surrounded by ant and termite hills, dense trees, underbrush, and tall elephant grass, Chivington took Beau on the first scout-dog maintenance run. Attached to Beau's working harness was a fifteen-foot leather leash, giving Chivington good control and the ability to limit the number of hand and voice commands. Yet he would be close by in case the dog came upon a tripwire or booby trap. Farther down the path, Beau would be released to work off-leash. Wilson was scheduled to work the night ambush run.

As they were approaching the first grading station, Beau caught an odor which sent him into a high-alert status. He stopped and sat, his good ear rigid and perked forward. His damaged ear made a valiant effort, but drooped at the tip. Chivington raised a clenched fist, as if to signal a halt. With his M-16 ready, he proceeded with caution into the dense underbrush.

About fifteen yards from Beau's alert, Chivington located the eye of a would-be killing zone of an ambush. Squatting behind a thorny, yellowish-green hedge was a young Vietnamese boy who had been recruited to act as a decoy VC on this training exercise.

"Chao ong [Good morning]," the boy said. "Duoc gap ong. [I'm pleased to meet you.]"

"Toi rat mung thoc gap ong [I'm pleased to meet you]," replied Chivington. "Ong co biet noi? Tieng Anh Khong? Xin ong cho biet ten? [Do you speak English? What's your name?]"

"Huang," the boy replied, giving his name. "Da coit thoi. Cho! [Yes, a little. Dog!]" he exclaimed, pointing a shaking finger at Beau. The three decoys had not been told much about the dogs, because Violette wanted as much realism as possible.

"Thua co, cho [Yes, a dog]," replied Chivington. "Ong muon...? [May I offer...?]"

Breaking in, the half-smiling boy asked, "Phong ve-sinh o dau? [Where's the toilet?]"

Chivington could see a small, round wet spot on Huang's black shorts, and a steady stream trickling down his left leg. Huang was petrified at the sight of this imposing, 120-pound black and tan canine with piercing eyes and sharp white teeth.

Smiling, Chivington walked over to the kid and rubbed his thick head of black hair while Beau licked his face. Huang's grin erupted from ear to ear.

Chivington and Beau had passed their first test with flying colors. Chivington praised Beau for doing such a great job. They were working well together. Violette had said that a bond would develop between handler and dog, and the strength of that connection would affect how well they worked together.

Chivington felt close to Beau, and he was pretty sure Beau felt the same way.

#

By day's end, all dogs had been promoted to the next phase of testing—night runs. Prior to hearing their critique, the handlers were able to treat the boys before they returned to their village. A chorus of "keo, si-cula [candy and soda]" reverberated throughout the compound as the boys enjoyed the candy, chocolate, and soda purchased from the BX. They even had some extra goodies to take home. After boarding the jeep, the boys waved goodbye, and their echo of "xin-cam on ong nhieu [thank you very much]" faded as they departed.

During the critical commentary, the handlers learned that most dogs had completed their first round with an "A" (average score), except for Beau. He finished with an "AA" (above average). One German Shepherd named Rebel came close to getting a "P" (poor), but the scorer changed his mind after a reevaluation.

From day one, that particular Shepherd had a lousy disposition. He tried to bite anyone who came close to him, even his own handler. Chivington once saw the handler slap the dog across the mouth, and that only made things worse. Luckily, Violette hadn't seen him do that.

Each maintenance run score sheet had a blank section for the scorer's comments, and Beau's was completed with one word: *Outstanding.*

The night runs were also satisfactory, except for Rebel. He had a few problems during the day run. Rebel rated "P" and needed more training. Wilson and Beau were again graded better than average.

Chivington was surprised and glad to see that Wilson was taking to the training. He worked well with Beau, and he even seemed to have a positive attitude about it. Although the strongest bond had been formed between Chivington and Beau, it was obvious that Wilson was getting along with the Doberman. When the training began, Wilson's verbal praise to the dog had sounded forced and insincere, but now Wilson seemed to enjoy working with Beau, and his words of praise sounded genuine.

Maybe Beau is whittling away at that chip on Wilson's shoulder, Chivington thought.

Wilson and Chivington studied in detail Appendix A of their briefing guide regarding the drawings and notes depicting typical VC and NVA mines and booby traps. The VC and NVA were very clever at creating all kinds of nasty traps. All of the handlers—both engineers and infantry—would face live mines on the next day's runs. They needed to be alert, or suffer possible injuries.

One of the most dangerous tripwire configurations was called the daisy chain. It consisted of three or more mines, grenades, mortar shells, and artillery rounds, all connected by a circuit of tripwires. Another booby trap was the dreaded punji pit—a hole eighteen to twenty-four inches deep, with sharpened bamboo spikes anchored at various angles. A tripwire six to twelve inches from the top of the pit would detonate a hand grenade, which in turn triggered an artillery round. Even if the explosives didn't go off, the fecal-contaminated spikes could inflict serious injury to the dog and his handler.

Because of the danger and seriousness of the live ordnance course, the scoring, according to Violette, would differ from the scout-dog evaluations. Dogs and their handlers would be rated one (very bad) to five (excellent). Canines would be graded for acuteness, along with speed of response and correctness of position. By the same measure, handlers would be judged by proper use of voice and hand commands, and the effectiveness of praise and correcting techniques.

"Both must fit together," said Violette.

Chivington didn't have to be told that things happened fast in the bush. He had already learned that the hard way. A lot would depend on how well he and Beau worked as a team.

Rebel went first. About fifty yards into the run, an explosion occurred, followed by ear-splitting yelps and a booming call for a medic. Rebel had wandered too far ahead of his handler and snagged a drag tripwire which appeared to be no more than a loose wire on the path. He had missed the scent.

Two dustoff choppers were on standby for this very reason. The uninjured handler and his wounded dog were transported to Doc Blevins at Cam Ranh Bay.

Before sending out the next team, which consisted of Chivington and Beau, Violette explained to the group that Rebel's pace was too fast.

"This is what happens when your dog gets too far ahead of ya. Ya must recall the dog and give 'im a *stay* command. Remember, keep 'im fifteen or so yards off-leash, no more. After the recall, have 'im *stay* for one minute, then *move out*. When his pace is right, give 'im lots of verbal praise."

Chivington was nervous when he and Beau started along the trail. He kept his attention on Beau's head and ears as they moved forward slowly. Beau worked the trail like a pro. Not only did he detect a kick-the-can type mine, consisting of a tin can with a pinless grenade, but he also discovered a tilt rod anti-tank mine designed to disable tanks. When a tank ran over the rod, it tilted a few degrees, setting off a charge under the belly of the vehicle.

Beau's most difficult detection came in the form of a simple-looking rock in the road called a stone mine. This was nothing more than a mixture of explosives and concrete, but it was destructive to man, machine, and beast.

As the day wore on, the entire class of dogs and handlers completed their live-ordnance runs without further incident. Violette was pleased with the results. The numerical ratings averaged 3.5. Beau's grade of 4.5 once again put him at the head of the class.

"By God," Violette said, looking at Beau with open admiration, "I guess Dobies can cut it over here, after all."

He said this class, except for the wounded Shepherd, was ready for graduation. He also mentioned that Doc Blevins had performed minor surgery on Rebel's front paws and his prognosis was good. After recovery, Rebel would most likely be returning to Bien Hoa for retraining.

"With a different handler next time," he added. "Those two just never got along."

He also reminded them of the farewell party to be held that night at the airmen's club.

"After ya take care of the dogs and clean up, meet me after chow at the club. I'll have your paperwork completed before ya head back to your assignments on Saturday afternoon. Y'all did a damn good job, and I salute Beauregard. He may be a Dobie, but he's one hell of a dog!"

That evening's gathering was joyful despite the one canine injury. The beer, music, laughter, and high fives carried well into the evening—and "Eleven O'clock Charlie" didn't crash the party.

#

Gray clouds hovered over the base the next afternoon as the handlers and their dogs boarded choppers that would fly them back to their respective base camps.

Returning to Phan Rang felt good to Chivington, even though the accommodations were not as "plush" as the ones they'd had at Bien Hoa. The troops at Phan Rang were still in tents and prefab housing, but it was home, like it or not.

After kenneling Beau, Wilson and Chivington presented themselves to their company commander in his sandbagged bunker. Both wore new patches above their nametags, showing the black head of a dog against a yellow background.

Their meeting was brief. Captain Wojtacha told them they had done a good job with the training, but he needed to address the incident with the helicopter at Bien Hoa.

"Warrant Officer Webb spoke to Colonel Ricci about bringin' you up on charges, Corporal Chivington."

"What for, sir?" Chivington asked, his heart rate picking up as he thought about a possible Article 15 (nonjudicial punishment).

"Endangerin' the life of his crew, for one thing," Wojtacha said, "and threatenin' to shoot Webb's door gunner, for another."

Chivington was trying to put together an acceptable reply when he got unexpected support from Wilson.

"Now hold on a minute, sir," said Wilson. "That chopper made an emergency landin' in our training area. We had just completed the chopper phase of our trainin' with Beau, and he did exactly what he had been trained to do. That's the kind of spirit he has."

Chivington stared at Wilson in surprise, then decided to add his own two cents' worth. "That's right, sir. That chopper invaded Beau's territory."

"Hell, I know that," snapped Wojtacha, "and so does Colonel Ricci. When Colonel Ricci got Webb on the field phone, he told that pussy how much this dog and his men mean to him, and he wasn't gonna let some ticket-punching asshole interfere with his mission at Phan Rang. He told Webb that as far as he was concerned, the dog and his handler acted in accordance with their training."

Chivington and Wilson both stared at Wojtacha in amazement.

"He did, sir?" Chivington asked.

"You bet your ass he did. He also told Webb to get fucked."

Wilson burst into laughter. "He said that, sir?"

"He did. I was right there. You're dismissed."

"Thank you, sir."

They saluted and did an about-face.

Outside, Chivington said, "Thanks, Sarge. I didn't really think you'd stand up for Beau like that."

"Well, fuck," Wilson said, sounding put off, "Beau's a pretty good dog, as dogs go. He hasn't sniffed my crotch or slobbered all over me even once—not yet, anyway. Mainly, I didn't want that asshole Webb to get any satisfaction. He's a ticket puncher, like Colonel Ricci said."

"Well...anyway..."

But Wilson was already striding off in the direction of his hootch.

"Thanks anyway," Chivington said, but Wilson was too far away to hear.

#

After taking showers—if standing on a wooden pallet under a 300-gallon water tank with a protruding pipe for a showerhead could be called a shower—and grabbing some chow, beer fueled the evening bull session along with a poker game. Chivington rambled on about Beau and the training at Bien Hoa. Wilson even tossed in a favorable comment here and there. Taut mosquito netting protected the gambling guzzlers from those vexing bloodsuckers.

As the night wore on, the story of the king cobra that had found its way to the kennels grew to gargantuan proportions, and they all got a kick out of the encounter between Beau and the Vietnamese boy, Huang.

"Where in the hell did ya learn to talk gook?" asked one of Chivington's buddies.

Chivington finished another Schlitz, thinking that warm beer wasn't really so bad once you got used to it. "Since I had a knack for language in high school, I took German. So after basic training, they sent me to the Defense Language School in Monterey, California. I figured I was headed for 'Nam anyway, so I asked to study Vietnamese, figuring I'd get a plush job with the Spooks. The instruction is done by native speakers and it's total immersion."

"Ha!" his buddy laughed. "I guess that didn't work out so well."

Chivington shook his head. "Because of my own stupidity. I fucked up and got arrested in a drunken, off-post bar brawl. That ended my studies. I did learn to speak a little gook, though."

Chapter 15

At the Sunday morning ecumenical service, attended by many Protestants as well as Catholics, Colonel Ricci received Holy Communion from Father Rizzo. He was only a part-time Catholic, but he had been practicing a little more diligently since arriving in Vietnam.

Major Mario Rizzo, better known as Padre, was intelligent, complex, and a no-nonsense career chaplain. Ricci had discussed the war with him, and he knew that Padre was motivated by the same Domino Theory that inspired his commander in chief, LBJ, and his predecessors, JFK and Ike. As a result of his Jesuit training at Fordham University in the Bronx, Padre was schooled in the "just-war thesis" as espoused by the two pillars of Christianity, Saint Augustine and Saint Thomas Aquinas. For Padre, America was fighting the "just war." Padre saw himself as one of God's messengers, chosen to "execute wrath upon him that does evil..." (Romans 13:4). In his mind, he had been sent to help rescue the poor and deliver the downtrodden out of the hands of evildoers, the Communists.

Prosecuting this war was therefore foreordained. It became a religious crusade much like that of his hero,

General Stonewall Jackson, who felt the same about his role in the Civil War. General Jackson believed that God was an omnipotent Confederate and greeted any news from the battlefield as "good." Even bad news was evidence of God's divine plan, according to Jackson.

Being a transplanted Virginian steeped in Civil War military history, Padre was inspired by Jackson's love of God, country, and his being a fervent observer of the Sabbath. Like Jackson, he was a Christian soldier doing God's will. Both had been deprived of familial love which helped to shape their personas as dogmatic, blind followers—not only to God and the Ten Commandments, but to country as well. Like Jackson, Padre was also shy and introverted. Determination became the centerpiece of their lives.

Padre loved Jackson's Book of Maxims which Stonewall started writing while at West Point in 1842. Two of these maxims gave Padre strength to overcome many of life's obstacles: (1) *You may be whatever you resolve to be*, and (2) *Never make a friend, only acquaintances.* Because of the emotional pain, both feared the death of a friend. The loss of an acquaintance assured less grief.

When he thought about Marilyn, which was often, Ricci was inclined to agree somewhat with Padre's rather bleak outlook. It stemmed, he thought, from their upbringings, as both Padre and Jackson had been orphaned. Jackson's mother gave him away at the age of five, and Padre, who grew up in a New York City orphanage, never found his biological mother.

But Ricci knew that unlike Jackson, Padre never learned to love another human being. Being an Army chaplain, he combined his love of the military with his love of God and country. He was proud of the white cross sewn to his collar. His job was to nurture the living, comfort the wounded, and honor the dead.

In his Sunday morning homily, Padre told the attending 62nd Engineers, "You men are here to help make amends for the wrongs inflicted upon the innocent people of South Vietnam. It is our job to advance good over evil with the objective of securing peace and punishing the Commies. We're fightin' a 'just war,' according to God. Peace be with you." He made the sign of the cross.

Ricci could see that Padre, like some of his superiors, had fallen prey to tortured logic.

When Padre accompanied his troops in the bush, he was always armed with his Bible and a Steve McQueen-type sawed-off shotgun strapped to his hip—despite the fact that chaplains were not authorized to carry weapons. McQueen had portrayed a bounty hunter in a late 1950s TV series, *Wanted: Dead or Alive*. It, along with *Gunsmoke*, was one of Padre's favorite westerns.

Padre, like Ricci, was a stocky, muscular Italian-American. He was ten years older than Ricci, though, and his close-cropped black hair was graying around the temples. His spare moments were spent penning metaphysical poetry, some of which Ricci had read. Padre's writings underscored the awareness of the Inner

Self; he believed this brought peace of mind and health of body. Padre felt the study of Zen helped one to better "know thyself," a basic Socratic idea.

When angered, Padre used expletives with the best of them. Afterwards, he would always say, "Father, forgive me." (Padre was influenced, in part, by Mark Twain who said that under certain conditions profanity provided a relief denied even in prayer.)

#

On Monday morning, Ricci ordered Wilson to coordinate assignments with his company commander regarding the three K-9 teams designated to help protect Phan Rang's perimeter.

"In light of recent intelligence reports," Ricci told Wilson, "K-9 detection of probes by VC sappers is a must. Base construction is underway and the protection of my men and equipment is top priority. The 62nd's time will be split between tactical combat support and base development. Most of your patrols will be at night within a designated area. Keep that in mind."

"Yes, sir," Wilson said as he saluted.

Little did Ricci know at the time that another enemy had already made its way into his base camp. Wilson had barely cleared the doorway before Sergeant Young hurried in. He showed Ricci one of many notes from the Bitch Box. This message cautioned that "Ralph" was in residence and being overworked.

"Who the hell is 'Ralph'?" Ricci asked, puzzled.

Young hesitated. "Sir, that's a term referring to a shotgun that…well, sir, we may have the beginnings of a drug problem."

Ricci shook his head. "No way, Young. What is this shit?"

"Sir, 'Ralph' is a twelve-gauge used to inhale marijuana. They put a bowl inside the chamber and suck up the smoke from the end of the barrel. It's like an Indian peace pipe."

Ricci heard enough. "Find Padre and bring 'im back here."

"Yes, sir."

Within a few minutes, Young returned with Padre. Puffing a cigar, the priest sat in one of the visitors' chairs across the desk from Ricci. Ricci waved Young into the other chair and got right to the point.

"Padre, I want advice. We've got a potential problem here. I want to nip it in the bud, ASAP."

Padre took the cigar out of his mouth and asked, "What's the problem, Colonel?"

"Sergeant Young tells me that we may have an incipient drug problem."

Padre lifted an inquisitive eyebrow and glanced over at Young. "Oh, yeah? What makes you think so?"

Young told him about the note from the "Bitch Box" (Ricci's suggestion box).

"I've heard nothin' in my official capacity," Padre said, "but I'm not surprised. I just read the *Stars and Stripes* about what's goin' on at home."

"What about confessions?" Ricci asked.

Padre frowned. "You know I can't—"

"Major, if you know something that could jeopardize my command, I'll…"

"You'll what, Colonel?" Padre snapped.

"Goddammit, Padre, I'll send your ass packin'. You're an officer first and then a chaplain. Don't forget that."

Padre didn't flinch. Studying the mangled end of his cigar, he said, "Colonel, I'll forget that we had this conversation, but I'll tell you one thing." His eyes returned to Ricci's. "These kids are likely to do anything to relieve the pain of bein' in this damn war. Most of 'em are barely out of high school. The fear of the unknown, of death, or perhaps boredom or stress or low morale—all of those things work at 'em."

"Dammit, Padre, drugs don't cure pain, and y'know that the 62nd has damn good morale. Maybe Aldous Huxley was right."

"About what?"

"In *Brave New World* he implied that our society would one day drug itself into some kind of zealous apathy and a forged sense of well-being."

Padre shook his head. "Colonel, marijuana isn't really toxic, and it does make you feel good for a while. It provides a temporary escape and a temporary high. It creates an induced fantasy world. Maybe it oughtta be legalized."

"'Scuse me? Legalized? What kind of bullshit is that, Padre? Are you some damn gullible rube?"

Padre shrugged. "I've tried it myself."

Ricci stared at him in astonishment. "You *what*!"

"Yes, I have."

Ricci turned to Young. "Sergeant Young, have you ever tried this shit?"

"No, sir, but I do know from readin' the data that it can alter brain chemistry. I also know that it can become addictive and lead to harder drugs like heroin and cocaine, and marijuana has some pretty nasty side effects, like bein' unable to sleep, and it can make ya sweat like hell. It makes ya lazy and it fucks up your memory and attention span, but the potheads who use it, they just don't seem to give a shit 'bout that."

Ricci expelled a breath. "From this moment on, I want any and all information about any of my men who are even *suspected* of using grass. Soldiers who smoke dope are no damn good to me or this outfit, and if you

205

know where 'Ralph' is located, I want that fuckin' thing in my hands. Do you read me?"

"Without fail, sir."

"One more thing," snapped Ricci. "We need to find the source. How does this crap get to my men?"

"I'll check into that, sir."

Ricci looked back at Father Rizzo. "Padre, you're free to go."

"Yes, sir," he said, getting to his feet.

Ricci turned his attention back to Young when a sudden squeal of brakes brought his eyes back to the open doorway through which Padre had just stepped. A speeding jeep skidded past Padre only a foot or so outside the door, barely missing him, then rumbled and belched to a stop, churning up a thick cloud of dust. Padre fell backwards, crashing into the bunker doorframe.

Ricci reached the door just as the jeep quit thirty feet beyond the bunker.

Getting to his feet, Padre screamed, "Goddammit! What the fuck do ya think you're doin'?" Then Ricci heard the priest mutter something under his breath. He thought Padre was asking God to forgive his blasphemous tongue.

After seeing that the priest was unhurt, Ricci walked briskly to the jeep, with Young close behind. The GI stumbled out of the vehicle attempting to stand at attention. His shoulder patch identified him as a Screaming Eagle.

Ricci stared at his blurred vision, and then at his nametag. "Private Mudd, what the fuck is wrong with you?"

"Sir, I…I…"

Padre caught Ricci's attention and waved him back a few feet. "You asked me about drug sources," Padre said, his eyes on the jeep driver. "Well, maybe you just found one."

Ricci frowned. "How so?"

"This soldier isn't drunk on booze. Not at this time of day. Look at his eyes."

Ricci turned to Mudd, who was leaning back on his jeep, still attempting to remain at attention.

"At ease, soldier," snapped Ricci. "Have ya been smokin'?"

The young man's brow furrowed as if he couldn't grasp what Ricci was asking. "Smokin', sir?"

"Yeah, goddammit, grass, marijuana, whatever. Who's your commanding officer?"

"Ah, sir, it's…" His voice faded.

"It's Colonel Hall, sir," said Sergeant Young. "He's an airborne jock from the First Brigade of the 101st. I know the Colonel."

Acting on a hunch, Ricci said, "Young, get Chivington and Beau over here."

"Yes, sir."

Fifteen minutes later, Chivington appeared with Beau on-leash. Ricci told Chivington that he wanted the dog to sniff out Mudd and his jeep.

After several minutes of maneuvering off-leash, Beau started whimpering and barking. Then he put his front paws on the hood of the jeep, leaving light claw-mark imprints in the olive-drab paint.

"Chivington, lift the hood," ordered Ricci.

As Chivington propped open the heavy metal hood, the dog lunged forward, sniffing at the engine. Then Ricci saw it: several packs of rolled reefers taped to the underside of the hood.

"Sergeant Young, get Colonel Hall on the field phone."

"Yes, sir." Young stepped back into the bunker to make the call.

Colonel Jeffrey Hall was a veteran paratrooper who had jumped with the 101st on D-Day and with the 187th in Korea. He was a gruff, no-nonsense disciplinarian who had zero tolerance for drug use.

Ricci's meeting with Hall was brief and to the point. Both agreed that Private Mudd would be put on report and given an Article 15. Hall apologized to the chaplain and praised Ricci's quick thinking.

"It was the dog," Ricci said, looking down at Beau and giving him an affectionate pat on the head, "and that's another reason why Beau is one hell of an asset to the 62nd Engineers."

Chapter 16

Late one afternoon, barely two weeks after Chivington, Wilson, and Beau returned to Phan Rang from their retraining at Bien Hoa, Wilson ordered Specialist Four Maddox, Specialist Four Bill Clark, a newly arrived medic, Chivington with Beau, and Private First Class Bruce Tomburg, another cherry just in from basic training, to assemble.

"Okay, guys, listen up," Wilson said. "We just got our orders from Captain Wojtacha. Colonel Ricci wants us to run a recon patrol in the direction of Au Phuoc, about nine miles from here. Colonel Ricci needs a sawmill, and he thinks that's the place to set it up. We'll be moving out first thing tomorrow to check it out."

"A sawmill?" Tomburg asked.

"Right. For construction of this base, but there are reports that certain elements of the 274 Dong Nai Regiment of the VC 5th Division are using that location as a rest area. There are two more regiments—the 27th and the 275th—all consisting of about 4,500 men. These are highly trained and disciplined troops, and we've gotta stay out of their way."

Wilson gave them marching orders: Carry two canteens, as well as Halzone water purification tablets, and enough ammo for the M-16s and an M-60. He reminded Chivington to bring extra water for Beau, as well as enough C-rats and dog food for three days.

Wilson also went through his routine about booby traps and told Clark to review the basics on stings, bites, tick control, and dehydration. Clark had recently completed his basic medical training at Fort Sam Houston, near San Antonio. A handsome, stocky youth with curly blond hair and an athletic build, he was eager to do this job, including sick call.

For his opening remarks, Clark started with reptiles. "As most of you know, there are a number of poisonous snakes in 'Nam—and I know all about that king cobra and Beau," he smiled, looking at Chivington, "but I'm more concerned about the ones that are less visible—namely the dark brown and black pit vipers. Their heads often resemble a javelin tip, and their venom can destroy your red blood cells."

"Why are they called pit vipers?" Tomburg asked.

"Because of the heat-sensing pit on the side of their head," replied Clark, "and their fangs can be two inches long. They're shaped like fishhooks. Once into your arm or leg, don't even try to pull away. Those fangs are locked for ten to fifteen minutes. Even if they wanted to, they can't turn loose until then."

"Hmm…okay," said Tomburg, sounding a little nervous.

"And watch out for water snakes if we have to cross streams," warned Wilson.

"What about ticks?" asked Tomburg.

"Just keep 'em off your ass," Chivington told him.

"I'll put a match to their ass," Tomburg said. A Midwesterner of medium height, Tomburg was plump, gap-toothed, pasty-faced, and nearsighted. Like Maddox, he wore glasses, often sliding down his nose.

"That's the last thing you want to do," Clark said. "You'll just drive 'em further into your skin." He paused, looking at Tomburg. "What would ya do for a snake bite, man?"

"I'd use my knife to cut cross incisions over the fang marks, then suck out the poison."

"That's Hollywood," Clark said, shaking his head. "If you do that, you'll flood the wound with bacteria."

"So what the fuck are we supposed to do?"

"Apply a tourniquet, mark the bite with cross incisions, then wash it out. Otherwise, your ass is in trouble." Clark cautioned them about one more thing: dehydration. "If your hands and feet start swellin', that's a danger sign. If you get an irritating rash, you've got blocked sweat pores, another sign of heat problems."

"So don't get dehydrated on this mission," warned Wilson. "We have no time for casualties."

"There's one more sign of dehydration," Clark said, "your piss. If it's getting dark, you're in deep shit."

Maddox laughed at that. "If our piss is dark, we're in deep shit. What happens if our shit is dark? Are we in deep piss?"

"If your shit is dark, it probably means you've got a bleeding ulcer," Wilson said. "One more thing: we may encounter VC as we get closer to the village of Au Phuoc. Local elections are in progress, and the VC are active during balloting."

"How come?" Maddox asked.

"They want to terrify local villagers, tellin' 'em that democracy doesn't work." He looked around. "Anything else?" When no one spoke, he said, "We'll move out right after breakfast, so get plenty of sleep tonight."

#

Despite Wilson's orders, Chivington didn't get much sleep. Beau was curled up on a grass mat next to Chivington. He would often moan, twitch, and jerk his front paws forward, as if he were digging at something. Maybe he was as anxious as his handler. Maybe Martinez's ghost was visiting them both.

When Chivington did manage to fall asleep, it was light and uneasy, populated by dreams that were too vivid to be mere dreams. In the early hours of the morning he finally dropped into a deeper sleep. He had a vivid image of himself hurrying to get someplace. He wasn't sure where—a birthday party, he thought. It all seemed very real, but his destination was vague.

Then he was inside a restaurant furnished and decorated like a garden, the tables arranged among masses of plants and beautiful flowers, but in among the vegetation were bamboo stalks and giant cypress trees. Bladed leaves of elephant grass rose above petunias and snapdragons like evil overlords.

Then the hostess appeared before him and led him to a large booth with wide, upholstered benches set off in a corner of the garden. He thought that it was unusual, dreamlike, for her to take satin pillows from a shelf and fluff them up, but when she leaned over to place them behind him on the bench, he could feel her hair brushing his shoulder and neck, so he knew he couldn't be dreaming.

The woman was radiant, and he suddenly realized it was Felicia from high school. He wanted to ask her where she had been, but then the woman turned and Chivington saw that he was mistaken. It wasn't Felicia at all. This woman's features had distinctly oriental lines. Short, jet-black hair framed her round face.

She served him a tall tropical drink he hadn't ordered, and the first sip made him lightheaded. It smelled of rum and flowers, and it had a licorice taste.

Then she slipped into the booth behind her, screening them off from the sight of the other diners.

When he reached out to touch her arm and shoulder, she smiled and nodded as if she welcomed this contact.

214

His hand caressed her arm, and he marveled at how exquisitely soft she felt. He looked down at her bare neck, surrounded by a thin gold chain, just inches away. It was very natural and beautiful to Chivington when she reached up with one hand to the thin strap around her neck, and with a delicate shrug, drew the top of her gown down to her waist. She sat still, but the gesture made her breasts swing a little from side to side.

Chivington found himself leaning down, wanting to press his lips to her nipples, but before he could touch her, she slid from the bench into the green vines that now enveloped the open end of the seats. He could hear her sigh, and then gay laughter tinkling like bells where she had gone.

He rushed toward her, falling deeper into branches and vines. He attempted to push them aside. In a frenzy, he tried clutching the girl as she was dragged farther into the plants. He awoke as his struggle ended.

The dream broke up, splitting into cracks of darkness and light. Fully awake, he realized the hand on his shoulder was that of Clark, the medic. Within the next hour they would be going out on patrol. The dream receded against the onslaught of harsh reality.

He remained on the cot for a moment longer, thinking about Felicia. At one time, with the passion and naiveté of seventeen-year-olds, they had thought they were in love for eternity, but Felicia's family had moved to Virginia the summer of their senior year, and after three letters, he knew that things weren't the same between them. Then he met another girl, and Felicia met the salesman in Virginia, and that was that.

As he lay there listening to the other men stirring around him, Chivington ached for a return to those fresh, carefree days. Had it really been only five years ago when he was dating Felicia, brushing her breast with the back of his hand as if it were an accident, feeling the soft, tentative probe of her tongue against his? It seemed a lifetime ago.

He turned onto his side and reached down to touch Beau, lying on the floor beside his cot. The dog shifted position, lifting his head up to stare into Chivington's eyes.

"Ya been dreamin' about girl dogs?" Chivington asked.

Beau whined softly, his right ear standing straight, the left flopping over at the tip. Chivington reached out and caressed the dog's head, running his hand over the floppy ear.

"That's your badge of courage, boy," he said, feeling a tightness in his throat. "Wear it proudly, Beau, wear it proudly."

Chapter 17

At 0500, under the cover of pre-dawn darkness, the patrol, with blackened faces and clad in olive-drab fatigues and boonie hats, moved out. Carefully in place were Wilson's binos, a dog-eared map, and a Lensatic compass. RTO Maddox would use the call sign "Timber Wolf," and base camp went with "Grizzly One." Radio contact would be maintained throughout the mission.

With Beau on-leash, Chivington walked ahead of the team. Wilson came next, then Maddox with his radio. Bringing up the rear were Tomburg with his M-60 and Clark. The field grass was brittle and the ground rock hard.

Chivington moved forward slowly, watching Beau's head and ears. Chivington paused every few steps while his brain sifted through everything his senses were telling him, looking for signs of danger. He glanced back often to get directions from Wilson, who kept his eyes on his compass and the trail to the right. Using hand signals, Wilson could gesture any change in direction.

For three hours they walked at an agonizingly slow pace. The grass gradually gave way to ferns, thick vegetation, and trees. The sounds of birds and flying insects were all around them. It hadn't rained for several days. Huge spider webs clung to tree limbs, draping from tree to tree. Chivington had never seen such monstrous spiders, giving him one more peril to think about.

At one point, Beau stopped, his right ear on alert, perked up as he stared straight ahead. Chivington, his heart pounding, thrust a clenched fist toward the sky and went down on one knee.

He saw what had grabbed Beau's attention. It was a deer-like animal with split hooves, long, narrow horns, and short hair with brown and white markings.

"Doesn't look too dangerous," Wilson said. "Let's keep movin'."

The animal peered at them. Its head was held high, ears erect. Then, as they resumed their movement toward it, the animal turned and darted away, vanishing into the woods.

As the morning sun rose higher, so did the temperature. Chivington welcomed a breakfast stop in a small, dusty clearing surrounded by trees of an old French rubber plantation.

After settling down, Tomburg began guzzling from his canteen.

"Sip it," Clark said. "Suck it. Pretend it's your girlfriend's tit. You're gonna need that water later."

Chivington used a small tin cup for Beau's water. He lapped it eagerly even though it was warm. After Beau finished drinking, Chivington checked him for ticks and found none. He inspected Beau's ears and pads for burrs or abrasions. So far, everything looked fine.

Kneeling and cranking up his radio, Maddox made contact with base camp, giving them grid coordinates of their location.

Tomburg fished a cigarette pack out of his thigh pocket and lit up, but killed it after a few drags. "Jesus," he said, breathing heavily, "that felt like someone was drawin' my breath outta me." The heat and humidity were sending him a message.

"Rookie," said Wilson, "listen to those of us who've been here a while. Discipline yourself. We're gonna need that gun if we get caught with bare asses, and the smell of tobacco in the jungle can give our position away."

"You can count on me, Sarge," Tomburg said as he tapped the M-60 and snuffed his cigarette.

"Check yourself for ticks and other critters," said Wilson, talking to all of them. He had seen Chivington going over Beau. "We've been lucky, so far: no gooks, no booby traps, only mosquitoes, flies, ants, monkeys, and one strange-ass-looking deer."

"Yeah, what the fuck was that, anyway?" Tomburg asked, pushing his glasses up. "I never seen anythin' like that in Kansas."

"We ain't in Kansas," Clark said.

"Break out the C-4, if you want hot chow," Wilson said.

After nature's call, they prepared their morning meal.

According to Wilson's map and compass they were right on target. He thought they would reach their destination by midday if all went well. That was the word he sent back to base camp.

Chivington remembered Wilson's warning the day before: they might encounter Viet Cong as they neared the village of Au Phuoc. He tried not to think about that as he poured a small amount of grease from his C-rats onto Beau's food and the remainder on the ground. He didn't want to encounter Ho Chi Minh's revenge this early in the day, especially with VC in the area.

Beau would eat well on this patrol, at least. Vacuum packed in tin cans, Composition D Burgers proved to be the ultimate dog food for this mission. They were unspoiled, tasty, and nutritionally sound.

After chow, they policed the area, then saddled up and proceeded forward with Chivington and Beau on point. As they approached the village, Wilson warned them again to stay alert. He kept a close watch on the compass bearing. Being off even a click or two would cost them time, maybe their lives.

Another two hours passed; a gentle breeze sprang up, making life a little more bearable.

Then Beau alerted by flicking his ears and tipping his head. Like a rocket from a launch pad, Chivington raised his clenched right fist, then knelt on one knee beside Beau. He followed Beau's gaze but saw nothing. He listened and heard nothing. He glanced back and saw that the rest of the team had also gone down onto one knee with weapons ready.

After a couple of minutes, Beau seemed to relax. Chivington decided to continue on carefully.

Beau moved ahead for another hundred yards or so, then alerted, with his right ear upright and the scarred left ear semi-erect. Again, Chivington signaled for a halt. They were approaching a small opening.

Seeing and hearing nothing, he signaled Beau to move ahead.

Beau refused. He sat rigid, staring at something.

Chivington looked closer. Then he saw it: a camouflaged tripwire about five inches above the ground and surrounded by grass. A light breeze hitting the wire tipped Beau.

Chivington's heart pounded, realizing how close they had come to dying. If Beau hadn't alerted, they would have blundered right into that booby trap.

Chivington gestured. Wilson moved forward to investigate. It was a VC-rigged daisy chain—a combination of Claymores, hand grenades, and mortars all connected by a complex circuit of tripwires.

"Good boy, Beau," Chivington said as he gently stroked Beau's head. He then handed him a chunk of pound cake saved from breakfast C-rats. Swallowing it whole, Beau licked his upper lip and looked around for more.

Wilson moved around the tripwires gingerly, snipping them with wire cutters. After disconnecting the daisy chain, he walked over to Beau and added his praise by slipping him another piece of pound cake.

"He came through for us." Wilson sounded a little surprised. "Good job, Beau. Good job!"

The time spent at Bien Hoa had already paid off. From their training they remembered that verbal praise was okay, but a food reward for discovering a major ordnance was more powerful.

The booby trap left no doubt about VC being in the area. From this point on, the patrol would be on high alert. Another hour of humping passed. By now, fatigue jackets and dragon towels were sweat-soaked. Maddox and Tomburg had trouble with steamy glasses, which kept slipping down their noses. Chivington decided early on to pocket his shades for the same reason.

As morning passed into late afternoon, the team reached a shallow stream, its surface covered with a crust of green algae. Clouds of mosquitoes swarmed above it.

"Watch for snakes when we cross," warned Wilson.

The stream was about twenty yards wide. Beau and Chivington stepped into the knee-deep water. Beau swam until he reached the other side. Not far past the stream, Beau alerted. Chivington again halted the patrol, but neither heard nor saw any signs of the enemy. Beau was nervous. Chivington felt certain that Charlie was watching them.

This time, Beau followed Chivington's signal to move forward. Beau then stopped and stood rigidly. His head and ears pointed to the left front. Chivington turned in that direction and stopped, raising his clenched fist. Crouching, Wilson made his way up to Chivington.

Pointing with his right index finger, Chivington said softly, "That looks like some kind of listenin' post."

Wilson raised his binos for a closer look. "It's a VC outpost, all right. I can't tell if it's new or old." He checked his compass and map. "Au Phuoc is less than an hour to the northwest." He turned to Maddox. "Report this information to base camp."

Maddox did so. Base camp warned them about a possible trap.

"No shit," Wilson said dryly. "They're so fucking helpful."

Chivington thought—Wilson was reading his mind. The ambush took out Martinez's patrol.

They moved on. Collective tension took its toll.

Another alert from Beau caused Chivington to halt the patrol. Everyone lowered themselves. Chivington realized the alert was for real. Thirty yards ahead, in a small clearing, six Viet Cong soldiers in black garb were preparing a meal. One was writing in his diary. Diaries were important to VC because they could not receive mail in the field. Even without binos, Chivington could see Ho Chi Minh sandals, high-water trousers, and a VC flag. The Viet Cong flag was red with a yellow star in the middle. One soldier wore a camouflaged pith helmet. The others wore brown boonie hats with thin chinstraps. Lightweight web equipment hugged their waists, along with extra bandoleers of ammo and AK-47 banana clips. Another VC carried a set of EE-8 field phones.

Motioning by hand, Wilson brought Tomburg up front with his M-60. He told Maddox to alert base camp for the potential need of a dustoff and an air strike.

Once they reached the edge of the clearing, staying back in the shadows, Wilson whispered to Chivington, telling him to use his M-16 on the youngest VC to his left. "Shoot 'im in the legs. If it looks like he might get away, turn Beau loose. I don't want 'im killed. I need some answers. He's just the gook to give 'em to me."

Chivington's mouth tightened. The soldier looked very young—even younger than Chivington's baby brother, still in high school.

"Tomburg, I wanna sweep of the others with the M-60," Wilson went on. "Cut 'em to pieces. We don't wanna give 'em a chance to use one of those field phones, or take cover and start shootin' back."

Tomburg acknowledged while gripping his gun. "Ya got it, Sarge. I'll make hamburger out of 'em."

Everyone locked and loaded. Chivington moved his selector switch to full automatic. Shivers tracked the length of his spine like melting bits of sleet trickling down a windowpane. As much as he hated doing this, he knew Wilson was right: they couldn't risk letting any of the VC shoot back or call for help. Chivington had a feeling that backup units were a lot closer for the VC than for their own patrol team.

He also knew that Wilson was rolling the dice. If this action alerted the main VC contingent, they were history, but if they could catch them off guard and capture the kid, they might be able to get enough information to get the Colonel his sawmill.

"Fire!" screamed Wilson.

Whack-whack-whack-whack-whack. The staccato bursts echoed through the forest. Viet Cong sprang to their feet looking around for cover, but they didn't have a chance. The M-60 erupted, cutting them down like chainsaws felling trees.

As the young VC started to run, Chivington clenched his teeth, took careful aim, and squeezed off three quick bursts, aiming below the kneecaps. Blood spurted from the wounds as the boy wailed and went down. Despite severe pain, he reached for his AK-47.

After Chivington's command, Beau flung himself at the soldier in a canine instant. As the VC landed on his back, Beau sank his teeth into the boy's right arm, causing him even more pain and labored breathing.

Chivington called the blood-spattered dog to back off.

Looking around, Chivington saw Tomburg had done a thorough job with his M-60. The results didn't look much like hamburger, though. Five bodies lay in strange, contorted heaps, with blood, flesh, and brains everywhere.

He looked away, feeling sick.

Wilson put Tomburg on watch. He ordered Clark and Maddox to wrap a nylon rope around the boy's feet. They tied his hands behind his back, then hoisted him upside down. His right pant leg had been ripped away. Chivington could see that a fist-size chunk of meat had been blown from above his knee. The bloody left pant leg was saturated.

Hanging by his feet from a tree limb and still bleeding, the young VC came face-to-face with a snarling Doberman ready to take his head off. Tears streamed from the boy's panic-stricken eyes.

Chivington moved over close to Wilson and said in a low tone, "Christ, Sarge, is this necessary? He's just a kid."

"Yes, it's necessary," Wilson shot back. "We've gotta get answers—answers that might save our asses, and don't forget that this kid would've shot your fucking head off if he'd had a chance."

Wilson either forgot or didn't care about the Geneva Conventions (Article 17), which prohibits "…physical or mental torture…on prisoners of war to secure information…." (Every soldier sent to Vietnam was given a one-day seminar on the Laws of War.)

The vehemence of his reply made Chivington back off. He could see that Wilson wasn't taking any pleasure from what they were doing.

"You're the one who can speak gook," Wilson said. "Ask 'im about Au Phuoc. I want to know what we might be comin' up against."

With reluctance, Chivington agreed. His interrogation began. While firing questions at the boy, Beau got in his face. Chivington was aware of this kid's agonizing pain. The boy was so terrified of Beau that he seemed not to notice. He kept saying, "Dung lai! Dung lai! [Stop! Stop!]"

It took time to obtain the information. Chivington learned that elements of the 274th Regiment had control of Au Phuoc. The minds and hearts of the villagers had been grabbed.

After completing the inquisition, the boy was lowered to the ground. His face was gray.

"What're we gonna do now, Sarge?" Tomburg asked, his voice sounding almost eager.

Wilson stepped back, his face grim. "Waste 'im."

Three short bursts ended the boy's suffering, leaving his crumpled body in a pool of red blood.

"Christ," Chivington exclaimed, turning away.

"I'd do the same for any animal with those kinds of injuries," Wilson said.

But Chivington wasn't just turning away from the boy's torn body. He was trying to shake free of the vision of those helpless Indians drowning in a sea of blood at Sand Creek in 1864, while Colonel John M. Chivington rode through the village making sure that no woman or child had managed to escape the massacre.

Maddox made contact with base camp, reporting what they had done. Base camp ordered them on.

After the bodies were tucked in the underbrush, the patrol moved on toward Au Phuoc. They made some progress. An hour later, Chivington, with Beau on-leash, raised his clenched fist. Near the edge of the tree line, Chivington saw thatched-roof hootches.

Shaded by coconut palms, Wilson scoped the village. After changing positions and wiping sweat from his eyes, he focused on something else catching his attention. Chivington spotted two trucks. He wasn't sure from the distance, but they appeared to be Soviet-built. Hanging around them were several black-garbed VC with rifles slung over their shoulders.

Where are the villagers? Chivington wondered.

He spotted a free-roaming pig, rooting around for something to eat, and a water buffalo, caked in mud, lolling in the shade. A mother duck appeared with several ducklings marching in lockstep. The ducklings reminded Chivington of a moment from basic training frozen in time. He could still hear the "tup-theep-fo, threp-fo-yolef-yolef-rye-lef," from the monotonous marching drills back at Fort Jackson.

With phone in hand, Wilson made contact with base camp. "This is 'Timber Wolf,' over." He listened. "Grizzly One, there are two Soviet trucks here, but not a civilian in sight. There are at least four VC with Kalashnikov AK-47 rifles. Our observation seems to confirm what we learned from the VC prisoner." After another brief silence, Wilson said, "Roger that," and signed off.

"What's happenin', Sarge?" Tomburg asked.

"They're sendin' in an air strike, ETA twenty minutes. Everyone move back and lay low."

It was a long twenty minutes. Beau was uneasy. Chivington gripped his harness. VC milled about the trucks as if they were waiting for something, too. Chivington could hear voices, although he couldn't make out what they were saying. Occasionally, one of them would laugh at something.

You wouldn't be so cheerful if you knew what's comin', you poor bastards, Chivington thought. He was tense, apprehensive, and full of angst.

Finally, he heard the whine of jet engines approaching from the south. The whine rose to a scream. A pair of Phantoms streaked through the still, hot air with their flashing, twenty-millimeter cannons tearing apart foliage, hootches, and people. VC scattered. The green-and-tan Phantoms zoomed in on their targets with amazing agility. One of the trucks went up in flames. Chivington heard the *whump* of the gas tank exploding. A few seconds later, the second one blew.

After the strafing run, the jets came back, dropping napalm canisters on the village. There was a dull thud and a sickening *whoosh* as orange, yellow, and black globs of liquid fire splashed through the foliage.

Figures in black fatigues began running from the flaming village. Chivington saw many screaming people burning alive. Wilson ordered his men to lay down a base of fire. There would be no escaping this inferno. Squealing animals ran in all directions. Even at one hundred yards, Chivington felt the heat.

The Phantoms flew overhead for one more pass, then looped around and headed south.

Beside Chivington, Wilson rose onto his elbows and started firing. Tomburg opened up with the M-60. More VC were attempting to flee the conflagration, most of them passing through the M-60 field of fire. Other civilians took refuge near the tree line. Struggling to reach safe cover was a burned, one-legged man on crutches. The M-60 caught him and spun him around before he dropped, his crutches flying.

"Not the civilians!" Chivington screamed at Tomburg. "For God's sake!" But it was hopeless. There was no way he could make his voice heard above the M-60s hammering roar.

Another man emerged from a blazing hootch, his body ablaze, arms and legs swinging wildly. High-pitched shrieks echoed across the ash-covered ground. Rounds from an M-16 on full automatic brought him down. He lay motionless, still burning like a grotesque campfire.

Fuck! Chivington thought, wondering how much more of this he could take. *Fuck, fuck, fuck.*

The M-60 stopped chattering. Suddenly, it was quiet. Black and gray smoke twisted up toward the sky. Chivington grimaced at a foul smell of jellied gas and burned hair and flesh. It was the stench of death and destruction.

"Let's go!" Wilson ordered.

They got to their feet and started moving toward the smoking ruins that had once been the village of Au Phuoc. They fanned out so they wouldn't form a tight target area—although Chivington didn't believe there was anyone left in the village capable of shooting at them. Dead animals and scorched bodies with burned-off faces and hanging, charred flesh littered the ground.

Not all were dead. One VC was crawling on his hands and knees, dragging his entrails. The sleeves of his black shirt had been burned away. Chivington could see nothing but white bones and joints. Chunks of raw, bloody flesh were dangling from his thighs and back.

For a second, Chivington was sure that the contents of his stomach would come up, but he managed to gag it down.

231

Wilson stepped behind this pathetic human remnant, raised his pistol, and fired into the back of the man's head. The bullet passed through, blowing out most of the man's face and leaving a large splotch of blood, skull fragments, and brain tissue on the ground.

Just as Chivington thought this horror show couldn't get worse, it did—in a way he could not have imagined. Coming toward them from a burning hootch was a shrieking woman and a young boy. The boy's chest was covered with blood that had run down and soaked into his black shorts, but it was the woman Chivington couldn't take his eyes off. Her clothes had been burned off, and her body was charred and smoking.

She collapsed ten yards from him, writhed for a moment, then lay still. The boy dropped to the ground and slumped beside her, holding her head in his lap.

As Chivington approached the boy, he could hear him moaning, "Ma, Ma, thuc day, Ma, Mathuc day. [Mother, Mother, wake up, wake up.]"

Kneeling beside him, Chivington winced at the woman's burned skin, singed hair, and open eyes. Napalm had melted her flesh to the bone, turning it white.

Then Chivington realized that the boy, too, was seriously wounded. Hot shrapnel left a gaping hole in his frail, bloody chest.

Wagging his stunted tail, Beau walked over to the boy and licked his teardrops. The boy lurched back, turning his head up toward Chivington.

Chivington froze in astonishment and dismay. "Huang!" he shouted. "What in the…" He couldn't find the breath to say more. It was the boy who had assisted them during dog training exercises at Bien Hoa. Chivington turned and shouted, "Clark! Get over here!"

Specialist Clark hurried over with his medic bag. "What's up?"

"It's Huang," Chivington said. Then he realized that would mean nothing to Clark. He gestured at Clark's bag. "I know this boy, goddammit! Do something for 'im!"

Clark looked at the boy, then shook his head. "Ain't nothin' I can do for 'im."

Chivington looked down and saw that Huang's eyes were open and staring at the sky. His labored breathing had stopped.

Chivington closed Huang's eyes, and felt tears rolling over his own cheeks. Beside him, Beau whined.

"What's happenin'?" came Wilson's voice.

Chivington opened his eyes and looked up at the sergeant. "It's Huang…from the training at Bien Hoa…"

"Aw, shit," Wilson said, looking at the dead boy. "How the hell did he get over here?" He shook his head. "He should've stayed put in Bien Hoa." He waited a moment, then said, "We got work to do here, Chivington."

There was, Chivington knew, no time for sentimentality. If a moment of grief were allowed for every person killed in this fucking war, there would be no time for fighting, no time for more killing.

He got up and wiped an arm angrily across his eyes to clear them, then carried Huang's body over to one of the few hootches that had not been burned. He laid the boy beside the one standing wall.

God, if you're up there, he said, with fresh tears spilling over his cheeks, *I hope you're ready to take this little boy, and I hope the fuck you take better care of 'im up there than you did while he was here on Earth.*

Drying his eyes, he turned and called for Beau.

The patrol continued through the incinerated remains of the village. Beau, off-leash, roamed in and out of smoldering hootches.

"Take a look." Wilson was peering into the twisted wreckage of the two Soviet-built trucks. Chivington came over and saw blackened containers resting on the remains of the truck beds. "They must've just got here with supplies and ammo."

Wilson ordered Clark to round up the walking wounded. He ordered Maddox to call for a medevac. The survivors from the village would be airlifted to Cam Ranh Bay for treatment, interrogated, then resettled.

Civilian casualties, or collateral damage, were an acceptable residual of this war—even if they were little boys.

Colonel Ricci will get his sawmill, thought Chivington.

He heard the medevac helicopter only after it passed overhead. He looked up as it banked hard right, almost standing on its side, and sank toward the ground.

#

Ricci, learning of the destruction of Au Phuoc through the rather emotionless report from Wilson, was pleased they had accomplished the task without a single American casualty.

He wasted no time. A week after the air strike, the dense, rich forest around Au Phuoc was under a new kind of siege. A Rome Plow and other land-clearing equipment had been airlifted to the site. With a protective heavy-duty cab and a special tree-cutting blade, the D7HE military tractor went to work.

This cutter was synonymous with land clearing in Vietnam. Manufactured by the Rome Plow Company of Cedartown, Georgia, the blade was designed to operate six inches above ground level. It cut vegetation at the top and left the root structure intact in order to prevent erosion.

The blade's edge was sharpened daily by a portable grinder. Angled, the plow cut was sent to the right. The leading extended corner of the blade cut trees with a succession of stabs and dozer turnings. Lieutenant

235

General Julian J. Ewell said that the Rome Plow was "the most effective device for winning the war."

Colonel Ricci was impressed with the tree-removal process. As for the small village of Au Phuoc, Ricci's civic plans included rebuilding living quarters and a two-room schoolhouse for the survivors. To advance the pacification process, U.S. Army engineers made important civic contributions. They constructed schools, public fish markets, a children's hospital at Quang Tri, religious buildings, hospitals, public buildings, and communications facilities.

Elements of Bravo Company would operate the sawmill until enough lumber was available for Phan Rang's essential buildings, so another temporary base camp was soon underway. One rifle platoon from the 1st Brigade, 101st Airborne was sent there for security reasons.

Of the three K-9 teams at Phan Rang, two were dispatched to accommodate the rifle platoon in this dangerous area. For Phan Rang, Beauregard remained as the only K-9 sentry.

Ricci wanted more K-9 units but was limited to what he had. Knowing that certain elements of the VC 5th Division were operating in and around the Phan Rang area, Ricci had gut premonitions about an attack.

Then came the news out of the Ia Drang Valley and the 7th Cavalry's battles at Landing Zones (LZ) X-Ray and Albany. Ricci's plans for the rock quarry were put on hold.

Only later did Ricci learn from first-hand reports how bad it had been in the Ia Drang. The carnage was staggering, the kill ratio overwhelming. Corpses were evacuated to Pleiku by the 228th Chinook Company. There, next to the mess hall, bodies were stacked like cordwood and washed down with hoses. After off-loading the dead, the Chinook's floorboards had to be scrubbed clean of bloodstains. Bodies were placed in plastic body bags for shipment home.

Like the Gulf of Tonkin Resolution before it, the Ia Drang campaign, which cost 234 American lives in November 1965, set the tactical stage for turning Vietnam into an American War of "foreign aggression," as defined in the April 18, 1965 edition of *The New York Times Magazine.*

The sonorous echoes of *Gary Owen,* the regimental battle song of the 7th Cavalry and General Custer's favorite, could still be heard from the river valley of death.

We are the pride of the Army

And a regiment of great renown.

Our name's on the pages of history

From sixty-six on down.

We know no fear when stern duty

Calls us far away from home.

It matters not where we're going

Such you'll surely say as we march away, and

Our band plays "Gary Owen."

Chapter 18

On Friday evening before the beginning of R&R, Chivington, Maddox, Tomburg, and Clark sat drinking warm beer and playing five-card-draw poker. A large pile of Military Payment Certificates (MPC) lay in the middle of a wooden box top used for a gambling table.

Chivington was having a good night. Early into his tour in Vietnam, he learned if he didn't drink as much as the other players and kept track of his cards, he often came out ahead, and the next morning's hangover was less severe.

In this particular hand, everyone had folded except Chivington and Tomburg who, despite his country-boy appearance, turned out to be a shrewd poker player. After upping the pot by five dollars, Chivington called the hand.

Tomburg held the winning cards: two aces and two eights, often known as "the dead man's hand"—the same held by the aging and flamboyant Wild Bill Hickok in Deadwood, South Dakota in 1876 where he was shot in the back of the head by Jack McCall, an angry young man who felt Hickok had maligned his mother.

"You beat my ass," groaned Chivington, throwing down his queens and sixes. Later, Chivington would reflect back on the irony of Tomburg holding the dead man's hand in what was to be the last hand of poker he'd ever play, but for the moment, Tomburg was chortling over his win and raking in the money. Then Wilson came over to the table.

"Captain Wojtacha sent me. I have some bad news."

"Yeah, what's up?" asked Chivington as he gulped the last of his beer.

"Get your ass and gear ready for an 0500 mission."

"Aw, hell," groused Tomburg, pushing his glasses back up where they belonged. "We're on for R&R as of 0500."

"Negative, soldier. It's canceled. Colonel Ricci got word of a downed 0-1 Bird Dog around the village of Vinh Hao, about sixty clicks south of here. The pilot's got important documents for the Colonel, and Vinh Hao is rumored to be in VC hands."

The 0-1 Bird Dog was actually a two-seat Cessna A-37 Dragonfly aerial recon and observation aircraft. Armed with only one 62mm minigun, it was without armor plating and did not have self-sealing tanks.

"Hopefully, you'll find the pilot alive," Wilson went on, turning back to Chivington. "You'll need a medic, an RTO, and a gunner." He made a show of looking around the table. "Well, what d'ya know, I see some likely candidates right here. The chopper will leave for the crash site at 0500."

"But—"

"You'll get R&R on the next rotation after you return. Take two day's rations. Colonel Ricci's not gonna leave ya out there very long."

"You've got more experience with this kind of thing than I do," Chivington said. "How come you're not comin' along?"

"Because the Colonel has complete faith in you, Chivington," Wilson replied. "Plus, he wants to keep me handy in case sappers decide to hit the base. That's his biggest worry right now."

Wilson briefed Chivington on the grid coordinates, giving him some idea of where the pilot had gone down; in effect, he was filing the patrol route with base camp.

Resigned to missing the much-anticipated R&R, Chivington and the others turned in early. Tomburg, meanwhile, had retrieved the ace of spades from the plastic playing card deck in order to leave a posted message for Charlie. The ace of spades was a bad luck symbol for the Viet Cong and was used by many G.I.s to tell the VC to give up or face death. This tactic was one aspect of psychological warfare used by many Americans in Vietnam.

#

The next morning Beau sensed that something was up. He was eager and willing to move out.

"You're a good dog," Chivington said, rubbing Beau's back.

He gathered his gear, using his checklist as a guide. His equipment included binos, a flak jacket, a gas mask, flares, some dog food and salted peanuts for Beau, and his C-rations. They all wore camouflage fatigues and darkened their exposed skin.

At 0500, in silent darkness, they boarded the UH-1B Huey gunship from the 4th Gunship Platoon of the 120th Assault Helicopter Company. Tandem seating put the pilot to the right of his copilot. Both were dressed in gray-blue nylon jumpsuits, dark flak jackets, and weighty white flight helmets.

Factory-installed armaments on this chopper included rocket pads, two forward-firing miniguns, a chin turret with 40mm grenade launchers, and a pair of M-60 C A-1 machine guns. The 40mm grenade launchers could be fired with pinpoint accuracy, whereas the 2.75-inch rockets were considered "free flight rockets." Fired in salvos of twenty or more, they were used to saturate an area, dispensing death-dealing phosphorus and shrapnel.

Once aboard, Chivington and his men settled in. Beau plopped down on the metal floor near the open door, hoping to grab the breeze he liked so much.

The crew chief and door gunner voiced apprehensions about a possible hot LZ, warning Chivington that the pilot might have to drop them—even without touching ground.

"Ya gonna be able to keep that dog under control in the air?" the crew chief asked.

Chivington rubbed Beau behind the ears. "He'll do just fine."

Upon completing the preflight check off list, the pilot's hand moved carefully over switches and circuit breakers. Glowing red instrument panel lights reflected off the Plexiglas-shrouded cockpit. Rolling the throttle open, the pilot squeezed the trigger switch on the collective stick on his left, setting into motion the turbine engine with its whining transmission and swishing rotor blades.

Resembling the roof light of a police cruiser, the blinking red signal beacon indicated that it was time for lift-off. The pilot revved his engine. Spinning rotor blades became a blur. He pulled up on the collective, and the Huey began its ascent, gliding forward, tail up and nose down. The pilot moved the cyclic stick between his knees in a horizontal direction. Fully airborne, the chopper leveled off at 1500 feet and cruised at a steady speed.

Kneading Beau's ears with care, Chivington spoke to him. "Nothin' better than a chopper ride is there, ol' buddy?" Beau barked his approval as the wind whipped his wet saliva back toward Chivington's hand.

243

Twenty minutes of flight passed without incident. The jungle below was a covering of browns and greens, with an occasional winding river or stream cutting the pattern into jigsaw puzzle pieces. Small bare patches of ponds or dried depressions were holes in the jungle floor.

The green-tinted cockpit dulled the glaring light of a new day. Holding the plastic-covered navigation maps upright, the pilot pointed downward. Yelling over the *whump, whump, whump* of the blades, he said, "Accordin' to the grid, we're close." He pointed north. "That vill—Vinh Hao—is a click or two over that way."

They made several wide passes over the last known coordinates of the missing airplane. Far below in the rich, green vegetation, patches of sunlight gave the quiet setting a haunted expression.

Then scattered aircraft wreckage appeared among broken trees and scrub jungle. The pilot began his descent, looking for a clearing. Chivington could see that the only available landing zone, a small opening in the jungle, would be rough because of stumps and scrub brush. It was the remains of an artillery shelling. Splintered trees and gaping holes would make a full landing impossible.

The pilot circled the area for a moment, then the front of the Huey arched back, and they were soon below treetop level. Chivington knew they would be jumping within a minute or so. With a racing heart, he told his men to lock and load. Then he grabbed the doorframe and stretched his legs out to touch the skid for the rest of the ride in. He didn't have time to think about what to do; his training and instincts took over as the forward movement of the Huey ceased and it began to hover. The pilot gave the exit signal.

Chivington jumped first, barely clearing the skid and dropping about five feet. Beau didn't hesitate. He leaped, falling feet first right on top of Chivington. Both disappeared in the tall, hurricane-whipped grass. Maddox, Tomburg, and Clark followed. They all hurried to the cover of the tree line; above them the Huey lifted off and vanished behind the trees, flying back to base.

It took only a moment to regroup. The search and rescue mission crept through the pike-edged grass. Chivington and Beau were on point, and Maddox on slack with his radio a few feet back. Clark and Tomburg followed. They moved with caution and silence. Everything that could clink and rattle on their rucksacks had been taped. All communication was by hand signals.

As they approached the wreckage, they entered an area where the jungle had been ripped apart from the recent artillery barrage. They collided head-on with a cloud of stench that made all of them gag. Even Beau whined. Stiff-legged and bloated water buffaloes and dismembered jungle animals were scattered throughout the area. Trees had been stripped bare of leaves and splintered like matchsticks. Small animals and birds littered the ground.

With Beau off-leash, the patrol pushed ahead. While walking along the tree line, not far from flooded rice paddies, they came upon a woman dressed in black pajama-like trousers and a white shirt. A small child rested in her backpack. Another tot walked behind her. The woman struggled with a rope wrapped around the nostrils of a wounded and stubborn water buffalo stuck in the muck of a rice paddy.

Frightened by the sudden appearance of American soldiers, the woman turned with a mirthless smile. Chivington knew that a Vietnamese smile often signaled a sign of capitulation. "Ai do? [Who's there?]"

Pantomiming the motion, Chivington put out his hand, saying in effect, "Be calm, it's okay."

"VC di Roi! [VC gone!]", she cried out with tear-filled eyes. "May bay Tha Bom. [Fear of more bombs.]"

"Di Roi [They're gone]," Chivington reassured her.

The woman continued waving her hands, lamenting, "My ban [killed by Americans]," "Dich ban [killed by VC]," "VC numbah ten, VC numbah ten."

Chivington understood that she lived in the village of Vinh Hao which had been devastated by both sides. He explained as well as he could that they meant no harm, and that they were looking for a downed American pilot. She shook her head and shrugged, either not understanding or not knowing anything about the pilot's whereabouts—or lying about it.

Chivington took the rope from her hand. Like a tug-of-war contest, they all started pulling on the bleeding water buffalo. Just as they began to feel some movement, the woman screamed. The toddler had slipped into the muddy water and was struggling to stay afloat.

Before any of them could react, Beau plunged into the pond, splashing water while swimming toward the drowning child. Clamping his teeth onto the boy's torn shirt, Beau swam to dry land, where Clark and Maddox pulled them up and out of the water.

Chivington applied CPR. After a moment, the child coughed up water and mucus, and cried with alarm. Chivington handed the tot over to his mother.

With tears running down her face, she cried, "Cam on ong, cam on ong, cam on ong [thank you, thank you, thank you]." Then she turned, pointing to Beau, her wide grin exposing stained, broken, and missing teeth. She laughed as he shook the remaining water from his coat.

"Atta boy, Beau, atta boy," Chivington praised. All four GIs gave Beau a job-well-done pat on his wet head, and Chivington treated him to some peanuts. Beau licked the salt off his hand.

"Did they teach water rescue in the trainin' school?" Clark asked.

"Hell no," Chivington replied, rubbing Beau behind the ears. "Beau's a smart dog. He figured it out on his own."

After a brief struggle, they were able to pull the water buffalo from the paddy. Clark applied minor first-aid dressing to the flesh wounds. The woman, her children, and the water buffalo wobbled down the edge of the paddy berm toward the village. According to Chivington's map, it was only a click or so away. He recalled Wilson's warning that the village was suspected of being in VC hands.

Using a compass, Chivington and his patrol moved past massive cypress trees and clumps of bamboo. There were no man-made trails in the area; Chivington knew that would be a plus. Brushing aside branches and limbs, he struggled to find a way into the crash site.

Finally, they pushed through brush and saw the airplane's crumpled fuselage and broken wing. It resembled a fallen bird. Severed pieces of fiberglass and metal were strewn over the area.

"Ya think the pilot could've survived this?" Tomburg asked, coming up behind Chivington.

"Doesn't seem likely, but I guess we'll have to find out."

Moving with caution and depending on Beau to alert them to any tripwires or other booby traps, they conducted a search, finding no trace of the pilot.

Then Beau stopped. His right ear rose. After a moment, he started moving forward with his nose to the ground, following a scent. Chivington and the others brought up the rear, weapons at the ready.

About twenty yards into the grove of trees, Chivington saw the sole of a jungle boot. Waving his hand around, they surrounded the small space. Beau crept closer to the empty, bloody boot, then stopped.

It must belong to the pilot, Chivington thought.

They found no other signs of the pilot. Moving in the direction of the village, they continued to follow Beau through the dense and prickly underbrush. Blood droplets dotted the scent trail. By now, Chivington had little hope of finding the pilot alive. With luck, maybe they could recover the papers Colonel Ricci wanted.

Beau stopped abruptly, turned, and placed his paws on Chivington's chest. Beau's message: *Caution! Something's wrong!*

"Whatcha got, Beau?" Chivington whispered. "Whatcha got?"

After searching the area, they moved in a bent-over position until the partially destroyed village came into view. Chivington motioned for Tomburg to set his M-60, with tripod and belt of ammo, in a clear field of fire. Everyone locked and loaded. (The M-60 fired one hundred rounds per minute.)

Suddenly, the distinctive, rapid pops of an AK-47 shattered the silence. Chivington reacted, hitting the ground and rolling behind a damaged hootch as bullets kicked up small clouds of dust all around him. He winced in pain and grabbed the upper portion of his left arm, where a round had grazed him. Small traces of blood appeared on the sleeve of his fatigue jacket.

Beau growled. His hackles stood; his head was down. Chivington held him close to the ground as his eyes searched the area for the sniper. Tall grass and trees blocked their view.

Without warning, Beau lurched and raced forward, yanking free of Chivington's grasp. There were more shots. Chivington raised his binos and saw Beau running toward something that he couldn't quite make out. A moment later, Beau disappeared into the tall grass.

Then Chivington heard a bone-chilling scream. Beau's growling had escalated into hard, vicious snarls. Through the binos, Chivington saw two black objects rolling in the grass.

With Beau's leash and his M-16 in hand, he waved everyone closer. As they approached the ruckus, Beau's menacing growls coupled with wailing put Chivington's nerves on edge.

Then Chivington got his first good look at the sniper, and realized it was a young woman. Somehow, she managed to stand. While she turned to slam her rifle butt against Beau's head, Chivington fired several rounds at her back without even thinking twice.

The woman collapsed, staring at Chivington. Pink bubbles gushed from her nose and mouth. Her blood spread across the ground, pooling in shallow depressions. She continued staring at Chivington with glassy eyes.

Not a woman, Chivington thought numbly, *a girl*. She was no more than sixteen or seventeen years old, a small female with short black hair and olive skin. She bore an eerie resemblance to the girl of Chivington's vivid dream. Imprinted graphically on her left arm were Beau's teeth marks.

"That's how he dragged this fuckin' bitch out of the well," said Tomburg, pointing to her arm.

Maddox strode up, put the muzzle of his rifle to the woman's head near the temple, and fired a magazine on full automatic. Her head vibrated with the impact of the rounds. Her bloody brains spurted out the other side of her head.

"For chrissake, Maddox!" Chivington exploded. "Why the fuck did ya do that?"

Maddox looked at him quizzically. "Why the fuck *not* do it? I wanted to make sure she was dead." In combat that's called "Double Tripping."

Maddox did it for the thrill of mutilating human flesh; there would be no point in debating the matter.

Peering inside the well, Chivington saw a rope ladder used by the sniper to elevate herself.

"Where's Beau?" Clark asked, looking around.

Before Chivington could call for him, they heard muffled, guttural growls coming from behind a barn-like outbuilding next to an animal pen. They started moving with care in that direction.

"Holy shit," Tomburg muttered. "What's that stink?"

251

It was a scent Chivington recognized because he'd smelled it before, but he kept silent and motioned for the others to do the same.

Moving around the corner of the wooden outbuilding, they came upon the snarling dog shaking a bloody, limp rat clamped between his teeth—but the smell of rotting flesh was not coming from the rat. Chivington found its source. Lying a few feet from Beau was a nude, white male staked out in spread-eagle fashion. He had apparently survived the crash, but just barely. The right side of his face was gone. Halfway between his wrist and elbow, bloody sections of bone extended from his right arm.

What had happened to him after the crash had been much worse. Rats had eaten parts of his ears and nose; his eye sockets were bloodstained, crusty, and vacant. White maggots feasted on his open, rotting wounds. His legs, feet, and genitals were purple and swollen like balloons. Large black ants swarmed over him.

"Goddamn," Chivington muttered. "Poor bastard."

Sickened by the sight, the others swallowed hard. Turning his head, Tomburg vomited.

After covering the pilot's body with a poncho, they heard a child's cry coming from inside the building.

Chivington ducked under the low doorway, his M-16 ready. Maddox stepped in behind him. A woman was nursing an infant, and two raggedly dressed old men huddled in a far corner.

"VC numbah ten," they said with conviction.

"Fucking A," Maddox said, lifting his M-16 toward them. The old men shrank back, holding up their hands as if that would protect them from the bullets. The woman turned away, taking her infant out of the direct line of fire.

Chivington knocked the barrel to the side before Maddox could pull the trigger. "What in hell are ya doin'?"

"Wastin' some VC collaborators," Maddox said, sounding surprised. "You gotta problem with that?"

No doubt Maddox was correct. These peasants were VC collaborators—no question. Maybe they didn't have a choice, but there had already been enough bloodshed, and Chivington's mind had again gone back to his great-grandfather's raid on helpless Sioux women and children during the Sand Creek Massacre. The Chivington name wouldn't be dragged through that sewer again—at least, not today.

Breaking the hush, the woman said, "Toi muon luong thuc: Sua, gao, ca. [I need food: milk, rice, and fish.]"

Chivington nodded, and told his men to dump their C-rats in the center of the dirt floor, including the pound cake.

"What!" Maddox squawked. "What the hell are we gonna eat?"

"We can eat back at base camp," Chivington told him.

"Fuck this," Tomburg said. "I'm not givin' any food to these gooks—"

Chivington spun around, facing him nose to nose. "We are not takin' a vote on this, Private Tomburg," he said. "I wanna leave these people some food, and you're gonna put your C-rats in the pile, like it or not. Do ya read me?"

His face flushed, Tomburg turned away, speechless, digging his C-rats out of the rucksack. The others followed suit. Beau's peanuts landed on top of the pile.

Chivington explained to the woman that he would seek more help. The woman indicated that all she had left were two pigs and the water buffalo. They needed food as well.

Chivington turned to Maddox. "Get on the horn with the chopper. Tell 'im about the Bird Dog pilot, first of all. Then tell 'im we need all the food they can scrounge, including dry milk and animal feed for a water buffalo and two pigs."

Maddox stared at him in awe. "You want a gunship to bring milk and foods?"

Chivington nodded. "Fucking A."

Maddox sighed and reached for his radio. "What a fucked-up war."

You've got that right, Chivington thought. He gestured for the Vietnamese to leave the building and start for their village. The hamlet seemed redeemable.

He then instructed his team to look for a yellow dispatch case that held the document Ricci expected. An hour of searching was to no avail.

In late afternoon, the gunship returned with Carnation milk containers, bags of white rice, bread, leftover mess hall meats, raw cabbage, and some hay.

After off-loading the supplies, the dead pilot was slipped into a plastic body bag. Everyone, including Beau, gagged on the stench escaping from that bag. The dead pilot would have to be registered with Graves Registration (GRREG).

Chapter 19

Once in flight, the copilot radioed Phan Rang that they were coming in with a body, but no documents.

As everyone relaxed, a heavy thud rocked the helicopter. To Chivington, it felt as though a giant flyswatter had struck it.

"We've been hit!" the pilot yelled. The craft, shuddering violently, slanted sharply toward the ground. "Gotta set it down!"

The Huey's soft underbelly was taking small arms fire, bullets coming in one side and out the other. Scrambling, Chivington grabbed Beau into his lap. Others instinctively looked for cover. There was no safe place inside the Huey.

As the pilot fought for control, the chopper rose and dipped in sickening waves. Chivington heard the pilot shout frantically, "Mayday, mayday," into his radio, giving grid coordinates.

By now the cockpit was filled with smoke. The floor was slick with hydraulic fluid. The Huey was bleeding to death. Chivington risked a look outside and saw the ground fast approaching. *Maybe the trees will slow us down*, he thought, as he scrambled to grab the "barber pole" (the rack to which the jump seat was attached).

The skids clipped treetops. The chopper then lurched sideways as the rotor blades cut into tree limbs. Jagged pieces of rotor housing ripped through the cockpit. Wreathed in smoke and flames, it crashed full force amid a grove of rubber trees.

Chivington, stunned by the impact, forced himself to move. He grabbed Beau's harness, telling him to "Go!" as he gestured outside. Then he turned back to the cockpit, fighting his way through black smoke, holding his breath until he reached the pilot and copilot, but it was a useless effort. Both had been killed.

By the time he was out of the chopper, his heart was like a hammer pounding against his chest. His head throbbed. He felt hot wetness spread across his left temple. It ran down his cheek, along his jaw, into his collar, but there was no time to worry about his condition. The enemy who had shot them down would be coming any minute.

Chivington looked around. Maddox emerged with his radio, his left hand weak and dripping blood. Clark was bloodstained, cut and bruised, but intact. Dragging his body away from the fiery wreckage, Tomburg, sustaining a fractured leg, lacerations, and burns, managed to hold onto his M-60.

"Door gunner and crew chief are dead," he gasped, as Clark went to help him.

Beau, standing rigid beside Chivington, whined anxiously, his eyes darting from point to point in the tree grove. Chivington couldn't blame him for being nervous. He, too, felt danger signals from every nerve ending. No matter which way he turned, his back was exposed to menace.

"I've got contact," Maddox said, behind him.

Chivington whirled around, still bent kneed. He took the radiophone and told base camp what had happened. The RTO at base camp said that help was on the way and to stay put. They had the coordinates, but shadows were already lengthening around them. Chivington knew that if help didn't arrive before dark, it would be the end.

He told Tomburg to set his gun and tripod in place. Clark and Chivington put M-16s on full automatic. All Maddox had saved from the fire was his .45.

A low, guttural growl came from Beau. Chivington looked down and saw that Beau's ears were forward, hackles raised, and teeth bared. Chivington followed Beau's gaze and saw shadows moving.

Beau pulled out of his grasp, lunging at the Vietnamese walking point. An NVA squad had come to investigate the crash, believing there were no survivors. Taken off guard, the point man caught the full fury of a singed, blood-covered canine warrior that went for his jugular. The NVA's netted, light green, grass-covered pith helmet flew off his head. He cried out in pain as blood spurted from his neck like a geyser, soaking his khaki shirt.

"Down!" Chivington screamed. "Get down!"

An engulfing mayhem broke loose. All of a sudden, the rubber tree grove surrounding Chivington's team was splintered by enemy fire. Chivington had managed to fit himself into the contour of the ground, where a small rise and a decaying log gave him some protection.

Tomburg wasn't so lucky. As he scrambled for cover, AK-47 bullets ripped at him, driving him violently, face first, into the ground.

Then Maddox screamed after a bullet hit his right thigh, sending him stumbling back against a tree. With a spray from his M-16, Chivington dropped two NVA soldiers, catching them chest high.

Beau sprang at another one, sinking his teeth into the soldier's forearm. The others retreated. As Beau and the NVA regular rolled together amid the dirt and grass, the Vietnamese stabbed at Beau under his neck. Chivington moved closer, firing a single round into his back. The soldier stiffened and fell. Beau rose unsteadily to his feet.

"Stay, boy," Chivington ordered. He wasn't sure if Beau had been wounded. He didn't want him running around attacking any more NVA in this condition. He would only get killed.

Clark attended to Maddox, who lay only a few feet from Chivington. In order to stop the bleeding, Clark applied a rag tourniquet above the open thigh wound.

"Better check on Tomburg," Clark said, nodding toward the fallen private. "I think he's had it."

Chivington cast another look around, then, staying low, hurried over to where Tomburg had fallen. He was still lying on his stomach, groaning faintly. Chivington winced as he saw four wounds angled from the upper left shoulder to the right buttock.

Chivington knelt beside Tomburg and turned him over as gently as he could, swearing under his breath. Tomburg's dirt-covered face was screwed up in pain. His glasses were nowhere to be seen—not that he would ever need them again.

"Fuck…it hurts," Tomburg gasped. He coughed. "I don't wanna die out here…can't breathe…." His eyes opened as he focused them longingly on Chivington. "Man, don't, don't let me die." He coughed again, and blood spilled over his pale lips, running down over his cheek in scarlet rivulets. "Man, I've never even, never been laid." Another spasm of pain hit him. He gasped. "I don't…don't…." He drew one final bubbling breath, let it out, took in a smaller one, and he was gone.

Tear-filled eyes blurred Chivington's vision. "Shit! Shit! Shit!" He stared through tree limbs at the darkening sky. "Goddammit, just take all of us right now! Why play games? If you're gonna kill us all, God, just get it fucking done!"

"Shhh!"

He looked over at Clark, who was still sitting with Maddox.

"Man, there're still gooks around here. No sense advertisin'."

"You think they don't already know?" Chivington demanded. "They'll be back, Maddox, and a lot more of 'em this time. We're all gonna end up just like Tomburg, so what the hell difference does it make if—"

He broke off, turning his head as a familiar distant sound filtered through the grief and fury, *whump, whump, whump.*

"Damn, that's a great sound," Clark said.

Forcing himself into action, Chivington reached for a smoke grenade, pulled the pin, and rolled it to an opening away from the trees. Even at dusk, the pilot ought to be able to see the white smoke.

In the area surrounding the downed chopper, the gunship pilot unleashed a torrent of firepower—rapid-firing miniguns and exploding 2.75 rockets. Chivington didn't know if the chopper saw enemy soldiers, or if they were just tearing up the place for the hell of it. Another sweep sparked a small forest fire a hundred yards or more to the west of Chivington's position.

Then another chopper arrived, a dragonfly against the darkening sky. Chivington knew it would be a dustoff. He looked up, waving at this manna from heaven. The dark shape drifted over the clearing and settled down on the brittle, brown grass.

Two medics used nylon litters to haul the wounded into the chopper. Minutes later, the medevac was in the air again, heading for the field hospital at Cam Ranh Bay.

#

Ricci, Babs Brewer, and Wilson were waiting when the first chopper arrived at the Cam Ranh landing pad. Ricci's heart seemed to be beating in time with the beat of the blades. He was elated that Babs had been able to join him.

The medical report was brutal: Tomburg dead, just a month into his tour; Maddox with a raw leg wound, recovery uncertain; the 0-1 Bird Dog pilot tortured and killed; the four-man helicopter crew, all dead.

Inwardly, Ricci broke up. First came rage. It was directed more toward fate than specific targets. What, he asked himself, was being accomplished by having all of these kids fighting each other with machine guns, hand grenades, mortars, gunships, and all the other fucking weapons designed to kill and maim?

Next came grief. That was worse. The pain and sorrow that had been dammed up in him ever since Marilyn's senseless death came pouring out like a burst dam. He sobbed.

In those moments of anguish, Ricci reached full understanding of something that was simple, yet profound. People have the power to love instead of hate.

People have the power to embrace peace instead of war. The potential is there, inside every human being. War is collective absurdity. Why is it so hard to live up to that potential? Why do people insist on hating and killing?

After emotions had run their course, leaving him weak and shaky, the second medevac touched down.

Chivington and Beau filed out first. Beau looked bloody but unharmed.

Chivington wore a blood-soaked bandage around his upper right arm; another wrapped around his head. He moved under his own power. From the haggard, hangdog look on his face, Ricci knew he was grieving.

Wilson saw it, too. He spoke with him for several minutes. Geno and Babs stood back, giving them privacy. Wilson then slapped Chivington on his good shoulder while taking Beau's leash.

Ricci suggested that Wilson take Beau to Doc Blevins for a checkup. Before departing, Wilson brought Beau to Babs. She knelt and hugged the big Doberman. He licked her cheek. His stubby tail wagged with excitement.

By the time Wilson reached the animal hospital with Beau, stretchers came out of the medevac. Sent on their way were the wounded and dead. Maddox was taken to the field hospital OR. Tomburg, the Bird Dog pilot, and the crew from the Huey were taken to the Saigon Morgue. Chivington and Clark walked to the ER for examination and treatment.

Ricci and Babs drove to the hospital. They were there when Chivington came out. A graze to his upper arm required a half-dozen stitches, and a butterfly bandage was applied to his head.

Babs led them to a small conference room with a table and armchairs. They found warm coffee. Chivington reported to Ricci on what occurred, starting with the sniper and the discovery of the dead Bird Dog pilot, then ending with the rescue following the chopper crash. Chivington shouldered more than his share of the blame for what had happened.

"Corporal Chivington," Ricci told him, "it's damned remarkable that *any* of you got out of there alive. If you hadn't kept your head—and I mean *you*, since you were the leader of that team—you could've all bought it."

Chivington's eyes shut solemnly, his head down. "Thank you, sir."

Babs returned with three cups of coffee on a small round tray, placing it on the table. She sat next to Ricci.

"I mean it, Corporal," Ricci said, reaching for a cup and stirring in a sugar cube. "I'm not going to let you take heat for what happened. You performed admirably. The men who made it back owe their lives to you."

"Thank you, sir," Chivington said again, with elevated spirits. While sipping coffee he added, "Beau deserves a lot of the credit. He really came through for us, sir. I wouldn't be talkin' to ya right now if it weren't for him."

Babs spoke up. "I always felt his loyalty."

"Yes, ma'am." Chivington's brow pulled down, his eyes returning to Ricci. "Sir, there's something I've been meanin' to talk to ya about."

"Now's as good a time as any," Ricci said.

"Well, sir, it's somethin' that came up during the trainin' at Bien Hoa. Our instructor, Sergeant Violette, said that none of the military dogs in 'Nam would ever be allowed to go back home."

"What?" Babs exclaimed. "They wouldn't do that, would they?"

"Have you heard about that, sir?" Chivington asked.

Forcing eye contact with Chivington, he said despondently, with a stiff-necked response, "That's SOP, Corporal."

"No!" Babs put down her cup with such force that coffee slopped out over the rim and pooled around the cup. "That can't be right. Why would they do that? Whaddya mean?"

Ricci drew a breath, then let it out in a long pause. "I've heard that there are canine diseases over here that we don't have in the States. The Army is afraid they'll be carried back with some of the dogs."

"Then we can screen 'em, give 'em tests to make sure they aren't carrying any disease."

Ricci agreed. "That would work, but that would cost money and resources. Besides, well…once a dog is trained, the Army wants to get as much out of 'em as they can. A dog like Beau is a valuable resource. They don't want to lose 'em by sendin' 'em back home."

"I get it," Chivington said, making no effort to keep the bitterness out of his voice. His hands were clasped around his coffee cup as if he were drawing warmth from it. "We wouldn't send a tent or a jeep home just because it had done its job well. We keep jeeps and tents here until they break down or wear out or get blown up. Same with dogs, right, sir? They're just expendable military equipment."

"Unfortunately, that's true. Believe me, I wish it weren't."

"We can't let that happen to Beau," Babs insisted. "We've got to do something, Geno."

He looked at her. "Like what?"

"I don't know," she said with chest-pumping fury. "Can't you pull some strings and get 'im shipped home when Corporal Chivington goes back?"

Ricci lifted the cup and took a swallow of the warm coffee. He didn't see how he could pull strings with this problem. This kind of policy decision was almost impossible to overcome.

"Maybe we can sneak 'im out, sir," Chivington said.

Ricci lifted an eyebrow. "Sneak him out?"

"Yes, sir."

"How would you do that?" Babs asked.

Chivington shook his head. "I have no idea, ma'am, but I'll bet I can come up with something."

Ricci looked at the young soldier with new respect. The boy didn't know when to quit.

"I don't want to know anything about that, Corporal," he said at last. "We never talked about this, and I don't want to hear anything about it again. Is that clear?"

Chivington looked at him with bafflement. Babs learned over, touching his arm.

"He means go ahead and do what you need to do. Just keep him out of it."

Chivington's face brightened. "Yes, ma'am... er, yes, sir. Thank you, Colonel—"

"For what?" Ricci interrupted.

"For—" Chivington caught himself, "for meetin' us here today, sir. It was kind of you."

That night, Ricci and Babs went for drinks at the officers' club. Ricci sipped his bourbon and ginger ale. Then he set his glass on the table and said, "When I got word about what happened out there today, well, it hit me pretty damned hard."

She nodded. "I can't imagine what it must be like for you. I know how much you care for your men."

"Sometimes too much, I think." He took another healthy swallow from his glass. He needed fortification for what he was going to say next. "Babs, I'm overdue for some R&R."

"Hmm," she mused, tipping her head and looking at him slantwise. "That's quite a coincidence. So am I."

"Really? Do you have plans?"

"Not yet. Do you?"

"Back at Fort Leonardwood, they would say you don't need a gob of money for…"

"For what?" she asked.

"For Thailand, of course, Bangkok! Is your inoculation record up to date?"

"Ohhh, yes," she said, smiling. "What is it they say about Thailand? Tour…the whole works."

"For fifteen bucks a day, you get a first-rate room and the whole works."

Looking affectionately at him for a long moment, she then said, "Will we be using just one room, Geno?"

His face flushed. "Well," as he looked down at his hands, "Babs I'm not sure…"

"It's okay." She reached over and took one of his hands and held it between her own. "Geno, you know how I feel about you, and I know what you've been going through since, well, for the past two years. I don't want to do anything to offend. Surely, you know that."

Muted, his mouth wouldn't form the words.

"I was only kidding about the room. We'll get two. We would have to for propriety's sake, anyway."

He nodded, and squeezed her hand. "I love you, Babs."

"I love you, too, Geno. More than you can imagine."

Chapter 20

Ten days later, dressed in fatigues, Ricci and Babs stepped aboard a C-130 shuttle for Thailand. After they were seated, Ricci took the silver unicorn from his pocket and hooked it around his neck.

"You brought it!" Babs exclaimed.

He smiled. "Of course!"

She pressed his left hand and smiled. Buckling up for five days of R&R, they took off for Bangkok.

"How's Corporal Chivington?" she asked once they were in the air.

"Fine. His stitches came out day before yesterday. I've got him and Beau on sentry duty. Things have quieted down a little, and we'll have a full moon for the next few days. Sappers like to work in the dark. I'm damned sure they're going to hit us before long."

"Sappers?"

He explained about sapper units and the tactics they used against U.S. air bases. "They're good at what they do. They hit fast and hard, and there's usually no sign that they're even around until it's too late. Of course, they almost always attack after dark, so I'm keepin' Chivington and Beau on night duty. I'm hopin' Beau will detect their presence before they get inside the wire."

"He's only one dog," she pointed out. "He can't be everywhere at once. Phan Rang is a large base. Don't you have other dog teams?"

"Just two others, and I've sent 'em over to another location—a sawmill that's critical to our construction efforts. Perimeter security is even more difficult over there, so I've let 'em have two teams."

She took his hand in hers. "Let's put work behind us. We're gonna have a wonderful time in Bangkok."

Holding hands during the rest of the flight, they talked about small things, mostly just enjoying one another's company.

Approaching Bangkok, they descended through the clouds. Ricci was impressed by the vastness of the city, the Chao Phraya River and surrounding environs, including Don Maung International Airport just north of Bangkok. A quilted patchwork of rice paddies dotted the Central Plains, a densely-populated region of Thailand.

After deplaning, passengers were met by a military escort. An orientation followed in the briefing room. A military officer prattled about the tours, currency exchange, tap water, no tipping, and practicing safe sex.

Twenty minutes later, Ricci and Babs were taxied to their hotel. Heavy traffic including cars, trucks, buses, and mopeds all jockeyed for position.

The taxi's brakes issued an unhealthy squeal as they stopped in front of the Oriental Hotel, located on the Chao Phraya. The air conditioning left something to be desired. The furniture looked old and tattered, but the place was far superior to tents and hootches in a war zone.

The lobby bustled with activity. Bellboys shuttled in and out with suitcases. The constant hum of conversation echoed in the background, along with the dinging bell beside the old, tarnished cash register.

Ricci and Babs checked in. They were taken to their adjoining rooms on the third floor. Ricci thanked the bellhop with an Abraham Lincoln greenback. After unpacking, cleaning up, and changing into civvies, they were ready to hit the streets of Bangkok.

As Babs stepped out of her room into the hallway, Ricci's eyes widened at the sight of her festive red blouse.

"Hey, how did you know that red is my favorite color?" With a wink, he added, "And I didn't expect to find the pyramids of Egypt in Thailand."

"Don't be silly," she said, blushing. "Let's go." She grabbed his hand and pulled him toward the elevator.

It was hot outside, with the heat radiating off the pavement and buildings. Along the canals, floating sampan markets laden with exotic fruits such as mangos, pineapples, bananas, as well as dried beef and fish, were jammed like traffic on a Friday afternoon in New York City.

"Look at how they sit cross-legged in those small boats," Babs said, "and look at those straw hats. They're a little different from the ones in 'Nam. Not as pointed, but flat, round-topped, and wide-brimmed."

Holding hands, they stopped every so often, peering into small shops and vendors' carts. When they came across a GI bar, Ricci suggested they break for lunch.

"That sounds great," Babs said, "I'm starving."

After being seated at a small, linen-draped table near the front window, they ordered a spicy dish called *gang pet goon,* a mixture of Thai curry, hot peppers, spices, and shrimp paste served with steamed rice.

"Whew, this stuff is hot," Babs exclaimed after her first bite. "I'm not so sure—"

"That's okay, girl," Ricci said, wiping his lips. "It tastes like good Italian food." He motioned to the white-jacketed waiter. "Bring us two more Singhas."

The waiter nodded.

Babs leaned closer to him and whispered, "Geno, I'm already feeling pretty tipsy. Can we handle two more beers? They seem a bit strong to me."

"Yeah, I know. It's about twenty percent alcohol." He laughed, "Almost formaldehyde."

The meal completed, Ricci paid the bill. Babs held Ricci's hand as she staggered a little. The afternoon passed quickly. Their straw bags were full of small gifts and trinkets.

"We'd best get back to the hotel," Ricci said, swabbing his brow with the back of his hand. "It's hot out here, and I'm tired."

"Me, too," she said.

At the hotel, they decided on a short nap.

"I'll pick you up around 1800 for dinner, okay?" Ricci said.

"Sounds great."

#

That evening, in a dimly lit restaurant a block away from the hotel, Ricci and Babs enjoyed dinner, drinks, and dancing. The bellhop had recommended the place. It was everything he'd said it would be: soft lights, sweet music, good food, and attentive waiters. Babs was wearing white slacks and a tight, gaily striped top which drew interested looks from most of the men in the place.

"Geno, how do you like real plumbing for a change?" Babs asked as they were taking a break from the dance floor.

"It beats those drums, that's for sure," he said. "It makes me feel like a human being again."

"And a daily hot, private shower. It's going to be wonderful."

He smiled. "That's why it's called R&R, dear Babs. By the way, I read my horoscope in the paper today." He pulled a torn piece of newsprint from the pocket of his polo shirt. Ricci was a Capricorn, born on January 19.

"Really? What's the message?"

"Well," he said with a furtive smile, rubbing the unicorn. "It says something about a Leo matching my intensity. It says to plan a sexy night. It also says that my relationship is a fascinating blend of conflict and excitement, and then it says to put off final decisions."

"Well, I'll be damned."

"I happen to have yours, as well," he said, pulling another scrap of paper from his shirt pocket.

She lifted her eyebrows in surprise. "You know the date of my birthday?"

"Of course!"

She smiled. "Okay, what's my horoscope?"

After a gulp of dark San Miguel beer, he said, "For a July 31 Leo, it says that you have gumption and an admirer. It also says that you must honor your own needs in a relationship by taking what you want. The key to your success is proper timing." He looked up. "That's what it says."

"Very interesting." She studied his face. "Geno, does this mean—?"

"It means I've got some good red wine to share back at the hotel," he said. "Interested?"

She smiled. "More than interested, Geno."

#

As they approached their third-floor rooms, Babs said, "I'll see you in a few minutes."

"I'll be there."

With a palpitating heart, Ricci hustled to his hotel room. He decided to take a quick shower, and again marveled at the luxurious feel of it, adjusting the showerhead from a gentle to a pulsating needle spray—a far cry from the primitive facilities at Phan Rang.

A few moments later, holding a bottle of red wine, he rapped lightly on Babs's door. When she opened it, he saw an erotic blond in a short, black, lacy negligee. As she turned to gesture for him to enter, the silky material pulled taut against her left breast, molding it sweetly. He felt a hot flush creeping up his neck.

"How 'bout a nightcap, Captain?" he asked, his voice a little shaky.

"Yes sir, Colonel. You're the offisuh in charge." She seemed much more calm than he.

Ricci drew a steadying breath and stepped into her room. This was Babs as he had never seen her, beautiful and sensuous. Her red lips, curvaceous body, and low-cut negligee sent blood rushing to all parts of his body.

He carried the wine over to the sitting area beside the window. There was a small sofa, and a coffee table on which Babs had already placed the glasses. She sat down first and thumped the cushion beside her. Geno followed. His dilemma: Was he ready for this?

He *wanted* it, that much was certain. Maybe that would be enough, but what if he choked when it came time for the big play?

The iridescent lights of Bangkok illuminated a portion of the open window. A warm, gentle breeze pushed the light blue curtains away from the window ledge.

"Well, let's have some of this wine," he said, reaching for two glasses. He poured hers, then his own. His hands shook a little as he gave a glass to her, then lifted his own and clinked it against hers.

"Are you proposin' a toast?" she asked with a halogen smile.

He nodded. "To us."

They sipped, and when they reached at the same time to place their glasses on the table, their fingers touched. Without knowing exactly how it happened, Ricci found his arms around her, their lips pressed together in a lingering kiss.

"Wow!" she breathed heavily as their lips parted. "I think we should do that again."

Leaning back, she smiled. Then she got up and stepped around the table toward the bed. He caught up with her in two long strides and put his arms around her from the back, marveling at the feel of her body. He looked down at the back of her negligee, to the point where the straps met at a V far down her back, wondering how it would look underneath.

"Well..." he managed to say, his throat dry, voice croaky. He placed his lips on the nape of her neck. He felt her arch her head up and back, her lips touching his ear; spinning her around, wrapping an arm around her waist, he pulled her close, and pressed his lips on hers. They were just as soft and moist as they had been a moment ago, but now he also felt the tip of her tongue.

"Mmm," she murmured, her mouth still against his.

She ran her fingertips along the side of his neck. Geno Ricci was blind with lust. He lifted the negligee, trying to pull it over her head. It was caught on something. He stepped back, waving awkwardly at it.

"Let's get in bed," he whispered. He went over and folded back the covers, then turned. She tossed the black negligee onto the floor. While he undressed, Babs moved closer to the bed.

It had all happened automatically and without thinking. He knew it was right. There was no reason to feel guilt any longer. Marilyn would want him to find love again.

She lifted the sheet and light blanket, threw them back and out of the way. They embraced in the middle of the bed. She turned on her side to face him. He could feel her belly against his, her breasts on his chest. Every part of Geno Ricci was alive and sensitive to her touch and smell and sight.

When she moved her arms to reach around and toy with his back, he moved his hands up her sides. She felt soft and silky. He looked down to see her body, all naked, marveling at her young, peach-colored skin. Fascinated, he watched his hands massage the baby fat by her armpits. Below, he could see the expanse of her breasts and caressed the edges where the light tan turned alabaster. He wondered how anything could be so wholesome and beautiful. His fingers moved forward along the curve of her side to brush the nipple.

She looked at him, a small smile playing on her lips, her eyes soft and affectionate. Embarrassed, he pulled her close, kissing her throat and holding her around the small of her back. His hands traced the flaring line from her ribs to her hips. He pictured the sweeping curves at her hips as he moved his hands up and down and then around onto her buttocks. He thought ahead to when he would slide his hand around to the front onto her belly and between her legs. The anticipation reminded him of their kisses and the softness of her lips.

He pushed Babs more onto her back, and moved half on top of her, touching her lips with a finger, tracing the oval. He lowered his lips to hers, tonguing the corners of her mouth. He felt her respond and began kissing her neck, then her breasts, moving lower, and still lower.

Babs shifted, raising her right leg and draping it across Ricci's back. She crooked her calf forward, pressing against his neck as his tongue fluttered her to new heat. The layered air of the hotel room smelled of musk and bodies.

Then he could feel her pulling him up, softly guiding his body with her hands, opening her legs so he could move between them. He reached under her thighs and pushed up, then felt Babs lift her knees way up, cradling him in between. When he felt between her legs, first stroking her thighs, then gently working his fingers into her, he discovered that she opened like a tropical flower, full and luxurious, and dripping with nectar. She pulled him closer, guiding him, and he entered her.

Afterward, they stayed in bed, playing and dozing for several hours. Ricci felt as though an incredible burden had been lifted. For the past two years, he was the one who had constructed emotional walls around himself. Now it was time for a new passion.

#

The next morning, sunlight streamed across the bed. Sheets were a tangled mess. For the first time in ages, Geno Ricci felt rock solid.

"You're awake."

He turned at the sound of her soft voice, found her watching him. "Have you been awake long?"

She shook her head. "Maybe a half hour."

"You should've woke me—"

"I enjoyed watchin' you sleep. Didja know that you sometimes smile in your sleep?"

He laughed, rolled onto his side, and kissed her. "I had no idea. It's probably a recent development." He kissed her again. "Feel like havin' breakfast?"

"Maybe." Her eyes were very soft. "Maybe a little later."

Two hours passed. They were both famished. Ricci curled back the sheets on his side. He dressed by retracing the short trail of brown, tan, and beige clothes he had shed the night before. He listened to Babs getting out of bed, getting dressed, his back to her, his brain on rewind, remembering the delicious details.

They walked down the hall, hand-in-hand, clinched in the elevator, and dashed through the lobby, animated and joyous. He mugged at her grinning face, loving her flashing, attentive eyes. Taking her hand, he danced her through the door to the hotel's restaurant.

While sitting together at a booth, they devoured scrambled eggs, toast, and Ricci's favorite, rice tapioca. As they ate, the two lovebirds stared at each other.

Tipping their orange juice, "Salud!" he said.

"To the future," she added.

Ricci looked around at the restaurant, taking in the relaxed, carefree atmosphere. Everything looked exquisite. His body, he thought, was aglow.

Was it love or lust? Or both? Or did it matter? Ricci knew that love had toppled kings, ignited wars, and changed the course of history more than once. Love, he thought, was responsible for life's greatest joys and sorrows. He also felt that the body and mind must come together spiritually in order to produce this fragile emotion.

He never forgot what his Italian mother had said about love: *"Amor vincit omnia."* Love conquers all. That was one tip he would never forget.

After breakfast they boarded the Air Force tour bus. A forty-year-old ex-sawmill worker named Chavalit Pomwat introduced himself as the English-speaking tour guide and welcomed them to Bangkok. His initial remarks covered scheduling for the remainder of the week. During this overview, he praised Thailand's forests of teak and redwoods and condemned deforestation.

Stops in Bangkok included the glimmering red roofs and ornate spires of the Grand Palace, home of Thai kings for two hundred years. Chavalit said the palace covered one square mile, and he pointed out that it was situated along the banks of the river of kings, the Chao Phraya, Thailand's greatest river. In comparison, Ricci told Babs, this palace made the White House look like a cottage.

Farther along, the tour bus turned off Ratchadamnoen Avenue and down a dirt road. Ricci pointed to several wooden houses set on stilts. Chavalit said that many people lived along the canals in order to carry on their sampan floating-market trade.

Beautiful sunny weather enhanced their tour. The next stop caught Muay Thai kickboxers in action. Muay Thai, Thailand's seminal kickboxing sport, emphasized the use of the knee and the elbow, which become lethal human weapons in order to destroy the opponent. As they fought, musicians provided background music using long drums and cymbals. Babs noticed people jumping, hollering, and clapping as they would at an American football game. Chavalit told her fighters wore amulets for protection and good health.

On the way back to the hotel, Chavalit pointed to spirit houses sitting outside most Thai homes. He told them Thais put incense and flowers near them in order to please the spirits. Happy spirits meant fewer troubles in their daily lives.

#

After lunch, Ricci and Babs decided to skip the afternoon part of the tour and head out on their own. As they walked down the congested streets, their eyes and ears fixed on traffic jams and blaring horns.

While waiting to cross a street, they noticed a red, white, and blue Pepsi sign inscribed in Thai lettering. Looking up, Ricci remarked, "It almost looks like home." After crossing the street, they came upon a disgusting scene. Under the eye of Thai police, sex tourists were negotiating a deal with a pimp and a pair of twelve- or thirteen-year-old girls. Dressed in long, black, silk dresses, the girls looked frightened and nervous.

Why aren't they in school? Ricci wondered. *Where are their parents?*

But he knew that in order to survive, many parents sold their children—and not all were girls. Young boys were also served up. Many were beaten, chained, denied food, and raped by their pimps. An estimated 250,000 child prostitutes existed in Thailand alone. This heinous business was rampant throughout most of Southeast Asia.

"Geno, this sickens me," Babs said. "Let's get the hell outta here. I'm ready to go back to the hotel."

"I agree," he said with aversion.

Chapter 21

Over the next few days, sightseeing included a one-day tour (as advertised over the American Forces Vietnam Radio Network) of the infamous River Kwai Bridge. The bridge was built by 61,000 British and Aussie POWs along with 250,000 Asian slaves. They were necessary in order to complete the Burma to Thailand Railroad during the Japanese occupation from 1943 to 1944. The next day Geno and Babs visited the center for training baby elephants used in the commercial logging industry. Chavalit's comment about forest destruction struck a chord with Ricci, since he, too, was a tree hugger.

Chavalit told them that as a result of the industry's excessive harvesting, Asian elephants were disappearing. Unscrupulous loggers often drugged these beasts with amphetamines, which allowed them to work until they dropped. Chavalit stated that when an elephant passed its worth and became ill, the animal was often abandoned.

To his credit, Chavalit was not the typical Thai guide. He deviated from the company line. Ricci appreciated his honesty, even though he hated hearing it. That was why he decided to give Chavalit a hefty tip at the end of the tour, even if it were against the rules.

Along the way, Chavalit remarked how elephant herds encroached upon farmers' crops. Once elephants found good farmland, they kept coming back. He said, for example, that one bull elephant could consume up to 165 pounds of finger millet in one night. As a result, many farmers set traps using deep pits. Some elephants were even electrocuted. Chavalit told them how one farmer dangled the end of a hot wire into a tempting bunch of bananas. When the elephant reached for the food, he was zapped.

The story sickened Ricci. He didn't want to hear any more, but Chavalit went on about poachers and water buffaloes. He mentioned how poachers sawed elephant tusks off live elephants for their ivory. Such heinous cruelty resulted in infections and eventual death.

Chavalit's animal stories finally shifted to a lighter side: the annual water buffalo races held in Chonburi, Thailand, about forty-five miles south of Bangkok near the River Kwai Bridge Museum and war cemetery. He explained how 1,800 pounds of hair, horns, and hooves charged about twenty-five miles per hour for 130 yards. This popular contest, according to Chavalit, was about a hundred years old and attracted as many as 150 to 200 entrants in any given year. Intrepid rice-farming jockeys sat atop their steeds with only a rope for an anchor while urging the buffalo on with a bamboo riding crop.

Ricci likewise discovered that dishonesty and bribery were commonplace in Thai politics. Corruption was endemic in the bowels of Thai government where bureaucrats took bribes as a traditional aspect of Thai society.

Ricci and Babs spent their final hours of R&R shopping at the huge Air Force Base Exchange in Bangkok. As a gift for Babs, Ricci bought a .35mm Minolta camera with all the accessories. While on her private shopping spree, Babs found a beautiful Rolex Submariner for Ricci, dirt-cheap. This stainless steel diver's watch would look great on Ricci's wrist, complementing the unicorn.

That evening, after their parting candlelight dinner in a restaurant in the well-known Patpong nightclub district, they went back to her room. His place hadn't been getting much use, after all. As a tribute to their first night here, and to celebrate their time together, they again shared some red wine.

"Babs," Ricci said, leaning back into the cushions of the small sofa, "you can't imagine what this trip has meant to me."

"Oh, I think I've got an idea," she said. "I feel the same way."

He shook his head. "You can't. What I've been through the last two years…well, I realize now that it was guilt, Babs. I should've been there for her. If I hadn't been off in Guam, the accident that night might never have happened."

She took his hand and held it in hers. "Do you think that's how Marilyn would feel?"

"Hell no," he said. "I realize that now. Marilyn would be the last person in the world to blame me, or want to see me torture myself like I have. I've just been…" His voice broke, and he paused to draw a steadying breath. "Well, I couldn't allow myself to love anyone again, but with you, I didn't have any choice, Babs."

She leaned over and kissed him. "I know, Geno. It's like that with me, too."

"I feel almost as if, well, as if we've been brought together for a reason." He paused, looking at her. "You're gonna think I'm crazy, but I feel almost as if Marilyn had something to do with it, as if she wanted me to be happy, so she brought us together."

Babs set her glass on the table, then took his glass out of his hand and placed it beside hers. She leaned over and kissed him so softly, so lovingly, that he felt his chest tighten with emotion.

"Babs, I love you so much," he said, pulling her close.

"I love you too, Geno," she said, "and I do believe we've still got a few hours of R&R left."

#

Rapt with enthusiasm on the return flight the next day, Geno and Babs reflected on their five enchanting days in Bangkok. After landing, they boarded a chopper shuttle to Cam Ranh Bay, and from there, another chopper returned Ricci to Phan Rang.

A greeting party consisting of Young, Padre, Wilson, Chivington, and Beau awaited Ricci's return. As their commander stepped down from the helicopter, the men stood tall and saluted.

"At ease," said Ricci as he walked down the line, shaking hands. As he approached Beau, the dog sat and raised his paw. While grabbing his foot, Ricci laughed and patted his head. "Good boy, Beau, good boy."

Chapter 22

Under a quilt of stars and whisper quiet, Chivington looked down at his illuminated dial. It was past 2300. The night was unending. Drowsiness plagued the handler and his dog.

Ricci ordered all perimeter floodlights turned on after 1900, both at Phan Rang and the sawmill. Residents of both places were edgy. Double shifts for the K-9 Corps were a given. Rumors of sapper movement around the sawmill concerned Ricci.

Beau, off-leash, roamed about twenty yards ahead of Chivington, looking back frequently. Before he knew it, Chivington saw Beau pause while looking at one of the shadowy areas along the fence. Standing rigid, Beau peered through the tangled barbed wire. As Chivington approached, he saw Beau's raised hair and twitching nose. The right ear was erect and pointing forward; the scarred left one struggled to do the same. It was a strong alert.

Chivington dropped to a knee beside him. "What is it, boy?" he whispered. "Do ya see somethin' out there?"

Beau turned his head to one side, then bolted, running down along the fence line to another area of deep shadows about thirty yards away. Chivington readied his M-16 and followed Beau in a crouched run.

He saw movement, then heard Beau's snarling attack. While cutting through the concertina wire, a satchel-carrying grease-covered sapper wearing only a loincloth caught the full thrust of Beau's throat plunge. The jugular vein erupted like a broken water main, splashing blood all over Beau's face and down the front of the now-dead sapper.

Entering through another section of wire, two other sappers of the three-man squad met their fate head-on in the smoking, full automatic of Chivington's M-16 and exploding Claymore mines. These sappers, wearing black silky shorts, flip-flops, and floppy brimmed hats with chin straps, left their blood-drenched remains, including a severed hand, hanging on the wire like Christmas tree decorations.

It was 2245.

The hollow click of incoming RPGs sparked a full-scale attack on Phan Rang. Watchtower guards and sharpshooters reacted. Scanning the fence line, they released a massive volume of M-60 and M-16 fire. Illumination grew dim as AK-47s and 82MM mortars shattered floodlights. Heavy explosions shook the ground.

Provoked, Chivington thought of the motor pool and heavy equipment area where a number of vehicles were parked.

Mortars pounded the partially constructed airstrip. B-40 rockets hit the troop barracks. Another sapper cell crawled through an opening near the listening post. Dense brush covered much of the Juliet area, making sappers' concealment easier.

With Beau off-leash, Chivington, adrenaline flowing, advanced along the perimeter's edge between towers J-3 and J-4. A dark shadow lurked in their direction. Beau alerted. On full automatic, Chivington's trigger finger froze as Wilson identified himself.

"The Old Man wants you and Beau at the CP," Wilson confided.

Chivington wasn't surprised. Following their usual tactics, sappers go for the command post, killing ranking officers and pilfering military documents such as top-secret reports, equipment rosters, and the like.

The dog team hustled toward the CP. Ricci had ordered an air strike. At this time, the USS Midway was stationed off the coast of Cam Ranh Bay. Four roaring A-4E Skyhawks left their carrier. Guided by trip flares, the 4-Es crossed Phan Rang's perimeter, leaving a brilliant 4th of July fireworks display in their wake. By now, incoming mail had subsided and elements of the 274th VC Regiment were retreating. The A-4ES had done their job. It was 2350. Phan Rang was fixed in the black of night.

Chivington and Beau took up their position outside the command post bunker while Wilson went back inside, closing the door behind him.

Inside the CP, an uneasy calm existed. Ricci, Young, Padre, and Wilson hunkered down. Chivington and Beau would soon join them. Meanwhile, two three-man sapper cells were smuggling their way toward the CP. Malodorous perspiration permeated the interior.

Like flashlights stabbing holes in the dark, the red glare of a dog's piercing eyes contended with the sappers' secluded entry. All hell broke loose. AK-47 rounds flashed like rockets. The smell of gun smoke wafted to the low ceiling. Beau's growling fury and shark-like teeth ravaged the lead sapper.

"Hayako your ass, ya gook bastard!" shouted Chivington, as he wrestled another sapper to the floor. Plunging cold steel into the sapper's gut, Chivington yelled, "Die, shit face, die! VC numbah 10—no fucking good."

Ricci, Wilson, and Young emptied their 45s. Padre bellowed, "May God have mercy on your sorry-ass souls!" his shotgun blasting two sappers point blank.

A squeaking yelp reverberated throughout the room. Beau, losing lifeblood and lacerated, rolled across the floor with the remaining sapper zealot. Sensing Beau's trouble, Chivington speared the sapper's chest cavity then dragged his own bleeding body to Beau's side.

#

Backup generators provided enough artificial light to assess the dead and wounded.

Captain Wojtacha dispatched a couple of medics to the CP. Once inside, with flashlights in hand, they saw the carnage.

"Christ, Chivington, you're really hurt," said one of them.

"Forget it, asshole. Attend to Beau. Stop his bleeding, goddammit!"

"We'll get 'im a dustoff," Wilson growled. "We can't leave 'im here."

Chivington staggered through the bunker door, but once outside collapsed against the front wall and slid towards the floor. Ricci eased him down.

"We'll take care of you," Ricci said, getting a closer look at Chivington's shoulder and arm. "You're wounded real bad."

Chivington shook his head. "Knife."

"All right," Ricci said crisply. "Don't talk. We've got to stop that bleedin'."

"Beau," Chivington gasped. "How…"

"Medics have called for a chopper."

Chivington saw Padre and Wilson moving through the entrance, carrying Beau between them.

"He's in fucking bad shape," Wilson said as he lowered him to the floor beside Chivington. The front of Jim's uniform was dark with Beau's blood. "Looks like he's been cut pretty bad in three or four places."

With an effort of will that brought beads of sweat to his forehead, Chivington reached for Beau and gently brought the Doberman partly into his lap, cradling his head. Beau's brown eyes were fixed on his master.

"Hang in there, boy," Chivington whispered, tears sliding down his cheeks. "We'll take care of ya, boy. Just hold on for a few more minutes."

Ricci reached for a first-aid kit in his desk. With a small pair of scissors, he cut Chivington's shirt away from his shoulder, pressing a thick cloth bandage against the injury. Agonizing, Chivington pushed his hand away.

"Beau...use it to stop his bleeding."

In desperation, Chivington found strength, plucking the cloth bandage out of Ricci's hands and placing it against the worst of Beau's wounds, on his left side. Breathing in short, whining gasps, Beau labored.

Like a sponge, the bandage was soaked with blood. That is when Chivington realized it might be over for Beau. Throwing the bandage aside angrily, he leaned over Beau, bringing his own head down next to Beau's. Feeling Beau's sandpaper-like tongue on his face, weakly licking away the tears, deepened his sorrow.

"Beau," Chivington gasped, "I love you, Beau. You're a good dog, my buddy."

Just then, a familiar *whump, whump, whump* was heard, and the chopper landed, shining a beaming spotlight on Beau and Chivington. Medics placed Chivington gingerly on a poleless nylon stretcher, then loaded Beau in a litter basket wrapped in a blanket.

The chopper lifted and soared toward the field hospital and the veterinary clinic.

Ricci's, Padre's, Young's, and Wilson's superficial wounds were treated at the bunker. Padre, in the meantime, rushed to the Aid Station, providing spiritual comfort.

The following day, with trepidation, Ricci, Wojtacha, and Young reviewed damage reports. The Rome Plow and sawmill were intact but at a price: ten members of the 101st rifle platoon KIA; two dog teams KIA; fifty percent of the heavy equipment beyond repair; and Phan Rang nearly despoiled by elements of the 274th and sapper cells.

"Those fucking sappers had enough explosives to blow this base to oblivion—if it weren't for Chivington and Beau's initial alert," Ricci remarked with clenched teeth. "Those two caught hell for us. We owe 'em, and I lost my two other dogs, their handlers, and ten other good men, goddammit!"

\#

Captain Brewer attended to Chivington. After two transfusions, ninety-six sutures, and all the morphine she could dispense, his lifeline slowly resurfaced. In and out of consciousness, he demanded information on Beau's status. He likewise wondered about the aftermath of the well-planned assault on Phan Rang. What he didn't know was the extent of his wounds. Chivington's head injury was more than blunt force trauma.

Captain Brewer understood that Chivington would soon be air-evacuated to Japan, then possibly to Walter Reed Army Hospital in Washington, D.C. For openers, plastic surgery was a delicate procedure. Head injuries were something else.

Worst of all, officer rotation, like changing weather patterns, would cloud their immediate future: Babs, Geno, Doc Blevins, Padre, and others associated with the 62nd. Captain Brewer's departure was close at hand. She wondered what would happen to Beau.

Back at Phan Rang, Ricci had to deal with base repairs, Chivington, Beau, and his own return back to the world. As he lay in bed that night, he wrestled with his thoughts: *I can't leave this base at this point. It will be a shit load of work, but I can put it back together.* Chivington would be shipped all over the world, but he would get the best of help.

What about Beau? I love that damn dog. If I don't take care of him, who will? The Army might euthanize the poor bastard rather than take the trouble to treat him. Would he make it? If he did, would the fucking

Army make him go through this again and again until he suffered an agonizing death? The Army's war-dog policy sickened and enraged him. *Those cruel fucking bastards. Doesn't anybody sense what these dogs go through?*

As he tossed and turned, a solution evaded him.

With nowhere else to turn, he asked God for help.

As Ricci awakened at 0400 the next morning, an idea emerged. It was against his better judgment, but he didn't care. *Fuck Army regs. Without Beau, we would be in VC hands.* Ricci shivered as he thought of what they might have done to him as the commanding officer. *They might have tortured me for information. Castrated me for fun and then decapitated me. Beau is a war hero. He deserves some goddamn loyalty. We must honor uncommon valor. I'll call in a favor and extend my own tour of duty if I have to. I'm gonna save this war dog.*

At peace with himself, Ricci fell back to sleep.

In the next couple of days, Ricci ordered Young to complete paperwork recommending military decorations for all those who sustained "injuries in armed combat against enemies of the United States." This meant Purple Hearts for a lot of people in the 62nd and 101st. The Purple Heart, originally called The Badge of Military Merit, was first awarded in 1783 not for wounds but for meritorious service. Maybe a Bronze Star was also in order for Chivington and a promotion to sergeant. Ricci further contemplated honorary medals for Beau and the two other service dogs KIA at the sawmill. By Army regulations, they were at least entitled to a number of citations for bravery.

Following that procedure, Ricci prepared letters home to mothers and wives of those killed in action, a difficult task for any CO.

Geno wore ribbons of valor, including two Purple Hearts and a Bronze Star for his laudable service in Korea.

#

Two weeks passed. Thanksgiving had come and gone. The Christmas season was upon them. Captain Brewer's estimated time of separation left Geno with a gut-wrenching, vacant feeling. She had spent the final two weeks of her off-duty time attending to Beau. Doc Blevins' replacement was on his way. Airman Slater had already rotated back to the world.

After a blood transfusion and numerous sutures, Beau was still weak and not eating well. Not even ice cream and peanuts interested him anymore. Chivington's departure left Beau despondent. Beau didn't know it, of course, but Chivington had lapsed into a coma and was being air-evacuated to Walter Reed in Washington, D.C. There he might end up in the Snake Pit, the area of Walter Reed reserved for the most serious cases.

While Phan Rang's repairs were humming, Geno decided it was time to visit Cam Ranh Bay. He must attend Babs's farewell party and visit Beau. Bob Hope's Christmas show was set to debut after Geno's arrival.

Upon arriving at Cam Ranh, the festive holiday mood was dampened by sandbags which reminded him of the war and thoughts of the wounded and KIA—not to mention Babs's exit and Beau's weakened condition.

G.I.-made Christmas trees and other such ornamentations, however, buoyed his spirits. Geno appeared at Babs's ward where the party was in full swing. She did not see him at first. He viewed the ceremony with heartfelt pride and love for this woman.

"Captain Brewer, because of your extraordinary service at this hospital and to your patients, we present you with this farewell gift. Your promotion to Major has my signature," said her commanding officer, Lieutenant Colonel Nancy Schidemantle, as she handed Babs a brightly-wrapped gift with a large, red bow anchored on top of the package.

Then a chorus sang an off-key version of "For She's a Jolly Good Fellow," accompanied by harmonica and guitar. A thunderous round of applause followed. Then a quiet settled before a recording of Elvis's "Blue Christmas" over AFVN dedicated to Major Barbara Brewer played through a couple of radios. Her deep-blue eyes were floating. A quiet tear dropped from Ricci's face.

Waxing lyrical during the mood-altering din of Christmas music, the wounded, the disabled, one amputee, and a G.I. with tubes hanging from his gut, all rose in slow motion to give their Florence Nightingale a salute *au revoir*. Colonels Ricci and Schidemantle joined them.

#

At the helicopter pad, Geno walked in the direction of Babs, who was all gussied up in a starched white uniform. He pulled her close to his chest. A bear hug followed, then an all-embracing kiss. "Babs, I love you. Duty calls, but I'll be comin' home soon. I want to take care of you for the rest of our lives."

Clinging desperately to him, she responded in a soft and affectionate voice, "I love you, too. Please make sure Beau gets well and the hell out of this place, Geno. Please, promise me. I'll write just as soon as I get back to Alexandria. I'll be waitin' for you."

"I promise," he shouted as she boarded the chopper for Tan Son Nhut airbase and her flight back home. Waving goodbye, the *whump, whump, whump* of the rotors and the hot, swirling sand could not obscure the image of her loving face as the chopper gradually disappeared over the placid South China Sea.

Back at Phan Rang, Ricci tried to restrain his emotions. *What to do now?* he thought. Scuttlebutt had Chivington in a deep coma destined for Walter Reed. Beau's condition was going south. Padre listened to Geno's pain. Wilson was due to rotate any day now.

Wojtacha's replacement was already aboard. What a blue Christmas—white-knuckle time. Geno's level of anxiety twisted even higher. On a positive note: base repairs were nearly complete.

Soon after the holidays, Ricci went beyond the call. He remembered after Marilyn's death the sympathy card from the Republican Senate Minority Leader Everett Dirksen and his note: "…if I can ever help you…"

Geno knew politics to be a whore's game, but he had no choice. Marilyn Ricci, prior to her marriage to Geno, had worked for the senator as a staff secretary. Geno and Marilyn had met at a Capitol Hill party when he had played for the Washington Redskins.

A cleverly couched letter to Senator Dirksen explained Geno's quandary regarding Army regs and military dogs. Geno knew full well that if the letter ended up in the chain of command, his ass would be grass and his career ended. Senator Dirksen's clout with Lyndon Johnson, however, was legendary—and LBJ was a dog lover. Following this logic, Geno's plan, though a long shot at the proverbial best, seemed possible.

Geno spoke of all the heroics. With Chivington in Walter Reed's "Snake Pit," and Beau dying, Geno told Dirksen he wanted to bring the dog home in an effort to save Chivington. Both were war heroes and deserved some exception. He even mentioned the notion that after Beau's recovery, he could be used as a procurement recruiter for needed dogs in Southeast Asia.

#

Three weeks passed. Six-foot-five-inch Senate Aide Macklin Brown delivered Colonel Ricci's letter to the senator. With black-framed glasses, light hair aloft, and that booming basso profundo voice, Senator Dirksen called Lyndon Johnson. In response, LBJ told the senator, "Ev, bring that dog home, goddammit!"

Before Beau's return back to the world, Doc Blevins packaged Beau's medical records and medications, sending them with a rather frail Doberman and his medic to Bien Hoa for processing and a brief quarantine. Any contagious diseases had been ruled out.

During Beau's confinement, Ricci turned his beloved command over to his successor. His traveling orders were special. Young and Wilson, along with Padre, accompanied their Old Man to Tan Son Nhut for his flight home with Beau.

After arriving, Ricci spotted the intrepid black-and-tan Doberman, bandaged but standing tall like a true canine warrior. The nurses from Babs's old unit had outfitted Beau with a custom-made black saddle-like blanket. Resting across his broad back and hanging down over his bandaged ribs, honorary corporal stripes adorned the left and right sides of the quilted garment. An additional row of seven ribbon-like citations for bravery were affixed above the stripes. His working harness did not encumber his ability to walk on-leash.

Finally, an honorary Purple Heart was pinned close to his throat.

The colonel walked over, taking the leash from the medic. After seeing and sensing Geno, Beau licked his hand as Geno petted his broad forehead.

"This has got to be the first war dog goin' home by presidential order," said Wilson eagerly.

"May God bless, Colonel," Padre said. "We have all gone beyond the call, and as for you, Beau…God bless you, too."

As the colonel and his decorated warrior walked through the wide belly of a C-130, Young, Wilson, and Padre saluted Ricci and Beau for the last time.

"*Arrivederci*, Colonel and Corporal Beau. Godspeed and *con amore*," said Padre.

Geno returned the salute and waved goodbye.

The C-130 lifted like a huge dinosaur vanishing into the azure sky. Beau held his water until Clark Air Force Base in the Philippines. Then he traveled on to Travis Air Force Base near San Francisco and another short quarantine period before proceeding to Andrews Air Force Base outside Washington, D.C.

Upon deplaning at Andrews on a cold, blustery afternoon, Ricci and Beau were met by a bevy of media. Reporters from the major television channels 4, 7, and 9; the press, including the *Washington Post* and *Evening Star*; and a film crew from the Humane Society of the

United States gathered around the colonel and his war dog.

Flashbulbs and microphones sent Beau on alert. Ricci held Beau firmly on a short, taut leash in his left hand. "Easy, Beau," Geno said in a soft, comforting voice.

"Colonel...Colonel Ricci, it is our understanding that this is the first war dog returning from Vietnam by presidential order," screeched an upfront reporter.

"That's correct," replied Ricci. "We're on our way to Walter Reed..."

"What's the purpose?" interrupted another journalist.

"That's classified at this time," said Ricci. "Please excuse us," Geno bellowed as he and Beau snaked their way through the crowd to an awaiting military vehicle.

The next day, a crowd gathered at Chivington's bedside in Walter Reed: his mom, dad, sister, Senator Dirksen, Major Brewer, Colonel Ricci, the chaplain, Chivington's military doctor, Captain Neufang, Chivington's Army nurse, Debbie (who had secretly fallen in love with Chivington and was also an animal lover), and, of course, Beau.

"If he doesn't come out of it soon, he'll die," said Dr. Neufang. "He may have some brain damage."

A loud silence hung like a cloud. Several minutes later, still no sign of revival.

Chivington was a pale imitation of his former self. Geno took Chivington's hand, allowing his fingers to glide gently over Beau's black silky fur, then onto his head and wet nose. Beau remained stoic but was beginning to break out in a crescendo of motion when he felt Chivington's touch. Moments passed. Without warning, Chivington's twitchy legs began to move. His cotton mouth, crusty lips and waxen tongue collided with watery tears streaming down his ashen face, spotting the white pillow case. His head turned slowly, and matted eyes rolled open, looking at Beau.

Ebullient, Chivington's well-wishers hugged and cheered. Beau's front paws landed near Chivington's face. "Beau…Beau…Beau…" he cried.

There was not a dry eye in the room.

"The best place to bury a good dog is in the heart of its master."

—David Van Hoogstrate

Vietnam Veteran Dog Handler